Untouchable

By Jennifer Waldvogel

Dedicated to my grandmother, Laurine, who lived fiercely & wrote about her personal adventures in a way that has always inspired my own

One.

I was angry with my friend;
I told my wrath, my wrath did end.
I was angry with my foe;
I told it not, my wrath did grow.

-William Blake, "The Poison Tree"

September. Senior Year.

Anger lingers in my heart like an overdue houseguest. Shadowing every thought, every emotion. And in these shadows, I worry that I can't see the light.

By now, I've realized that anger isn't about those who've wronged us. Not the things they've said, not the betrayals, not even the careless disregard for everything we are. It's about how much we're willing to let that kind of cruelty chip away at our souls.

Anger is a parasite. And I'm tired of letting it suck the life out of me.

Two.

"This is the debt I pay / Just for one riotous day"
-Paul Laurence Dunbar, "The Debt"

Flames grew like wildflowers along the edges of the chalky, white walls. Licking the dusty air, they swirled around me in an orange-coated haze. I choked as thick soot stung every tiny fiber inside my rapidly contracting lungs. Staring down at my hands, I searched for the fire; they felt like they were on fire. Gasping, I scanned the room, eyes desperately seeking a door, any way out. Nothing. I crouched, grasping my knees, bearing the weight of the room, crushing my chest. I had to escape.

In the distance, I heard a tinny voice calling. "Andie…"

A girl's voice, but I couldn't see her. Blocking my vision, thick smoke rolled along the floor like waves. Here and there, spots of red glowed as embers moved, pulling pieces of the room to their demise.

"Andie." The voice was louder now, migrating from the back corner of the long, L-shaped room, somewhere near the giant steel shelving unit. Shelves full of athletic equipment. Rows and rows of never-again-to-be-used aluminum bats, gloves, helmets. All melting away.

Dropping to my knees, I sucked in a pocket of clearer air and began crawling across the floor, pulling my body, inches at a time, toward the voice. "Where are you?" I coughed the words, sucking in layers of smoke as I stood upright for a moment, trying to search.

"Andie..." The voice seemed a bit louder now. I could barely discern the outline of a figure, slumped to one side, head twisted awkwardly on a shelf full of round objects. A single hand reached weakly toward me.

I stumbled forward, reaching her, noting the long, straight hair cascading across the floor. She was striking, even now. Veronica, my best friend.

"Andie," Veronica croaked, pulling herself up on one elbow. She coughed once, spilling the space between us with fear. "I have to tell you..." Straining for breath, she shifted her face downward, away from the smoke.

I slid my arms beneath her small frame, pulling Veronica to a half-sitting position. "Gotta get out of here..." I groaned, working to upright the delicate limbs of her body. She suddenly lurched forward, leaning closer to me.

"Andie, no!" The shrillness of her words reverberated in the curves of my ear. Surprised by Veronica's abrupt forcefulness, I stopped. As I paused, the smoke cloistered between us, heat oppressive, transforming my clothes into a slick, second skin. The air grew thicker by the minute, and I felt my muscles betraying me. This dizzy, cool air floating above Veronica's head- was it a mirage? I shook my head to clear the haze, eyes desperately searching the edges of my vision for a way out. Veronica grabbed the edge of my shirt's collar, focusing attention back on her fading form. "Andie...it's important..."

She stared up at me, eyes swimming and then jerked my arm toward her so that my left ear was now close to her lips. Her grip was a vise. I couldn't move without hurting both of us. Frantic, I tried to reason with her. "We've got to move." I tried my best to speak calmly, but I knew she could see the panic in my expression. Veronica shook her head rapidly.

"Please just...." She gasped violently, coughing until she slumped forward.

"No!" I pulled her to her feet, throwing her limp arm over my shoulders, sliding her legs along the floor as I shuffled across the room. I could see a tiny shaft of light a hundred feet ahead of me. It had to be the door.

I can do this.

Resolved to fight, I pulled her with me. Eighty feet. Her breath rasped in my ear. Sixty feet. My calf muscles burned. Forty feet. Smoke thickened along the floor like a dingy, shaggy carpet. Thirty feet. A tiny shaft of light illuminated the path beneath my feet. Twenty feet.

Veronica's head lolled onto my shoulder. Body crumpling, her weight now slammed against my side. She was out. Out of breath. Out of energy. Out of will. I cradled her head, laying it gently on the concrete floor. *Was she breathing?* I couldn't think about that right now: we were nearly there.

Leaving Veronica on the floor, I raced the final feet to the door. Throwing the weight of my body against the solid wood, I pushed and pushed, agonized that after finally making it to the exit, we were still trapped.

The door finally groaned in response, bending beneath my force. In one final grunt of effort, I shoved the door open, grabbing a box near the opening to shove inside the doorway, something to hold it open so I could pull Veronica through. Turning, I ran back to the spot where I'd left her. Only...she wasn't there anymore. How could she? Where could she be? I never meant to lose her.

"Andie..." a voice reached out to me. The words were so clear, and yet, far away.

I never meant to lose her.

"Andie. Andie." More insistent now, the voice echoed all around me. *Where was it coming from?* I couldn't place it. And I couldn't find...

"Andie! Hello? Andie!!" Strangely, my right forearm began shaking on its own, moving in a consistent bobbing rhythm. Then my head. I felt the hair on the crown of my head swirling in circles.

"Andie!" Sharper now, the voice traveled directly into my eardrum. Almost as if someone was....

Right there. I cracked an eye open, swathed in the warmth of sunlight streaming across my face. My mother's large brown eyes stared at me in scrutiny. *Mom? It must be Saturday.* I felt a tickle on my toe. Then a snarffle. Almost like.... "Kermit?" A large, thumping tail whopped me in the face. One cold, wet nose digging through the lavender-tinted feather-down layers of the blanket on my queen-sized bed.

Bolting straight up, I nearly knocked into my mom. "Andie- I've been trying to wake you for ten minutes. You were sleeping like death." She clucked once with her tongue, rolled her eyes and walked across the room to pull the shades wide open on the bay window. The light on my bed expanded, filling the entire room with soft, yellow hues. From my vantage point on the bed, I could see neighborhood kids playing in the street. So it was a beautiful day, I guess. And yet I felt frozen- cold from another nightmare. These dreams had become my new normal. When Veronica first left, I was too hurt to even think about what happened. Now, my subconscious was working overtime to digest what I'd been avoiding. Shivering, I pulled the comforter closer to my chest, hugging the downy squares, settling into the daylight reality.

"Andie, baby?" My mom's face moved into view, blocking my stare past the outline of my cherry wooden desk, locked onto the swaying branches of the birch tree I could just make out along the edge of the window. "Are you all right?" She sat down next to me, plying the edges of the comforter with her soft, pale hands. I could hear the concern in her voice, but I didn't know how to fix that. I didn't know how to fix me.

"Mmmhmmm...." I tried a tiny smile. "Just slept hard, that's all." The lies rolled off my lips smoothly now, having had lots of practice. It was so much easier just pretending things were okay, especially to my ultra-nosy parents. Having a mom as a shrink definitely had its drawbacks. Every look, every word, every silent moment was constantly being scrutinized by my well-meaning, but incredibly sensitive mother. I knew she was good at what she did- I'd seen enough strangers wave and smile at my mom to know that she was working her magic around town- but on me, well...that was just unfair. Girls should be able to have secrets from their parents. They didn't get some kind of pass just because they'd earned doctorates in Psychiatry. If anything, they should back off even more, just to compensate. But she was still my mom, and if I didn't want her watching my every move, sometimes it was easier to just lie. "I'm fine- really."

Mom didn't look all that convinced, but her brow did unfurl a little. Instead, she tried another tactic. "I'm going shopping today. Wanna come?" Her face erupted into a big grin. When I didn't immediately respond, she wiggled her eyebrows and crossed her eyes. It was our old trick. Whenever one of us was feeling down, we'd make silly faces until the other one cracked. It usually didn't take long.

I laughed as she broke into a series of truly horrible dance moves, snapping her fingers to whatever crazy beat she happened to be following inside her head. "Okay, okay. I surrender." Raising my arms over my head, I rolled my eyes in one quick, motion. Kermit barked in affirmation, wagging his tail ferociously, pointing his snoot toward the ceiling. He might not be the brightest dog, but he was certainly one of the happiest. "Give me half an hour to clean up?" I brushed a hand through my thick, auburn hair, testing the frizz factor. Not too bad. Could probably get away without a wash this morning. Besides- the thought of putting all that effort into a morning routine seemed exhausting. I was still recovering from my dream.

"Sure, sweetie. I'll fry up some French toast for ya, hmmm?" *Of course. Sugar.* Aside from talk therapy, sugary goodness was among the top cures on my mom's quick-fix list. Our pantry was a smorgasbord of delicious treats. Coconut butterscotch cookie bars. Powdered sugar donuts. Cinnamon bread. Cranberry-walnut muffins. Mint Oreos. And for those really terrible days: Godiva truffles. That's how I always knew when to steer clear of mom. If I saw the truffle box come down from the top shelf, watch out. Level Five Crisis.

"Thanks, mom. Breakfast sounds good." Better not alarm her. Forcing a smile, I stretched my legs and swung them over the side of the bed. Maybe a shower was just what I needed. Time to clear my head.

As soon as Mom shut the door behind her, I breathed a sigh of relief. I was glad to be alone, but now all I could think about was my dream. *What was it this time?* Veronica had been so close to telling me. Some nights I heard her speak, some I didn't. This was one of those cryptic ones. All I wanted to know was when this would end. It'd been months since she left town, but I still couldn't get her out of my head. Not that I wanted to, really. We'd been so close. But things had changed so much between us.

I rubbed my eyes, clearing the sleepiness. Maybe today would be that day that turned everything around. Downstairs, I could hear Mom banging pots and pans in the kitchen, making me nervous. My mother was a notoriously bad cook. Not only did she love to experiment with weird flavors- trend cooking, as I liked to call it- but she had developed a pretty bad track record for burning things. I don't know how many scorched pots and ruined dinners Dad and I'd suffered through just because she "wanted to try this new thing." Thinking about a few of her more infamous disasters, I gagged inwardly. Maybe I could convince her to run through McDonald's this morning before our shopping venture. Anything was better than her French toast.

Hours later, after leaving a serious dent at *Serena's*, a clothing boutique in town, I sank back into my dream. It was still hard to believe that my best friend, and our friendship, was really gone.

Veronica's family had just picked up and moved in a matter of weeks. Tired of all the rumors, I guess. At first, it was a relief not to see her every day. Seeing her was just a reminder of what we didn't have anymore. Not like before, when we'd fantasize about the way we would change things if we could. Not like before, when the last thing either of us would do is make the other cry.

Three.

Whoever you are, holding me now in hand,
Without one thing, all will be useless,
I give you fair warning, before you attempt me further,
I am not what you supposed, but far different.

-Walt Whitman, "Now in Hand"

January. Junior Year.

It was the night of the big basketball game against Brenton. There was a huge party afterward, and I was going because Veronica forced me into it.

"I'm not even invited," I played with the corner of the white, cotton, eyelet blanket that covered her bed. It clashed with the *System of Down* posters plastered along her wall, but that was Veronica: walking contradictions.

"Andie," Veronica leaned down to flash her large, green eyes in my face. "You're ridiculous. Who cares what anyone else thinks or doesn't think? It's about having fun. And since you're going to be *my* date," wiggling her eyebrows at me, "hell, yeah, you're havin' fun!" Veronica stood up tall, smoothing her short, denim skirt, walking back toward her dresser, "Now get dressed!"

Silky fabric flew across the room and hit me squarely in the face. I mumbled in response.

"What? Hey- Earth to Andie. Put that on! You'll be gorgeous," Veronica affected her best British accent, throwing her nose in the air like she used to do when we played *Where in the World is Carmen Sandiago?* so many years ago.

"Okay, okay. But no guarantees on the gorgeous part." I walked into Veronica's adjoining bathroom, pulling off my plain navy tee, trading it for the silky purple halter she'd thrown my way. "Isn't purple supposed to clash with hair like mine?" I shouted toward her.

Veronica popped her head into the doorway. "You're not a redhead, you idiot. Auburn's like a whole 'nother shade of brown." She sighed. "Stop pretending you'd rather wear a potato sack than something sexy. If you want Mario to notice you- and who the hell wouldn't- then you've gotta *try* sometimes..." Mario was a sophomore I'd had my eye on for the past few months. We met at a tennis match. Veronica was competing and he was cheering on his older sister. Mario always had a steady stream of girls looking his way, so I doubted he'd ever notice me. Besides, he seemed a little glamorized by the party elite. Not sure if he and I would have much in common.

"What happened to being loved for our brains and sparkling personalities?" I smirked.

"That's great for school and work, but I'd *also* like to get lucky sometime this century." She looked pointedly at me. "And *you* could stand to be kissed once in awhile. I've seen the way you stare at the screen when Zac Efron appears. I can practically *feel* the drool." Veronica smiled wickedly.

I threw my navy tee, missing her head as she ducked. "Look- I do...*maybe*...want to be noticed by a certain guy," I smiled, feeling myself turning red, "but I hate parties. You know that, V. Why go through all this effort when absolutely no one will even notice?" I put my hands on my hips, defiantly.

Veronica raised her eyebrows. "Uh, Andie. In that top- believe me- people are going to notice." She walked toward me, turning my shoulders toward the mirror. "Look!" she demanded.

I felt stunned a moment. The silky fabric hugged my curves in the most feminine way. The bright color emphasized the olive tint of my skin. My eyes traveled the length of the halter top, admiring the way the line of the silk drew attention along the sides of my body and up toward my face. It *was* very flattering, that's for sure. Veronica had already commandeered my face for a make-up session and tousled my hair with mousse into something she liked to call Big Sexy Hair. I had to admit, the total effect was *very* different from my regular Oxford/cable-knit sweater look.

Veronica smiled, watching me look in the mirror. "I told you! Now tell me how genius I am...." Veronica suddenly scrunched her brows, walking closer to me as I turned to look at myself from the back. "Your bra straps in the back- it's going to ruin the whole look. Sorry, girlfriend...no can do." She stared pointedly, waiting. I stared back, waiting. If this was a battle of wills, I was going to win.

"Andie..." Veronica gently grasped my arm, turning my body so I could gaze again at the image in the full-length mirror hanging on the back of her bedroom door. "You look beautiful."

I sighed, smoothing the sleek fabric hugging the sides of my waist. The top *did* look really good.

Sensing my hesitation, Veronica continued, "Hot...Smokin'...Fire."

I cracked a smile, watching Veronica's eyes gleam as she geared up for what would, no-doubt, be a stream of ridiculous flattery. "Bomb squad hot."

I raised an eyebrow. "Nuclear warhead hot."

I felt nervous- wearing a top like this- so form-fitting, so revealing. And without a bra, that was bolder than I would *ever* normally be. But a tiny part of me felt a little dangerous tonight, and that was exciting. It was exhausting being the good girl all the time. My parents rarely even asked where I was going anymore. They didn't check my grades, call my teachers, set a curfew...nothing. Maybe that sounds like every teenager's dream, but really, it was just pathetic. To be predictable, to never rouse suspicion was so…boring. Determined, I reached my hand behind my back, unhooking the clasp of my light pink, cotton bra.

Tonight, I wouldn't be so boring. Tonight, I'd be more than the awkward seventh grader who won the regional Science Fair. More than the embarrassed eighth grader who knocked over the entire podium of diplomas during eighth grade graduation. More than the shy girl who stood in the corner, dreaming that everyone would one day see past the surface, past the grades and studying and awkwardness to something so much more.

Veronica plopped triumphantly onto her bed, eyes gleaming, "I-just-ate-a-ghost-pepper-and-I-have-no-water-hot." She smirked, daring me to challenge her.

"Okay." I turned and looked determinedly at my best friend. "Tonight, I'm all in."

Veronica squealed with delight, jumping up and pulling me toward her in a giant bear hug. We landed in a heap atop a mound of pillows piled along the edge of her bed. "Mmmshing me," I mumbled into a velvety blue pillow.

"What?" Veronica moved her arm, uncovering my face.

Laughing, "I said, 'You're smushing me.'" Sensing a swath of curls now covering my forehead, I puffed air quickly out my mouth, trying unsuccessfully to budge my wayward hair.

Veronica reached over, uncurtaining my face. "Enough play time." She looked at her watch. "I told Lonzi we'd pick him up about ten minutes ago. You know how he bitches when we're late." Lonzi, short for Alonzo, was my best guy friend. He'd earned the nickname in the third grade when he'd decided his full name was too stuffy for the imaginary IceCapades we played on my driveway every day for three weeks.

"Right." I loved Lonzi to death but he was truly a pain in the ass sometimes. Being late was only one of the many ways to set him off on a rant. And no one wanted that. His rants could be epic. Just when I thought he had finally dropped it, Lonzi would find some way to tie in my latest comment to his complaint. And then we were in the same argument over again.

Ten minutes later, we were honking in Lonzi's driveway, watching him strut down the walk with a clear look of annoyance on his face. Veronica turned up the radio and began singing. She winked at me. This would hold him off, at least a little bit.

Ten more minutes and four ear-blasting songs later, we pulled up to a long, winding drive. The sign at the end read "Bronson". I turned to Veronica, shock written across my face. "You didn't tell me this was Jared's party." I could feel my stomach start turning somersaults.

"Huh. Really? Could've sworn I did…" she trailed off nervously, suddenly absorbing herself in looking for a place to park. The drive was already half full with a stream of expensive sports cars carelessly wedged between BMWs and Lexuses. Veronica's Honda Civic looked ridiculously out of place, but she seemed to care less, choosing a tiny space next to a Porsche to park. Turning off the car, she stared straight ahead, avoiding my eyes.

"V- I definitely would have remembered hearing that this party is hosted by one of the biggest assholes in school." I turned in the seat to face her. "Don't you remember freshmen year?" I felt humiliated just thinking about it.

"Andie, I know. Believe me, I do care. But…" She hesitated, biting her lip. "I don't want to let the past…" She paused, "I don't want to live forever in that moment. Okay?" I sucked in a big breath, trying not to feel overwhelmed by what Veronica was asking. The flip-flops in my stomach were now moving faster and faster, threatening to pull me under. I could feel my heart quickening and I willed my body to just slow down, to just breathe.

Veronica leaned closer, grabbing both my hands, "Andie, I love you, you know I do." She stared pointedly into my eyes. "But that was two *years* ago." I watched the green swirls in her irises, idly noting how they reminded me of the trees outside my bedroom window. Home sounded so good right now. I could just leave this house, this parking lot---spend the night with my journal, curled up next to that bedroom window. Going home would be easier, but isn't that what I always did? I never took risks, never stepped outside my comfort zone. I always felt so *afraid* of what might happen if I did. Safe. Maybe the reason my parents never worried about me had nothing to do with them at all. Maybe I was the boring one. It was depressing to think of my life that way. To imagine that it was all my doing.

Veronica spoke softly, "We can't live in the past forever. I don't want to...to avoid all the fun we could be having just because..." Suddenly, she rolled her eyes, "Andie, they're not *evil*. Okay? Some of them are even kinda cute---like Mario, right?" Veronica nudged my arm, smiling, trying really hard to lighten the mood. "Anyway...it's just Jared's *house*. He won't even be around. You know he'll be too busy scouting out the latest freshmen to even notice you." Seeing my pained expression, she changed her tone. "Sorry, bad choice of words. But..." Softer now, "It's just a party."

Illuminated by the light blue glow of his cell, Lonzi poked his head between the seats, no longer content to sit silently in the backseat. I noticed how his dark, wavy hair was meticulously gelled in place. Wearing a crisply ironed, navy collared shirt and fitted, charcoal pants, I could see how much care he had taken to look good tonight. Licking his lips, he announced, "Ladies, this could be..." dramatically extending one hand toward each of us, "...the most exciting night of our lives." He winked at me, devilish expression on his face.

I forced a tiny smile. Swallowing the fleet of butterflies in my stomach, I nodded. "Okay, I mean, I am 'ghost-pepper' hot tonight, right?" I tried my best to channel that empowered self I'd watched in Veronica's bedroom mirror. The one who was determined not to blend into the background anymore. The one who wanted to be sexy confident, not geeky plain.

Veronica grinned widely, excited once again. "Let's go, girlfriend."

The walk toward Jared's front door stretched into a trail of memories. Moments splashed against the foliage lining the Bronson property. Girls pretending to be my friend so I'd do all the work for their school project. Whispers of "Nerd" and "Prude" in the halls at Birchfield Prep. Loud, raucous laughter when I asked Brad Kingsbury to dance at the Fall Formal. Fake invitations to the birthday party everyone else was going to attend. And for what? For their amusement? I'd never done anything, said anything to make myself a target. But maybe that was the point. I'd never really done anything. Being the Shy Brain, no one expected me to ever say or do anything besides what my parents or teachers requested. The kids at Westlake only cared about themselves. About how much money their parents made and who had the most expensive toys and which ladder they could climb fastest to become the most popular or most powerful. Playing with someone like me, a scholarship kid, a No-Namer, a girl who didn't follow the path of Search and Destroy...well it must be fun for them. That's the only way I'd ever been able to understand it. Because it didn't make sense. That kind of cruelty just didn't make sense.

Music pounded as we walked up to the door. I could see lights flickering through the panes of glass in the front room. Foyer. Vestibule. Whatever. *Here we go.* My confidence waned, fading like the will of that tiny helpless ant, squirming beneath the magnifying glass, seconds away from frying in the sun. Who would hold the magnifying glass tonight?

Veronica pushed open Jared's front door, sending a stream of warm, perfumed air floating back into my face. *Moment of truth.* I sucked in a breath, straightened my shoulders and walked into the house, instantly rubbing shoulders with two giggling sophomores, sloshing red plastic cups of beer on the Persian rug running the length of the hall.

The house was beautiful. It dwarfed mine and I thought a little guiltily of how much I wished my life was a little more Cinderella. Mom's voice was in my head, reminding me that happiness isn't about *things*, it's about people. Right. Well, these *people* would never give me the time of day without all the stuff that filled their lives. *Money can't buy happiness?* I scanned the room, soaking in the laughs, the smiles, the hugs, the kisses. Seemed happy to me.

I felt an elbow in my back. Turning sharply, I threw a dirty look. It was Jensen Bell and she was completely wasted.

"Oh, it's just you," she giggled, stumbling forward, grabbing my arm as she slid toward me. Her magenta striped top threatened to fall off her body, a single, thin strap placed on her shoulder. Half of the shirt was sliding down, revealing a hot pink bra. I could feel Jensen shift her weight onto me. Like I was nothing more than a post on the wall. Jensen smiled up into my face, breathing hot, drunken breath on my cheek. Maybe I had her wrong. She was definitely drunk, but also kinda harmless. And then she spoke, lifting wide eyes. "I thought it might be someone important." She stared for a moment, open-mouthed, a daze in her eyes. Then dropped my arm, straightening to stand.

I waited for the smirk. There was always a smirk. But when she just walked away, I felt even worse without it. Jensen wasn't trying to hurt me. She was stating the truth.

Feeling sick, I turned back toward the door. Coming here was a mistake.

"Not leaving yet, are you?" The voice was warm, inviting. I turned, smiling. Startled when I saw it was Jared, understated in a black v-neck sweater and jeans.

"Just looking for Veronica." My voice was flat. "Seen her?" I felt nervous. Normally, I tried to care less what he thought. Especially about me. But the way he was staring was reminiscent of a moment long ago.

"Surprised to find you here." Jared smiled, raising one eyebrow, waiting for me to share. I didn't. "But I'm glad."

I rolled my eyes. "Right." Glancing over Jared's shoulder, I could see the edge of Lonzi's sleeve. Looks like they hadn't gone too far.

"Can I get you something to drink?" Jared walked closer, scanning my face. I felt a tingle in my stomach. Absorbing the way his cool, blue eyes pulled me in, just like they used to.

"No," I stammered a little, "thanks, but I'm not really thirsty." I scanned the room again, trying to keep track of my friends.

"Andie." The way he said my name was soft and warm. *Is there some kind of charm school training for that?* "You look really great tonight."

My heart raced a little, betraying me. I forced myself back to that place, the humiliation. "You think a compliment like that makes it okay?" Quickly, I swallowed the flutters in my stomach, transforming them to fire. "You were...awful."

Now it was Jared's turn to be nervous. He frowned, licking his lips. "I've thought about that night a lot, Andie." Closing my eyes briefly, I wished he would stop saying my name like melted chocolate. Jared ran a hand through his dark, wavy hair. "I was..." Embarrassment wafted from his body like thick cologne. "If I could go back in time and erase that moment, I would."

I didn't know how to feel. The Jared who had become one of the most influential voices at Westlake didn't apologize. That Jared was cold. That Jared was selfish. This Jared was staring at me like I mattered. Staring at me like he actually felt remorse.

"Why should I believe you?" Everything in my body longed to walk away, but I was curious too. At one time, I had felt such sympathy for Jared.

Laughing awkwardly, "Maybe you shouldn't." The storm of his eyes was raging. "I get it. It's too late to say I'm sorry..." Jared bit his lip and shook his head. "But that doesn't mean I don't care." Jared dropped his head slightly, scuffing his foot on the sleek, hardwood floor.

How could I even *think* about feeling sorry for him? But somehow the tiniest part of me did. Mostly because he looked so wounded. Just like he had that moment I saved him. "Even if I'm willing to acknowledge that you're not a complete monster..." The corners of Jared's mouth twitched in an almost smile, "you're not someone I trust. At all." I tried my best to emphasize how much I *didn't* want to talk to him. Not now. Not ever really.

Silence languished between us. I had imagined this moment a million times. The ways I would eviscerate him if we ever found ourselves alone again, but the possibility now just seemed silly. What was the point?

Better to move on, leave him to his shallow world. "Goodbye, Jared." I walked forward, sliding past his left shoulder, into the central corridor of his expansive home.

"Do you believe in second chances?" Jared's voice was low. He had stepped backward so that we were now standing shoulder to shoulder. My left to his right. Music pulsated from the rooms ahead, a muffled echo here in the front entryway.

My mind swirled with images. Dozens of moments packed into the last two years. Jared doing whatever he could to make himself seem smarter, funnier, better looking than everyone else at Westlake. Freshmen year felt both like yesterday and a million years ago. I'd changed. Was it that hard to believe that someone like Jared could've changed too?

"I do..." The words were out of my mouth before I could think twice.

"Then, can I show you something?" I could feel the warmth of Jared's shoulder melding into mine. *Say no. Say no. Say no.* The words beat like a mantra.

Yet, curiosity was tingling every nerve in my body. "What is it?" I stepped to my right, building distance between us.

"Follow me." Jared began walking down the taupe tinted hallway, weaving and winding through a crowd of cheering teens. He turned left, pushing open a set of swinging doors into a large, stainless steel kitchen. Navy blue fabric lined the tops of a set of deep cherry cabinets. Four large picture windows showcased a glass-enclosed terrace adorned with twinkling white lights.

I walked in after Jared, stopping next to the large island in the center of the kitchen. Looking out the windows, I could see rows and rows of vibrant flowers set in colorful planters. "Wow. Beautiful garden." A large, wooden bench and giant telescope sat among them, partially hidden from view.

"Thanks. It's one of my favorite places." Jared took down a crystal glass from a buffet cabinet. Muscles pulsed beneath his shirt as he moved. "Nobody uses this kitchen, so I've usually got it to myself." Jared handed me a glass of lemonade. "Wanna check it out?" Jared motioned toward the terrace doors.

I hesitated. "I should really get back to Veronica. I haven't seen her at all…"

Jared pressed, "It's just a moment." He smiled warmly, with the slightest hint of boyish uncertainty, trying to reassure me.

"Okay," I relented, "just for a moment."

As soon as we stepped onto the terrace, I was absorbed in citrus, lilac, and honeysuckle. The air was incredibly warm, artificially heated to the ideal temperature for blooming flowers on cool nights. It was comfortably humid. Just enough to feel like cashmere on my skin. I breathed in deeply, inhaling the sweet floral scent. Noting the beautiful contrast between a sea of flowers here and a blanket of frost just outside.

"Nice, huh?" Jared commented, walking toward the bench next to a large telescope. "It's my little hideaway. A place to escape from my mother." He glanced toward me, "You remember how she...can be." Jared coughed awkwardly. He sat down on the bench, stretching his legs out in front of him, motioning for me to sit too. "It's even nicer over here." I raised my eyebrows, staring warily at the spot beside him. Jared touched the telescope lightly. "The only place to see the stars." He patted the spot again, waiting for me to move.

What was I doing? My head screamed "turn around and walk away". But that other part of me, the one who'd always lived just on the outside of everything, that part of me was curious. Reluctantly, I crossed the terrace and sat on the edge.

Jared turned the lens of the telescope toward me. "Here. Take a look."

Placing my eye to the lens, I squinted, trying to focus. "What am I looking for?"

I could feel Jared turning dials, hands close to my face. "Ok, can you see the lopsided pentagon? That's Orion's body." I searched the starscape before me, feeling lost. "Toward the bottom of the pentagon, three of the stars are really close together: that's his belt."

Suddenly, I saw it, surreally transported by the natural grandeur, by the realization that life here was so very, very small. "Wow. That's beautiful."

We sat in silence for a few moments, taking turns looking at the night sky. I leaned back against the bench, staring upward and Jared coughed softly, moving his hand toward his mouth and then laying it next to mine. I could feel his skin warm and sturdy against my own.

"Sometimes I wish I could just live up there." Jared's voice was soft and low next to me. I turned to look at his face, shadowed with a stormy look. "Everything I do down here is for everyone but me. When do I get what *I* want?"

"Maybe you should just be yourself." I stared straight ahead, but I could feel his eyes on me now.

Jared's face softened. He leaned close to me. "It's like…" He ran a hand through his hair in frustration, "…everyone expects me to be this certain way and sometimes I just give in to it. I play along because that's what my friends expect to see. And it's not just my friends." He stood up suddenly, pacing, "It's my parents and my parents' friends. They all have this protocol, this stupid code of behavior that's…exhausting." Jared turned to face me again, "Can't I just be who I want to be? Isn't that okay?"

Suddenly, Jared leaned down, chest inches from my body. I felt his heart beating so fast. Jared reached for my chin, cupping it in his left hand, pulling it

upward, just a little, to meet the angle of his lips. I
pulled back, afraid. What did this mean? "I don't
understand. You acted like you didn't care…like you
could never care… and now?" It was hard to form
coherent thoughts with his nose brushing mine, with
the lashes of his two perfect seas gently grazing my
cheekbones.

And then he was kissing me. Soft, warm lips
pausing on mine. His kiss was slow and teasing. I felt
my arms drop to my sides, taken aback by the tingling
across my body. Jared pulled me closer to him,
wrapping his arms around my back. His kisses became
more frenzied. I felt a hand reaching down to graze the
edge of my backside. I pushed it away. Jared ran his
right hand down the side of my body, sliding the silky
fabric through his fingertips. I felt his hand begin to
move upward, toward my chest, and I slid it away. He
groaned a little, grabbing me tighter, guiding my body
down onto the bench. I felt my breath catch. I didn't
want to lie down. This was going fast. I started to
move upward, trying to right myself, but he pressed
me down, laying his body heavily on top of mine. I
tried to speak, muffled beneath his kisses,
"Jared…stop."

"No one understands me. No one wants me," He
mumbled into my neck. I softened a little. Maybe he's
just caught up in the moment. I hadn't expected to be
here either.

Placing one hand on either side of his face, I met his gaze. "Just slow down, okay?" He responded by kissing me, melting my words into his lips. It was soft again. Good. I felt my heartbeat calming.

"I need this. I need this to happen," Jared whispered in my ear, running his tongue along its edge. With his left hand, Jared traced the skin on the nape of my neck. I felt his fingers move down toward my chest, tightening his right hand on my back. He was moving me down again, lying on the bench. I struggled against him. "Jared, I can't move."

He wasn't listening. Jared pulled at the bottom of my halter top, raising it up, palming my naked chest. I panicked. This isn't what I wanted. Especially not here. "Andie, shhh."

"Jared, stop." He kissed me roughly in response, running his hand along the zipper of my pants. With his body wedged on top of mine, he unzipped my jeans, exploring the absolute edges of my comfort zone. Heart palpitating, I knew that this was the last moment I might have to myself. What was about to happen could never be undone. With strength from beyond, I shoved Jared as hard as I could, pulling down my shirt at the same time.

He looked shocked. Flushed. Wild-eyed. "You wanted this," he said crudely. "This is exactly what you were hoping would happen."

I felt sick and stupid to believe Jared was sincere. That he was sorry. That we were actually connecting.

"What? Nothing to say?" Jared's face was crimson, sweater twisted, every hair on his head askew as he furiously ran his hands through it again and again. Suddenly, his expression changed, shades drawn across his eyes. A smirk. "When I saw you walk in the door, I thought you'd be an easier target."

Numbly, I watched him dust his designer jeans. So casually. As if nothing had happened.

"I'm going back inside now." Jared looked pointedly at me. "Gotta be plenty of other girls who'd actually enjoy my company. I'm sure I could find one who'd enjoy a good *fuck*." He drew out the last word harshly, looking me up and down dismissively.

I wanted to cry. But I couldn't. Not in front of him. I just stared, trying to give him my most evil look. Inside, I was crumbling. The humiliation two years ago paled in comparison. This was *true* degradation.

Jared turned and walked inside. I waited until the door slammed to break my pose. Head in hands, I let myself go. Tears streamed down my face and my breath came hard and fast. How dare he? How could he live with himself being so aggressive and then so dismissive? All the feelings I'd had toward him multiplied in that moment. I hated him. Hated how he'd manipulated my feelings. Hated how I'd let him kiss me…make me feel pretty and desired.

I slid off the bench to sit on the chilled floor, searching for something, anything to ground myself. It was such a beautiful night that I felt the painful contrast of Jared's actions even more. Looking at the stars sprinkled across the sky, swimming in the fragrant bouquets of the gardens, I couldn't find a bright spot. Right now, there was only one thing to make me feel better: I needed my best friend.

Four.

Veronica would know what to say. Veronica would know what to do. I don't know how long I'd been sitting out on the terrace, trying to pull it together, but doing it alone was nearly impossible. I needed my best friend.

Wiping my face, I walked inside to find her. The party was really going now. So many people. Bumping up against each other. Grinding to the blaring house music. Smoke filtered through the room, stinking the air. I searched and searched, running my eyes around the room. I didn't see her anywhere.

Frustrated, I looked for Lonzi. Moving to the next room, I spotted him. Leaning against a tall, stone fireplace, he was talking animatedly to Brock Larson, a cornerback on the football team. I could tell Lonzi was into him. The way he laughed with his mouth wide open, touching Brock's arm lightly to emphasize his pleasure with the joke. Brock looked tipsy, but surprisingly interested. As much as I needed a friend right now, the idea of interrupting was out of the question. Lonzi was one of the few openly gay guys at Westlake. I'd sat through enough school dances with Lonzi to see how devastating this was for him. As flustered as I felt, I couldn't bring myself to interfere. I'd just have to continue looking for Veronica.

I moved from room to room, calming as I walked. I felt less stunned than angry. Really angry, in fact. Relieved to feel less vulnerable, I just wanted someone else to share my frustration. V was the one I could count on to understand. Trekking up the winding staircase, I pushed past couples making out on the stairs and in the upstairs hallway. Remembering the way Jared had ignored my pleas, how he'd nearly… my stomach turned. I needed her right now.

Suddenly, I spotted a familiar face. Jesse Millen. Sports Editor for the *The Howl*, my favorite school publication and the dedication of countless hours of my time. Grabbing his arm, I blurted, "Have you seen Veronica?"

He turned slowly, buzzed from the cup of beer in his hand. "Hey Andie. Didn't expect to see *you* here." He laughed warmly, "Having fun with the other hellions?" Jesse looked at me expectantly.

I didn't have the time or the energy to explain just how wrong Jesse was. "Sure. It's great. But seriously, have you seen Veronica?" I looked at him hopefully.

"Would've thought she was with you." Jesse turned, calling out to a girl summoning him from across the hall, "Melinda, wait a sec." Squeezing my shoulder, "You know, I think I saw her a few minutes ago with Jared Bronson actually."

"Oh!" I tried to keep the panic out of my voice. "Do you know where they went?" I tapped my foot nervously, trying my best nonchalant smile.

"Well…" Jesse winked at me. "I think they were going somewhere to be alone, if you know what I mean." He smiled easily, as my stomach twisted.

"Thanks, Jesse." I moved past him quickly. "Uh, have a good time, okay?" Scanning the rooms before me, I tried to breathe. Veronica was much less skeptical about anyone, let alone someone charming like Jared. One of my favorite things about her was how open-minded she was. So her Jared-radar was going to be definitely less acute than mine. And considering how easily he'd manipulated me into feeling sorry for him, Veronica was in trouble.

I walked down a hallway of doors. Probably bedrooms. In this giant house, it was hard to be sure. They had to be in one of these.

Taking a deep breath, I opened the first door. I heard rustling on the bed, but I couldn't see who was there. "Veronica?" I whispered into the dark room. A muffled reply. "V? Is that you?" I tried again, leaning farther into the doorway.

"No!" A pillow shot across the room toward my head. "She's not in here, okay? Now shut the door, you perve," I recognized the nasally tones of Jensen Bell. Fine. Serves her right for insulting me when I walked in the front door. Just to be a brat, I left the door wide open. Angry shrieks filtered through the doorway as light flooded the once private room. Couples walking by in the hallway snickered as a shirtless Anthony Montano rushed toward the open door.

I felt a *little* bad about Anthony- he was actually a nice guy- but my annoyance with Jensen and her bitchy attitude overrode any real remorse. I smiled a little to myself.

Continuing down the hall, I began to get more nervous. *What if I couldn't find her in time?* I hated the thought that Veronica might be tricked, or worse, forced into something she didn't want to do. I was used to being an outsider at Westlake. But Veronica floated among all the social groups at school. She prided herself on that. Being taken in by Jared would make her question everything. I couldn't let that happen.

I opened three more bedroom doors but no Veronica. *Where could they be?* Spotting a small staircase at the end of the hall, I moved toward it.

"Hey- what are you doing?" A whiny voice called out as I placed one foot on the landing of the stairs. Turning, I could see Lindsey Bronson, Jared's sister, standing with her hands on her hips, scrunching her brow in annoyance.

"Trying to find my friend," I called hurriedly over my shoulder, climbing the second step.

"You can't go up there!" Lindsey shrieked, jumping in front of me on the third stair, wedging her body between mine and railing.

Raising my palms, I tried to reason with her. "I get it. This area is off-limits. But I've looked everywhere else, and I really need to find my friend. I promise not to touch anything."

Lindsey's nostrils flared in anger, "No! That's Jared's private studio. He'll kill me if I let anyone up there." Her eyes widened, panicked. "This is *my* house and you're not going up there unless I say so!" She stretched out her arms across the span of the stairway and planted her legs wide across the aisle like a human barricade. *Was she kidding?* I tried to slide past, but she wouldn't budge.

"Listen!" I leaned forward to stare her directly in the face. "I'm pretty sure my friend is with your brother and I need to find them immediately. So, get out of my way. Now." I pried the fingers of her left hand away from the railing, squeezing past her, climbing onto the next step.

"You bitch!" Suddenly, I felt my left arm viciously pulled downward. I lost my balance, tripping on the stair, my black boots losing footing. "This is *my* house. How *dare* you tell me what you can and can't do here? Who do you think you are anyway?" Fire stoked in her eyes.

Rubbing my sore foot, I looked up from where I'd fallen, meeting Lindsey's eyes, "Someone who's not leaving her friend alone with your pervy brother. That's who."

"Oh, I get it…" Lindsey's laugh was harsh and clipped. "You've got some kind of… *thing* for my brother. He probably wouldn't give you the time of day and now you're all upset." She sneered. "Stealing guys from your girlfriend…" Lindsey leaned in close. "You're pathetic."

I couldn't help myself. I lunged forward up the stairs, shoving Lindsey as hard as I could to get past her. Climbing two at a time, I reached the door of Jared's studio.

It was locked. Knocking fast, I called out Veronica's name. No response. Frustrated, I turned back toward the stairs, just in time to see Lindsey rubbing her head, talking furiously to one of her friends. The two of them were glaring up at me. It was only a matter of time before she continued her rant. *Great.* Then, the lock clicked behind me.

Jared's face filled the doorway. Seeing his sister and her circle of friends at the bottom of the stairs, he called down to her, "Linds, it's fine. Go back to the party." He waved at them, an easy smile across his face. I watched them walk away, heels clicking angrily down the hall.

As soon as they were gone, Jared's expression shifted dramatically. He stared at me with ice in his eyes. "What do you want?"

What I wanted couldn't fit in this universe. Instead, I said the only thing I could manage, "I want Veronica." The words croaked leaving my mouth.

At this, Jared's lips smirked, but his eyes remained cold. He leaned in to whisper, "What a coincidence, I do too." The words hung heavy between us. Jared moved so close to me, I could feel the bile rising in my throat. "You know, I think I'll keep *wanting* Veronica, a little longer. Sounds fun." His eyes were pure ice.

I bit my lip, forcing back the tears. This night I would survive, but watching the two of them together, again and again...what kind of game was he playing? "You wouldn't."

"No Andie, *you* wouldn't." I suddenly realized that while a part of Jared might be that vulnerable boy I met freshmen year, that part of him was small. So small it could never match the need to be noticed, to be in control, to get exactly what he wanted. And right now, what Jared Bronson wanted was exactly the opposite of what I wanted.

"Just get out of my way so I can see my best friend." Jared opened the door wider. I could see Veronica standing before a mirror, smiling to herself. She had no idea I was watching her.

"Go ahead," he whispered in my ear, "Tell her what happened. How you came onto me. How I pushed you away---"

"What?" I fumed, ears ringing. All I wanted to do was grab Veronica and get out of this house. Standing here even one minute more felt like suffocating.

"I can spin the story any way I want to, Andie, but no matter what, Veronica's the one who'll be hurt if you open your fuckin' mouth." I glared at him, feeling like vomiting and punching him in the face all at the same time. "Maybe next time, you'll think twice about saying 'No' to someone like me.

He'd said it aloud. The real reason he could be so cruel. Jared couldn't stand that he'd let down his guard and been rejected. Heavy price for me to pay for *his* wounded ego.

I gritted my teeth, "I don't care what you say. Veronica is my best friend and she will believe anything I say. And whatever…feelings…she might be experiencing now will fade away the second she realizes what a manipulative asshole you are."

Jared leaned his body against the doorframe, blocking Veronica from my view. "You can try that…but I'd think very hard about the consequences." Jared grabbed the back of my head, whispering harshly in my ear. "I can let her down easy, or I can make things very complicated. For both of you."

What was I supposed to do now? Veronica was my best friend. The damage was already done with Jared. The only thing left to decide was how badly things would end. My stomach churned. All I wanted was to make Jared suffer. To humiliate him the way he'd humiliated me. But to do that might mean losing any opportunity to save V from public scrutiny. I knew all too well what it felt like to be at the mercy of the Untouchables. And that was just a joke. I couldn't imagine what was in store for V if Jared was seeking *Revenge*. She wouldn't survive.

I looked into Jared's eyes with as much disgust as I could muster. "If you hurt her, I'll make you pay." Fury lined my voice.

"Oh, Andie," Jared laughed. "What are *you* going to do to *me?*" Unless…" He moved toward me again, "you tell anyone what happened on the terrace. No one rejects me," Jared set his jaw with these words. "And as far as anyone's concerned, no one ever has." He looked at me pointedly.

So that was all? Lie about what a complete asshole he was and pretend he hadn't tried to…? I cringed at that idea. But Veronica…I couldn't let her enter into some kind of emotional chess game with this guy.

"Fine. You keep your word, I keep mine."

The door closed and with it, a part of me closed too. Somehow I would have to bury this story, lie to my best friend, and pretend to be happy for her newfound love interest. The amount of impossible needed to fill that task couldn't fit inside a football stadium. But I loved her. And that was everything.

Numbly, I walked down the stairs, desperately searching for a distraction. People passed me by, talking, laughing, and sloshing cocktails in glass goblets

no doubt stolen from the extensive cabinets in the
Bronson kitchen. I didn't care. An hour and a half ago,
I would've gawked at the shallow, wasteful ways of my
classmates, but now, it seemed so trivial.

A tap on my shoulder startled me. I turned to stare
blankly into the smiling face of Lonzi. "Hello?! Earth to
Andie! I've been calling your name for five minutes. I
had to walk all the way over here and you *know* how
much I hate to leave a good scene!" He knocked my
arm playfully, waiting for me to smile.

I had to smile. If Lonzi thinks something's wrong,
he'll annoy me all night until I tell him. And that
would unravel me. Blowing a quick breath out of my
lungs for courage, I straightened and gave him my best
version of a smile. "Must've just been in a daze. This
party is somethin' else," I rolled my eyes as two guys
tried to hold the feet of another as he shot beer into his
mouth from a keg in the mud room.

Lonzi giggled. "Yeah, it's something all right. But
I've got big news, Andie baby." He grabbed my arm,
steering me to a corner of the room for privacy. "Big
news. Huge news." His eyes gleamed.

"This wouldn't happen to involve Mr. Larson,
would it?" I smiled at him for real this time. It was
hard not to get caught up in Lonzi's energy.

He grinned even wider. "Yessss! Oh, he is so hot,
Andie. So hot. But listen-"He lowered his voice, "I
don't think he's out yet, so keep this quiet, 'kay?"
Lonzi furrowed his eyebrows with concern.

"Can *you* keep this quiet, Lonzi? From here, it seems like you're barely containing yourself.'

He wagged his finger at me. "Are you criticizing me? I seem to remember a certain someone going on and on about Mario something or other..." He stepped back, smirking and waiting for me to defend myself.

"Okay." Hands up in the air. "Point taken. Now tell me about Brock."

Fifteen minutes later, I'd heard more than I ever wanted to know about Brock Larson, when I spotted her: Veronica. She and Jared were walking down the hall together, looking very close. She laughed at something he said, fluttering her eyelashes.

Jared caught my eye as she leaned down to fix the strap on her shoe. Placing a hand on the small of her back, he winked at me.

The nerve of him. I looked away to keep from spitting fire from my eyes.

Lonzi never even noticed my distraction. He kept blabbering away, so I nodded and "Mmmhmm"-d on and on.

Suddenly, I heard Veronica's voice in my ear. "Hey, superstar." She leaned down to whisper in my ear, "I'm having a great night. How 'bout you?" She pulled back to smile at me, cocking her head in her best *I've got a secret* expression.

"Umm...okay, I guess. Not what I expected." *That's for sure.* "You ready to go soon?" All around us, people were dancing. The music was blaring again, and my head was starting to pound along with it. "Not really my scene, I think." I pleaded with my eyes. The room was starting to feel small as the size of my secret pressed on my chest, my head, squeezing from all sides. I could barely breathe with Jared standing so near.

"You sure?" Veronica turned, admiring the dance party behind us. "Wanna dance a little first? I've barely seen you tonight." She wiggled her hips, moving to the beat of the music. "This'll be so much fun, I know it." Veronica grabbed my hand, pulling me to my feet. I allowed myself to be led, to fall into the beat of the music rather than succumb to the pounding in my head. Moving farther into the living room, I could sense Lonzi to my right, swinging his arms wildly to the tempo. I watched my arms, hips, feet moving as if I was watching someone else. For just a moment, I wanted to forget this night. I closed my eyes and gave in to the feeling of dancing, ignoring the way Jared's eyes were locked on me. I repeated to myself: *You're strong. You're strong.*

I really hoped so.

Five.

Monday… Tuesday…Wednesday…The days passed slowly as I struggled to keep my secret. Every time Jared walked by, my chest tightened. I felt the inside of my stomach violently churn whenever he reached for Veronica's hand, slid his arm across her shoulder, pulled her toward him. I nearly told her a dozen times, but then Jared's harsh words would descend, stopping me cold.

Thursday at lunch, Veronica surprised me with a proposition. She waited until we were seated at our regular table, one of a dozen square, wooden tables tucked into the South corner of the cafeteria. The best tables, long and rectangular, lined the wall of windows on the East side of the room. Outside the windows, rows of birch trees flanked the side of the building. Pink, flowering bushes nestled between the trees, close enough to nearly touch on days the windows were open. These tables were populated by the Westlake elite, but Jared didn't have lunch the same period as Veronica, so I was spared the embarrassment of trying to fit into his crowd during my only break in a jam-packed day of advanced classes and stress-inducing college prep planning.

"So, who's my favorite little librarian?" Veronica loved to tease me about my after school job at the public library. She enjoyed a good book as much as I did, but you'd never catch her hanging out in the library. Libraries were quiet and Veronica couldn't stay quiet if her life depended on it.

I rolled my eyes. "Fine. What do you want, V?" She was holding a sleek black tray- piled with sushi and wild rice- in one hand, lightly bouncing from one foot to the other, some kind of kick-ball-change pattern. Whenever Veronica was eager to talk about something, her whole moved in excitement. Teachers hated this about her. If Veronica had something to say, she'd literally be bouncing out of her seat until they called on her. It didn't take long for her to be the one guiding the entire discussion. It was just easier that way and, usually, she'd be so caught up in an idea, the rest of the class was energized too, talking over one another.

"Andie!" She pulled me out of my chair, looping her arm in a wide circle above my head, forcing a twirl. "Don't be such a grouch." She stuck out her tongue and crossed her eyes, making such a ridiculous face I couldn't help laughing.

"Okay, okay." I smiled, trying to sit back down as I felt the smirks of several dozen faces across the cafeteria. As hard as I tried not to care about their impressions of me, I was still so easily embarrassed. V, on the other hand, never seemed embarrassed by anything at all.

"I've got the perfect idea. The *most* perfect idea in the world. Maybe even the universe." She grinned wildly, wiggling her eyebrows as I waited in suspense.

"All right- you've got my attention." I stopped thinking about the Physics homework I'd been trying to finish and faced her expectantly.

"A double date!" Veronica grabbed both of my hands in hers, squeezing. "Jared's cousin is flying into town for the long weekend and he suggested that we double. Isn't that great?"

Instantly, I felt sick. I moved one fist in front of my face, trying to hide the bitter expression I knew was near. But there was no way out of this one unless I wanted to confess what happened the night of the party, and the longer I waited, the more awful it felt to have kept it from her at all. No, there was no way I could ever tell her. So...I guess I was going on this date. At least then I could keep an eye on Jared even if it meant downing Pepto like there was no tomorrow.

"Yeah, V. Sounds great," I put on my best smile, hoping Veronica wouldn't notice the hollowness of my expression. I'd always been so easy to read, wearing every emotion like a reader board across my forehead.

Glancing up, I saw shiny, pink lips beaming in one of her "movie-star" smiles. No, I was definitely good on this one. There was no way she'd notice my hesitation now.

Six.

"So then *I* said, 'Not if the shark finds you first!'" Jared slapped his hand on the table, laughing heartily at his own barely amusing anecdote. The more time I spent with Jared, the more I realized how obnoxious his typical behavior was. I coughed up a sympathy laugh, rapping my nails lightly on the white linen napkin. Jared's voice carried across the crowded restaurant, causing a few heads to turn above the din. The rose-tint from the low-hanging lamps cast a crimson glow across Jared's face as he swaggered through the meal. *You look just like the devil you are.* I smiled to myself, thinking of all the horrible ways I could inflict pain on Jared as I sat across from him. He looked at me, registering my smile, and threw me a saucy grin. *If only I could erase his touch from my skin.*

I looked away from Jared, and my eyes fell on Ethan, my mysterious double date. He was staring into his salad, absentmindedly picking at a cherry tomato with the tines of his fork. As I watched him, Ethan lightly licked his lip, and I felt a single butterfly flutter in my stomach. He was undeniably sexy with caramel hair that kept falling carelessly across his forehead and eyes that smoldered in such a wide array of colors I could hardly capture even one. All throughout the meal, I'd found myself wondering how it'd feel to be the napkin, the fork, the glass that kept touching his deliciously appealing lips. But then I'd see Jared- his cousin- and remember the world Ethan came from. Thinking of this now, I frowned, until I felt a sharp kick on my shin.

"Ow!" I darted an accusatory look at Veronica. *What the hell was she doing?*

"Oh, Andie, I'm so sorry. I must've kicked you by accident. It's just so exciting listening to Jared's stories…" She flipped her long, honey hair away from her shoulder, squeezing Jared's arm at the same time. "I guess I just got carried away."

She looked at me pointedly, communicating in the way that only two best friends can. It was a look I knew well, but one I was certain Jared couldn't read in a million years. A look that most definitely said, "Knock. It. Off."

Well, sorry, V, but I make no promises. "It's fine, V. Must've been so enthralled in these tales at sea that I drifted away there myself." I flashed Jared a smile. "Of *course* I'm interested in the things you say, Jared."

He winked at me then: one quick, subtle move that only I could see. I felt my jaw set but held my ground. *Only a matter of days now. He can't stay with her much longer, can he? How much time would he invest in a fake relationship?* Then again…I'd never imagined how slimy he could be, how he could slither his way into my best friend's heart just to punish me for saying 'No.' He was a snake.

Ethan's arm brushed against mine as I reached for my water glass the same time he picked up his spoon. "Sorry about that," he murmured in a low tone, smiling out of the left corner of his mouth.

I felt myself blushing. "Not a big deal," I tossed out casually. I'd been trying so hard to avoid my attraction to Ethan all night, but with Veronica hanging all over Jared, it was hard to sit mute and talk to no one at all. I'd learned that Ethan was only in town to visit because his parents were thinking about buying a house in the area. He didn't sound excited to leave his old home. I think he was hoping to convince them to stay.

Frankly, I'd been shocked when Ethan first walked in the door. Not by his attitude, but by how little he and Jared had in common. The one thing that had been guiding my every thought leading up to the date was how heinous he must be. If Jared was willing to spend time with him, if Jared was *related* him, he had to be awful. But after just ten minutes in the same room together, it was hard to believe he and Jared were even close. They hardly talked.

I felt Ethan's eyes on me. *Was he talking to me just now?* I shook my head, returning to the table. "Hmmm?" I looked across the tablecloth, trailing up toward his hazel eyes. *Damn, he had pretty eyes.*

He chuckled. "I was just wondering about this plan of yours..."

"My plan?" *Was this guy out of left field or what?* I picked at my napkin, extending my paintless index finger along the lines of the fabric.

"Your escape plan." A smirk gathered at the corner of his mouth again.

"Uhh…" I felt a blush creep across my face. It was impossible for me to hide almost anything. Emotionally, that is. I kept quiet enough when I wanted to. Veronica was loud enough for the two of us, usually. But something about this guy really unnerved me. He wouldn't let me be. He read my face and actually *called* me on it.

Ethan laughed. "Didn't mean to catch you off guard." He swept a hand through his chestnut hair, gently pushing away a few long strands that had fallen across his face. I watched the slow, smooth movements of his hand, noting the strong lines and lean muscles running down along his forearm.

"Yeah, right." The response was snarkier than I'd intended. Veronica looked away from Jared for a moment, just to shoot me another glare. I bit the edge of my thumbnail, squinting my eyes at her: *my* version of the "back off" look. She lifted her eyebrows, shrugged her shoulders and re-immersed herself in all things Jared. *Fine. As long as I didn't have to listen to his stupid stories.*

Ethan tried to cover his smile with his right hand. "Okay, so maybe I did mean it. Just wondered what you were thinking about so intently…kinda hurting my ego a little here, ya know..." He looked serious for a moment, and I softened.

"I'm sorry..." I began quietly, "I *am* distracted, but it's not your company." I gave a quick glance across the table as Jared pulled Veronica in for a lingering kiss. "Trust me." I couldn't help keep the grimace out of my voice, and for a moment, I didn't even care that Ethan was Jared's cousin. I didn't care if he knew that I thought Jared and Veronica were a terrible idea. Keeping up this charade was exhausting.

Seven.

Two weeks later, Jared texted Veronica to break up with her. After watching them flirt in the hallways at school and sit near each other in the cafeteria, I was ecstatic that he'd followed through. I'd been battling mini panic attacks since the party, certain he was going back on his word. The thought of having to break Veronica's heart myself was agonizing.

I tried my best to comfort her, but she was more upset than I'd seen her in a long time. *What was the big deal, anyway?* He'd only been talking to her for a short time. Veronica had had many boyfriends and Jared couldn't even be considered that, could he?

She said he was different. That she felt different with him. But I think that she really just liked the spotlight. Being with Jared Bronson meant being part of the inner circle. Veronica had been sucked inside their world. Even I knew how powerful it could be. Those few moments at Jared's house - before he turned into a scum-sucking asshole - were intoxicating. To be admired by someone who had everything made you feel valuable. It was hard not to have your head turned by someone who seemed to be unfazed by the world. Veronica had been Jared's muse - if only for a moment - and now she didn't want to go back.

I felt it a few weeks after their "break-up."
Veronica and I were supposed to go Valentine's Day
shopping together. We'd decided to buy t-shirts that
said "I Don't Heart Valentine's Day" to wear to school
as a protest for the materialistic Love Fest that usually
accompanied the holiday at Westlake. It was like some
kind of sick competition. Every guy had to prove to his
girlfriend that she was the most loved in school. And
apparently- the only way to do that was to lavish
truffles, teddy bears and roses on your girl. My
favorite part was the way every admired girl's friends
would pretend to be excited while throwing dirty
looks about the gift receiver in the background. *Nice.* I
guess it was only okay to be happy for your friend if
you were the one with more flowers at the end of the
day.

Veronica and I had always made fun of the
Untouchable girls and their gifts. The way the guys
cringed as the holiday approached, knowing they'd be
judged by everyone based on one single day. But she
was different this year. Sullen.

"What about these?" I held up two pairs of socks
with skulls and cross bones. "Nothing says 'I love you'
like the symbols of death, eh?" I laughed until I realized
Veronica wasn't laughing with me. "What's wrong?
You seem down today."

She sighed. "I don't know…I guess I wish I *did* have
a valentine this year…" She looked up at me with wide
eyes. Veronica was even *dressed* down today.

Normally, she'd doll up for a shopping trip - Veronica believed there was no point spending money to look good if you didn't already feel good, but today she'd donned a ratty purple sweatshirt, grey yoga pants and a faded, Westlake baseball cap.

Desperate to cheer her up, I smiled widely, pulling her into a bear hug. "Hey - I know for a fact there are *plenty* of guys who'd absolutely *kill* to have a date with you. Why not give someone new a try?" I leaned back to look at her face, "I hear Trenton Styx is free. I guess he and Liz broke up recently." I wiggled my eyebrows at her.

She smiled the tiniest smile. "It's not that, Andie. I could check out other guys, but when I said I wish I had a valentine, well…" Veronica squirmed a little, "I guess I meant a particular valentine…a particular someone…I already have in mind." Her sheepish grin could only mean one thing. It wasn't like Veronica to be secretive about a guy unless…

"V!" I spoke sharply. Realizing I'd raised my voice, I glanced over my shoulder before continuing, "This isn't about Jared again, is it? I thought you were moving on."

Veronica's eyes glistened, misty with regret. "I can't help it. I can't stop thinking about how I felt when I was with him. Like flying or something. So fizzy, tingly, you know?"

Sadly, I did know. But I pushed those thoughts away. I'd made a deal with the devil and I wasn't going back on my end of the bargain now. I just had to keep Veronica away from him.

"Look," I softened my voice, "I know that you really liked him, but it seems like he's moved on. I saw him with some sophomore the other day, holding hands by his locker. If he was still interested, would he be getting close to someone else?"

She leaned onto the edge of the sales rack, idly plucking the edges of a wool skirt. "I know you're right, Andie. It's just…I don't feel the same about school after being with Jared. He opened my eyes to this whole other Westlake." She bit her lip. "And I liked it."

Waves of disappointment pulled me under. This wasn't the Veronica I loved. The girl I loved was so much stronger. She didn't need guys to make her feel confident. Dating was an exciting pastime, not self-affirmation. Veronica had never needed to be popular to feel good about herself, but now things seemed different.

Veronica continued, "Maybe I've just been thinking about things more. About ways to get involved at school to make a bigger splash, ya know?" Her face brightened the way it always did when she was about to embark on an adventure.

Okay. This sounded more like Veronica. "What kind of things?"

"Just…something big. Something that says 'Here we are'. I'm tired of sitting in the background. I saw things from the other side, and maybe I just don't wanna go back." Veronica set her jaw and looked me straight in the eyes. "It's good over there, Andie. People look up when you walk into the room. People make way for you. They listen. Really listen when you talk. And it just sucks to return to…" She waved a hand over the racks of clothes, "this."

That stung. Did she include me in the ways she was now disappointed? I couldn't deal with that. Not after all I'd done to protect her: keeping my mouth shut, enduring the smug looks from Jared in the halls. It was bad enough the way those guys ruled the school. To see them getting away with treating girls this way was disgusting.

"Oh." I dropped my eyes to the floor, rubbing one foot against a corner of navy and gray specked tile. What was I supposed to say to this?

Veronica leaned closer, squeezing my arm. "Not you, babe- you're the cheese to my baked potato," she whispered playfully.

"The whipped cream to your pumpkin pie?" I volunteered.

"Oh, definitely. The salt to my fries, chica." She grinned and swung her arm around my shoulders. "I want you to see it too, Andie. It's fun being on top. Really fun. And how hard can it be, anyway? It's just all about perception." Veronica broke away to look at a satin tank top, humming as she walked.

It was good to see her hopeful again, even if the idea was a little crazy. How were we- I guess I was in this now- going to become part of the elite? I wasn't coming into a small fortune anytime soon and money was the great equalizer at Westlake. Honestly, I didn't care all that much about who knew me and who didn't. It'd be nice to see the Jensen Bell's of the world take a step down, but was it really worth more heartache? Shivering as I thought about that horrid deal I'd made with Jared, I followed Veronica across the store. I'd help her again, of course, but at what cost this time?

Eight.

A few days later, I caught a glimpse of what Veronica was talking about. Suddenly she'd taken interest in two of Westlake's elite clubs: Debate Team and Student Council. Great. She wasn't starting slow. These were the two groups most coveted by the Untouchables because they were most likely to get noticed by the Ivy League and, of course, concerned two of their favorite topics: politics and power. It was pretty much guaranteed that if you elected to Student Council, you were also accepted to the Debate Team. Campaign speeches for the 'regular' students were a joke. When you're going up against a team of professional speakers, it's hard to really get anyone else to listen. So I guess Veronica had set her sights on the top. Literally.

"Wait--- you're running for President?" I watched her pick up the application form and almost choked. "Wouldn't it be better to start with something a little smaller? Like maybe Senior Representative?" I couldn't imagine this being a successful campaign.

"Andie," Veronica turned to face me, a confident smile on her face, "go broke or go home, right? This'll be great. I've already got the endorsement of your peeps at *The Howl*." Veronica knew how much I loved writing for our school newspaper. "That counts as the popular vote, doesn't it?" She smirked at her joke.

"Ha ha." I paused, wondering how to broach this delicately. "I just don't want you to get your hopes up and then..." I hated to say it aloud.

"And lose? Well, well. Not the best attitude from my campaign manager is it? Maybe I should find someone else to run things for me. Someone who actually believes in me." Veronica pushed out her lower lip in a gigantic fake pout.

"Okay. Okay. I'm in, but no crying if things don't work out, 'kay? I've run out of Kleenexes for you on Jared Bronson." I stared pointedly at her, hoping that she wasn't doing this in some lame attempt to get him back.

Veronica flipped her hair over her shoulder and looked me straight in the eye. "Jared's old news, Andie. Way old news," she rolled her eyes for effect.

I wasn't so sure. But I was hoping so badly that she was right, that things would go back to normal now, at least in regard to V's usual style. This campaign was more ambitious than she'd ever endeavored, but I was her best friend, and unconditional support, that's what BF's are known for.

The next few weeks flew by, but I could feel something brewing. Lately, I'd noticed Jared and his close friends, Hamilton and Brad, whispering a lot more whenever Veronica was around. They were planning some evil deed- I could just smell it. And I wondered if it was because they were nervous. Veronica had rallied a lot of support from the girls at Westlake. She was the first female student to ever run for student council. Auditions for the debate team had been a disaster, though. Veronica was articulate and fresh. She stood up for the feminist issues that she knew and loved. Problem: that didn't sit well with the Untouchables or their parents. No one wanted an investigation of the long-held traditions less than Westlake alums.

I'd overhead Mrs. Kingsbury talking to Dean Brauer at the last basketball game and it didn't sound good. It wasn't my usual gig- covering an athletic event for *The Howl*- but Jesse had the stomach flu, so I was just a fill-in. Bored watching the two teams pass the ball back 'n forth in a penalty-less period, I'd wandered out into the hallway for a soda. Glimpsing Brauer and Mrs. Kingsbury, I couldn't resist eavesdropping.

"She's a menace, Nathaniel." No one ever called Brauer by his first name. I was shocked to hear him addressed so casually. "I know she hasn't got a chance, I mean, obviously." She swept her perfectly coiffed blonde locks over her shoulder. "But it doesn't look good. Not at all. The last thing we want is someone trying to stir things up."

Dean Brauer squirmed uncomfortably. "Evelyn…" he began, and then backtracked quickly in response to her disdainful glare, "Mrs. Kingsbury, I see your concern, but I assure you- Westlake traditions are not in danger. She's just a naïve girl, trying to win an election. She won't be successful because she doesn't have enough of a following. Nothing is at stake." He opened his arms, spreading his hands out in front of him.

Mrs. Kingsbury leaned in close. "That's just it, *Nathaniel*. Everything's at stake. Brad's going to make it to the top here, just like his brothers. And so will his friends…your other top donors, I might remind you. She may be a nobody, but she's a pesky nobody. This pot keeps getting stirred and suddenly, anybody can be a leader here. There isn't room for anyone else at the top. Do I make myself clear?"

Dean Brauer stepped back, avoiding Mrs. Kingsbury's pointed finger in his face. "Let's just remember protocol, Mrs. Kingsbury." Brauer raised his chin. "I'm not going to be threatened in my own school." He straightened his blazer, pulling at the bottom with both hands.

She laughed, stepping close again. "Nate, darling, you're so quaint sometimes. No, of course not." She lowered her voice, still smiling all the while. "That's not a threat. It's a promise." Brauer's eyes widened. She grabbed his arm tightly. "If Brad, or any of his friends, doesn't make it to the top, as many times as he tries, in as many areas as he desires…well, let's just say that I'm very, very good friends with the Board of

Trustees and suddenly, your time here at Westlake is looking *quite* short." With that, she turned on her heel and walked away, shoes clicking menacingly on the marble floor.

For a moment- the briefest possible moment- I actually felt bad for Brauer. To be held hostage by the parents of Westlake's richest kids must really make him feel inadequate. Wasn't he supposed to make and enforce the rules himself? What do parents know about running a school anyway?

Just as I was really feeling sorry for him, I remembered his words about Veronica. He'd called her 'naïve' and clearly didn't respect her as a real candidate. That had to mean something. Student council presidents worked very closely with Brauer on all social events and school policy concerns. If Brauer didn't respect Veronica at all, he must not expect to work with her. So…it really was a wash. In the beginning, I didn't actually think she had a chance, especially after she didn't make the Debate Team, but the more she campaigned, the better chance she seemed to have.

Later, when I told Veronica about the conversation I'd overheard, she just laughed. "Looks like I am making that splash, huh? Wow. So the fancy alums are all in a tizzy." She winked and danced in a circle. "Workin' my magic, aren't I?"

I had to laugh too. Maybe it wasn't that dangerous. *What could really happen?*

Nine.

Five days before the election, I found out. Veronica and I were planning her final speech, one that would be presented to the whole school at an assembly the day before elections. It was pretty good, too. Once she saw how Westlake women were responding, Veronica really took on the persona of the First Female rather than just Another Candidate. It was exciting to be around. Girls smiling in the hall, high-fiving and calling out for her to "Keep up the fight." But all the while, there were rumbles. The Untouchables, especially the guys, were definitely not happy. We were in a dirty looks epidemic with no foreseeable cure. Still, Veronica acted like she was immune.

That night, Veronica called me, but I could barely make out her voice on the other end of the line. Just sniffles and choked breath. For a moment, I thought it was a prank call, that someone had snatched her phone.

"V? Is that you?"

I got a snort in return.

"Veronica? What's wrong?" Worried, I pressed the phone closer to my ear, searching for any signs of life.

Sigh. Okay, at least a sigh was some sign of life. It was followed by one deep, ragged breath. "Hey…"

Oooh. Not good at all. And not like Veronica to be so quiet. Usually, I had to work hard to squeeze in just a word or two when she was upset. Veronica was never really the type to clam up. She never *im*ploded; she *ex*ploded. To hear her voice so tinny was unnerving. I was typically the one to keep things inside. This role reversal was killing me.

"Hey back." I blanked for things to say. This was new territory, so I just waited.

"I'm dropping out of the campaign." Veronica's voice was flat.

"What?! But…" I stopped myself. If she was dropping out, something serious had to be happening. And the last thing she needed was for me to freak out too. In a calmer voice, "I guess I'm just surprised." Pause. "It seemed like things were going well?" I could hear the question in my voice as I flashed back to dirty looks in the hallway and the heated talk between Brauer and Mrs. Kingsbury.

I heard a honk as she blew her nose. Then a sniffle. "Not exactly. Just, uh, not what I want to do right now. Just wanted you to know."

"Can I come over? We can curl up on the couch and watch reruns of *Ally McBeal?*" We had both become obsessed with the crazy, hair-brained attorneys on that show after binge-watching the series on NetFlix one lazy summer. Usually, just mentioning the show was a guaranteed laugh.

Veronica was quiet for a moment. "No. I've got homework to do." She paused, "It's not a big deal, Andie." Veronica's voice had gained strength but also a harsh edge. "Wasn't this some kind of game, anyway? Just to see if we could get everyone's attention?" She laughed bitterly. "And we did. So end of story."

"A game?" Confusion lined my voice. "I know this meant more to you than that, V...but if it's what you want, then, I support you." *What was she talking about?* Veronica didn't play games and she certainly didn't quit. Something else was behind her sudden exit, but for some reason, she didn't want to tell me. And I couldn't push. Not now. Not when she was sounding so bitter and so broken.

She cleared her throat. "Okay...I'm going to go now. Got a history paper. 'Bye." Before I could even respond, Veronica had hung up the phone.

I stared at the receiver. Dial tone buzzing loudly. *What just happened?*

Ten.

The next day at school, Veronica avoided me. Every time I caught her in the hallway, she told me she had to rush to class or some appointment. I knew that she couldn't really be meeting her counselor or dean that many times, but I went along with her charade anyway. If Veronica wanted space, I'd give it to her. At least for a little while. Sooner or later, she *had* to talk to me.

But the stares were driving me crazy. Jared and his boys had reverted to smirks in the hall. Every bone in my body knew that they were responsible for V's withdrawal. I just couldn't prove it. Not without hearing from her first. But it made seeing them unbearable. I imagined a million different ways to rip the smirks off their faces. Most of which included a sharp knee to the testicles. Screw 'em. I was so angry I could hardly see straight. They had nearly destroyed me before, but now, now this was about my best friend. I could feel a storm on the horizon.

Still, there wasn't anything I could do until Veronica started talking. So, I really only had one option: corner her until I found out the truth.

I had my opportunity the next night. Before she'd bowed out, Veronica and I had planned to meet at her house to go over her speech one last time. I knew that she wouldn't have any other plans, so this was the perfect moment of ambush. I hated thinking of it that way, but Veronica had been avoiding me so fiercely, I had begun to think of things in aggressive terms myself.

Pulling into her driveway, I searched for a light on in her bedroom. Dark. Deciding to take my chances that someone was home, I rang her doorbell. Her sister Margaret answered the door, confusion on her face.

"Veronica's not feeling well. Didn't she tell you?" I could see that she had no idea Veronica and I hadn't been talking much these days. So V wasn't sharing with her family either? Usually, Margaret was our annoying tag-a-long during the summer. Three years younger than Veronica, Margaret made it her mission to be involved with everything that involved being "grown-up". When I first met V, that had been completely obnoxious, but now that we were all in high school, it really wasn't that bad. At least for me. V still complained sometimes. I wished that I had siblings, though. Being the only one for your parents to focus all of their hyper-attentive energy on was exhausting.

"Yeah…" I fumbled to come up with an excuse. "She just asked me to bring something by for one of her classes. A History paper, I think?" I crossed my fingers that the paper hadn't been a lie and that maybe, just maybe, she'd shared that with her sister.

"Oh." Margaret opened the door wider. "I think she was working on something last night. I don't know," Margaret rolled her eyes, "she keeps to herself sometimes. Like I really care what she does online." Margaret seemed more than annoyed by her sister's secrecy.

I mumbled something in response, and then bolted up the stairs. By now, I'd grown crazy thinking about what might have happened to push Veronica away from the campaign. Had they threatened her? Offered something better in return? I groaned, hoping that getting back together with Jared wasn't part of the deal. She had better standards than that, didn't she?

Veronica's room was almost completely dark. All I could see was the faint glow of the television through the crack in her door. Pushing it open, I saw Veronica curled up on the bed, her entire frame wrapped tightly around a body pillow.

"Veronica…" I whispered, hesitant to wake her. But she wasn't asleep.

She turned immediately, and then moved her vision back to the TV. No words.

I walked over to the bed and plopped down next to her, pulling the comforter up to my chin. "Did you know- you're the peanut butter to my jelly?" I leaned over to brush a strand of hair away from her face.

She didn't answer, but moved her hand up toward mine, grasping it firmly. I watched her feet draw imaginary circles beneath the pile of blankets.

"And the cherry to my Coke?" I continued, waiting for her to respond. Her feet stopped moving. Like she was thinking. "But most importantly…" I paused for dramatic effect, "The thong to my leopard mini."

She cracked the tiniest smile and I knew I was in. "The chicken cutlets to my push-up…" Her smile widened just a little.

Just as I was about to continue, she whispered. "The pasties to your nips?"

I snickered, "Now *that's* a new one. Didn't know you were into that." I swatted at her arm.

Her smile faded. "Bet that's not all you didn't know I was into." Veronica turned away again, cradling the pillow tighter.

"Hey, V. I'm your best friend. You can tell me anything." I leaned over to catch her eye. "And I'll support you. Anything," I emphasized, squeezing her arm.

She raised herself up on one elbow and turned to look at me. "Anything? Big promises." Veronica threw off the blanket and walked across the room. "I think differently of me, so why wouldn't you too?" She sighed, running a hand nervously through her unkempt hair.

I stayed quiet. She was right on the edge of breaking this whole thing open.

"You want to know why I dropped out of the race. Why I decided to quit right before the end. And the truth is...telling people about that is the whole reason I stepped away. This deal I've got, this *situation* has me cornered. Because if I explain why I wanted to stop, I've played right into their hands. And I can't afford to lose my dignity too." Veronica sat down heavily on her desk chair, slowly swiveling back and forth.

I moved closer to her. "If you don't want to share this with everyone, fine. But at least tell me. It's *killing* me not to be close to you right now. And if someone's hurting you...point me in that direction, because they're going to pay." I brought my hand down on the desk hard, shaking the can of pencils on the second shelf.

Veronica laughed. "What are you going to do, Andie? Confront them?" She shook her head. "They'd just get off on that. They're in control, Andie. They've always been in control. And it was laughable for me to think I could change that. At all." She picked up a book and started idly flipping the pages. Anything to avoid my eyes.

"Who's 'they' here? Are we talking about Brad and his pathetic followers? Jared too?" I started pacing, feeling my body heat with anger.

Veronica shrugged. "If only...I could probably deal with those assholes myself, but it's not just them, Andie." She leaned in close to me. "It's everyone. Half the school. Their parents. The deans...We're totally overrun at Westlake. I thought I understood the power dynamics. It was the rich kids and then the rest of us. The kids who grew up with silver spoons and the kids who occasionally used plastic. But I was wrong. So wrong. This is way bigger than that. This is about an entire community. Setting the stage for their precious little spawn to take over the world. And let me tell you- they don't just hate to lose...they *don't* lose, Andie." Her eyes were wide and wild.

I felt my heart quicken. Veronica looked pale. She was breathing fast now and I watched her get up from her chair to move around the room.

"V, you're scaring me. Tell me what's wrong." I walked toward her, arms outstretched, begging her to meet my eyes.

"No." She crossed her arms and shook her head vigorously. "I'm not going to drag you into this too." She looked at me, intensity in her eyes. "No."

I sighed. Frustrated. Angry. I didn't know where to direct my anger. Everything in me wanted to embrace her, but the way she was keeping me out...it hurt. I thought she had more faith in me than that. What was I supposed to do now?

"Is it official, then?" I walked back toward her bed, sitting down carefully. "The race? Did you tell Brauer that you're not running anymore?"

Veronica laughed bitterly. "I hardly had to tell him...he already knew it was taken care of. The moment I walked in his office...I could see it in the smug expression plastered on his face." She leaned forward. "He's in this too, Andie. All the ways you imagined him to be an asshole, just magnify it by a thousand. He's *unbelievable*."

I felt nauseous. This sounded much more dirty than I'd imagined. Whatever was going on, I feared that it would turn my world upside down. But the anxiety I felt couldn't compare to the need I felt to know more. Whatever it was, I just wanted to keep her talking. If Veronica kept letting pieces slip out, eventually I'd have the whole story.

"If Brauer's involved, the parents must be too...does this have anything to do with the conversation I overheard between Brauer and Mrs. Kingsbury?"

Veronica looked startled. "I'd forgotten about that. Yeah..." She looked down, picking at her deep purple glossed fingernails. Veronica shifted in her chair. "They didn't want me to run...you knew that I guess...but I didn't know how badly. Until," She paused, biting her lip, holding back.

"Until..." I looked at her. She stared blankly back.

"Until Jared called." Looking relieved that she'd finally shared, Veronica leaned her head back against the pale blue walls.

So this *was* about Jared! Feeling annoyed, I hoped that Veronica hadn't given up the election just to get back together with that arrogant bastard. But...I hadn't seen them in the halls at all. In fact, Jared had been stuck like glue to a new girl in school, some girl with a weird name...Sienna, or something.

"What did *he* want?" I challenged, instantly regretting my tone.

Veronica squirmed some more. "That's the part I can't say, Andie. It's too...it's mortifying, okay? And I can't help it if I don't want my best friend to know something so awful about me." She looked up at me with pleading eyes. "I just want you to see me as the strong one, someone who wouldn't be so...stupid."

I tried to laugh, hoping to break the tension. "The smart girl? Oh, V, you know you stopped caring about that a long time ago." I chuckled again, half-heartedly, but she didn't break a smile at all. "Okay, sorry. Bad time for a joke. But seriously, I *do* think you're amazing." A tear glistened in her eye. "Even if you made a mistake. Even if it's a big one. Hey--"I dropped down to the floor, kneeling in front of her. "I've made plenty of mistakes. And what kind of friendship do we have, anyway, if we can't believe in each other? Love each other for the *real* people we are?"

She began to cry. Softly at first, but then the tears rained down more heavily. I held her as her shoulders shook, feeling my t-shirt soak with the force of her sorrow. All I wanted was to erase this feeling. To make her smile again.

Soon, her sobbing slowed. She began drawing in deep breaths, steadying herself. Veronica pulled away, wiping her face on a t-shirt she picked up off the floor.

"I'm just not ready yet, Andie." Veronica spoke softly.
"I'll tell you, but not tonight. Just not tonight."
Resolved, she lifted her chin, waiting for my response.

Really? Here we were, completely vulnerable, just
the two of us, and she still couldn't tell me. What had
happened?

I stretched my legs out in front of me, preparing to
stand. Suddenly exhausted. All of the worry I'd been
holding in all day oozed out of me. Not that I still
wasn't worried, I just knew that I couldn't ease that
anxiety today. Veronica was in pain, but she was still
holding back. I needed to get home, to escape for a
moment. I knew this wasn't about me, but I felt hurt
anyway. I'd laid it on the line, asking for Veronica's
trust. If she couldn't do that, how much did she really
value our friendship?

"You're going, aren't you?" Veronica asked, even
before I had a chance to say it.

"Yeah…it seems right." I looked at her. "I'm really
sorry, V, whatever this is." I hugged her again before
standing up.

"I know you are," She paused, "and I will tell you.
Honest. Just give me time, 'kay?" Veronica wouldn't
look me in the eyes. It was hard to believe her this
way. She'd never kept secrets before, at least not that I
was aware of. Right now she had me questioning how
much I really knew her. I couldn't imagine anything
awful enough not to tell me. If she had some kind of

skeleton, what would that be? My mind spun with the idea.

I shook my head, clearing it all away. "'Course you will, V. We're best friends, right?" I looked her in the eyes, testing.

She smiled, but something about it didn't feel right. "Yeah, Andie. We are." Veronica walked to the door, opening it for me. She reached over to give me a half-hug. "Careful going home, 'kay?" I could smell the sweat in her hair and I wondered how long it'd been since she showered. Veronica was usually meticulous about her appearance, but lately...

All the way home I thought about our conversation, looking for clues. The way she'd talked so intensely about the Untouchables and their parents. The way she'd included Dean Brauer in the mix. *What could they have on her?* I pondered everything. Grades. Scholarships. College admission. Everything I thought they could control somehow. Had she cheated on a test? Maybe, but that was so unlike her. Veronica was freakishly smart, mostly because she had a photographic memory that I'd envied forever. She didn't need to cheat. Scholarships, maybe. Maybe the "awful thing" was some kind of bribe. Did Veronica take a deal? Agree to bow out if they got her into the school she wanted? Maybe...but that'd be the kind of thing she'd laugh about with me. To prove that she'd got one over on them. No, if she couldn't tell me, it had to be something I'd hate. Didn't she say she'd changed? That she didn't want me to look at her differently?

Jared! I swerved the car as his name flashed into my mind. Returning to the night of the party, I thought about the way he'd been using Veronica. I'd kept it a secret- did that mean I was just as bad? At the time, I'd thought I was protecting her, but was I really? Veronica had mentioned his name, saying that his phone call had changed everything. Maybe he told her about coming onto me that night?

No…that didn't make sense. How would Dean Brauer be involved in that? There's *no way* Jared would do anything to make himself look bad…that was the whole *point* of him blackmailing me.

It didn't add up. Jared was involved, but how? I racked my brain all the way home, but when I pulled up in my driveway, I still had no answers. Lying in my bed, I tossed and turned, reliving every moment from the past several weeks. Every time I thought about Jared and what he was capable of, my mind raced back to the night of the Brenton after-party. To the way he'd tricked me. To the way he'd touched…I shivered, reluctant to return to that moment, but I couldn't stop the images worming their way into my consciousness. No longer able to sleep, I crossed the plush, cream carpet in my bedroom, sliding into the armchair near the bay window toward the front of the house. It was too cold to open a window, so I rested my cheek against the window pane, staring up at the moon, the stars…

"No!" Jumping up, I backed away from the window, remembering the smell of Jared's cologne as he sat so close, holding the telescope. Remembering his frantic kisses on my lips, my neck, hands sliding down my chest. My stomach lurched, and I ran into the bathroom, dropping down on my knees, retching into the toilet. Spent, I slid down onto the cool, white tile, full of such regret. How could I have ever kept this from Veronica? How could I let her *date* him? It wasn't like I didn't know…even before that night…what he was capable of. But stepping into the foyer of his house-that way he had of seeming so…vulnerable. It started when I let myself feel sorry for him again. I should have trusted my instincts, but I'd been thrown off course by Jared since the moment we met. Since the moments *before* we met, back when he seemed so harmless, so lost, so lonely. I never should have trusted Jared freshman year, but I'd wanted so badly to save him.

Eleven.

I dwell in Possibility —
A fairer House than Prose —
More numerous of Windows —
Superior — for Doors —

-Emily Dickinson

November. Freshmen Year.

Veronica's emerald eyes widened as her melodic voice rose and fell with precision. "Did you hear that she fell asleep *right* in the middle of the *exam?*"

"Really?" I mumbled distractedly. I could only half listen to her chatter. Normally, I'd be hyper-focused on my best friend, ready to laugh at the endless stream of anecdotes about our classmates' idiosyncrasies, or in this case, the epic downfalls of the adults in our lives.

"Yeah- Mrs. Lamberto of all people." Veronica paused to pull three sections of her flaxen hair into the beginnings of a simple braid. "I mean she practically strangled Eduardo Jimenez last week when he *sneezed* during the *Diary of Anne Frank* essay." Veronica leaned in conspiratorially, "I swear she mumbled something about the Fuhrer...not that Eduardo isn't devilish in his own ways."

Veronica winked, prompting me to groan as I momentarily tuned back in. Veronica had a habit of falling in love *at least* once per month, each time more dramatic and heartbreaking than the last. I couldn't understand it. From what I could see, high school was just a breeding ground for stupidity; hormones were the drug *du jour*; and every boy reminded me of a greasy, underdone, dive bar burger: appealing when you're really hungry but guaranteed to make you violently ill.

Every boy, that is, except Jared Bronson. I know how hypocritical that sounds, to dismiss all 9th grade boys as somehow *less than* and then tout the details of this new guy, but something seemed different about Jared. He was confident, that I could tell, but he also seemed a bit wounded. At least in the eight days I'd known him, which I realize, was a mere blip in the radar of life. Regardless, it was curiosity about Jared that had me sidetracked right now, barely listening to Veronica rail on about how her classmates had constructed a paper airplane landing strip atop Lamberto's sleeping form.

Instead, I watched Jared cross the library, pausing to ask Mr. Alysium, the charmingly awkward school librarian, a question. I fantasized for a moment about their conversation, about how he might be searching for a particular read. In my runaway thoughts, he was a Hemingway fan, someone who loved the understated simplicity of Ernest, someone who could relate to the hero's masculinity, someone who believed in loving deeply, passionately in the most unassuming manner. Someone who would grab me tightly, kiss me hard on the mouth, and not apologize for it.

The likelihood of this was slim.

Still...I was intrigued by Jared Bronson. When he'd arrived at Westlake last Monday, I'd watched him slide gracefully out of the passenger door of a silver BMW, a pained expression on his face as he argued with the female driver. Distracted, he'd stumbled once while walking the perimeter of the stone-lined circular drive, something that seemed to surprise him as he hardly took a moment to appear embarrassed, just kept surging forward. I'd watched him from my vantage point, a sunken spot of grass beneath the weathered willow tree flanking Door 12 - a mostly solitary spot since it only led to the maintenance corridor.

Something about that walk, and the slate-grayness of his frown, made me sympathetic. The careless tousle of his hair, the storminess behind his gaze spoke of worries far beyond the typical storyline of wealth, power, and entitlement so carefully carved into the walls of Westlake Academy. Maybe there was more to Jared's story.

So here I was, murmuring tiny affirmatives to appease Veronica, while simultaneously sneaking peeks at him from a carrel nearby. It was a rare opportunity because Jared and I shared only one class: Freshmen

Literature. It was one of the few classes I didn't share with Veronica. Normally, I'd be ecstatic to work with my best friend, but she could read me so well, and I couldn't risk even a hint of intrigue- Veronica would find a way to intervene in the most aggressive, yet endearingly persistent, way. Besides, Jared Bronson could just as easily be a narcissistic social-climber like everyone else around here. I wasn't interested in wasting emotional energy on that. At all.

Walking toward the stacks, Jared paused to read a posting on the Do-or-Socially Die Westlake calendar bulletin board. Mostly, the linen-lined, mahogany-framed board was papered with Student Council propaganda, but it shared a generous one-eighth space with club bids and community groups. Jared's pale blue eyes zeroed in on the bottom left corner of the board, then darted quickly away. Glancing warily around the library, Jared's gaze suddenly met mine. My eyes, which were embarrassingly locked on the contours of his broad shoulders, admiring the way his fitted, navy, Kenneth Cole t-shirt hugged the definition of his arms. Mortified, I tucked my head, picking at the fraying threads of my cowl-necked indigo sweater. In the background, I could hear the lilting cadence of Veronica's chatter. Silently, I counted to fifteen, praying that when I looked up again, Jared would be gone.

Not standing right in front of me.

"Is Bertrand Hall in the Bertrand Wing?" Jared, who was now close enough for me to drink in sips of citrus and sandalwood, was furrowing his brow in the most maddeningly adorable way. As I struggled to regain my composure, I must have paused a moment or two too long. His eyes shifted quickly from concern to annoyance. "Do you know or not?" he barked, leaning down to wave his hand in front of my eyes.

I could feel my face warming, tiny prickles singeing my cheeks, rising quickly from my jawline to the corners of my lips in a frenzied dance. "Listen, *you* walked over---

"---at the perfect time." Veronica's voice seamlessly sliced through mine, the cleanest whisper of shears through silk. Balancing delicately on the tips of her toes, she reached across the honey blonde wood of our study table to nudge my arm. "Andie here was just about to make her way to Bertrand Hall." Turning to stare meaningfully at me, "Don't you have a meeting with Ms. Sheraton?" Barely missing a beat, she purred, "I'm Veronica, by the way, but Andie's the one with all the answers. And I really have to be on my way." And just like that, she was gone, blonde braid sashaying against her back as she hummed "Dream a Little Dream".

Staring glumly at an imaginary point of interest, Jared shifted his charcoal Herschel Supply Co. backpack more securely on his right shoulder. Silently.

"So...I guess I'm going to Bertrand Hall," I muttered, stuffing my red Meade idea book inside the front pocket of my khaki canvas bag.

I walked quickly toward the library doors, then through the crowded halls of Westlake, weaving the slightest of paths for Jared, glancing only once to see that he was still behind me. Bertrand Hall was *not* in the Bertrand Wing. The benefactor, Arnold Bertrand III, was one of those donors who had always been ostentatiously generous. Tragically disappointed when his first donation, a research laboratory, was surpassed in prestige by Thomas Wittier's state-of-the-art STEM lab. Quickly, Arnold offered a second donation, which led to Westlake's third and smallest auditorium, Bertrand Meeting Hall, casually known as The Meet, mostly due to the constant parade of Timberwolves' meetings held there each week. As the donor wars continued, so did Westlake's stamping of Bertrand's name. To date, Westlake housed Bertrand Lab, Bertrand Hall, Bertrand Wing, Bertrand Sky View (atrium skylight), and Bertrand Knoll- the nicknames for *that* grassy spot of heaven fall somewhere in the seedy range due to its seclusion and ever popular make-out status.

So I wasn't surprised that Jared would be confused about Bertrand Hall, but I *was* a little curious about how someone who seemed so nervous and standoffish would be hanging out in one of the most social spots at Westlake. By now, I'd turned the corner directly in front of the large, mahogany doors. I felt relieved that my obligatory errand was over; the last thing I wanted to do was spend more time feeling mortified about my fantasies when the reality was far less romantic.

"Yeah, so here it is." I heard the sharpness of my voice and winced a little as I turned my back to leave. I felt bad because he was new, and I knew how hard it could be to be the new kid. For me, that moment arrived September of my sixth grade year. Dad had just taken a job teaching at Brookhaven College, so we upended our life to move to here. According to my dad, education was the most vital source of life, rivaling only food and air. So, rather than bask in the sunshine, or at the very least, devour a stack of fiction, I spent the summer before sixth grade writing admissions essays to every halfway decent private school in a 30-mile radius of Brookhaven College. Luckily, Fischer School of Excellence not only accepted me, but offered a scholarship, and for my parents, this was the golden ticket. We lived a comfortable life- Mom's counseling practice was thriving and Dad was that loveable, goofy professor who always managed to acquire a throng of groupies- but our bank account wasn't even in the same zip code as most of my peers at Westlake. I knew what it was like to feel like an outsider, and normally, I tried to make others feel comfortable, probably because I could hear the voice of my empathic mother in the background. But, this time, embarrassment was pulling the strings.

"Thanks," Jared paused, opening his mouth to speak, tip of his tongue clicking against the back of his front teeth, lost in some sort of internal battle. I saw that slate-grayness again, that stormy countenance that had first triggered my sympathy and felt my resolve waning. I really wasn't giving this guy much of a chance.

"Okay… 'bye," Jared blurted abruptly, halting my ride on the empathy train. He grabbed the brass handle of the heavy door, peering inside cautiously before striding through, no last glance or wave to acknowledge my favor, or even my presence. Just before the door closed behind him, a small platinum object slipped from Jared's pocket, clanging lightly on the polished, metallic kick plate before striking the floor. Peering closer, I noticed that it was not a coin, but a small medal. Only a tiny strip of red fabric remained along the top edge, clinging to a thin rod. The backside was smooth, color faded in the center; the front read, "North Conference Champs" with a tiny baseball bat embossed beneath.

If it was only a coin, I would've kept walking. But something about this medal seemed potentially significant. Sighing, I palmed the medal and opened the door to Bertrand Hall. Scanning the room, I heard members of *La Luna*, the art club, animatedly discussing their latest mural project, interrupted periodically by squeals from *The Howlers*, Westlake's theatre troupe, as they pantomimed a scene from "Go Tell It at the Starbucks". Not to be outdone, a small trio of *Moon Beams*, one of Westlake's prestigious choral ensembles, was working on an arrangement of "Ave Maria", most likely for the upcoming Winter Festival.

I didn't see Jared anywhere. Frustrated, I turned to leave when I spotted a door ajar at the back corner of the auditorium. Shaking a wayward curl out of my face, I walked purposefully toward that door, determined to return the medal and then move on with my afternoon. As I neared the small meeting room, I heard an adult female voice welcome the group, reminding them that confidentiality was integral to building trust in the group. On cue, the face of a slight brunette momentarily appeared in the doorway, pulling the door closed too quickly for me to determine whether Jared was sitting inside. The only thing I did see was a single word written on the chalk board behind the speaker: Alateen.

Twelve.

"Ok, class, let's take out our copies of *The Odyssey* and prepare to discuss." Mr. Cannon paused amid the cacophony of backpack zippers and rustling pages. "Today, I want you to reflect on how Odysseus's pride interferes with his journey home. Find a partner to begin your discussion. Together, I expect you to cite four references from the text." A tiny sea of groans swept the classroom. Mr. Cannon smiled. "Better get started- we're going to discuss this as a class in exactly twelve minutes."

I glanced over my left shoulder, looking for Priya Shah, my go-to partner for these kinds of things. Her desk was woefully empty. Turning half-way around in my chair, I scanned the room, assessing the Who's Who of partner availability. It seemed like in the short time I'd checked for Priya, everyone else had found another person to share the workload. Maybe Mr. Cannon wouldn't mind if I worked alone. No one to impress. No one to argue with. A competition-free moment at Westlake sounded like a dream.

I settled into the text, flipping through the lines, quickly hunting for the best examples of Odysseus's arrogance until I felt the heat of a stare. Lifting my eyes, I noticed Mr. Cannon awkwardly signaling with his eyebrows, directing my attention to the far right corner of the room. In the back, Jared was hunched over his desk, left hand buried deep in his chestnut hair, grasping the roots like a fraying rope, clawing dejectedly through the pages of his copy of Homer's words. I guess I wasn't the only one without a partner, which apparently, Mr. Cannon was not-so-subtly trying to rectify. Guiltily, I thought about the medal burning a hole in my backpack. I'd had it for two days now, avoiding another awkward encounter with Jared Bronson.

Sighing, I picked up my book and made my way across the cream-carpeted room. I could catch the subtle hints of sandalwood again as I neared Jared's desk. The moment my feet appeared next to the corner of his desk he jerked his head up, annoyed. "Yes?" As pretentiousness dripped from his voice, I quickly tallied a second mark in the "Typical Westlaker" category, a.k.a. "Who's Who to Never Talk To" list. Right after I return his medal.

"Mr. Cannon thought you might need some help. You look like you're drowning over here," I spoke in a voice just loud enough to arouse snickers from a few students working nearby.

To my surprise, Jared cracked a smile. He stretched his arms in front of his body, leaning across the desk. "You always tell people exactly what you think?" The cool water of his eyes focused intensely on my face, waiting for a response.

I frowned, nervously grabbing the curl closest to my face, shoving it behind my ear. "No..."

"Oh, just to me, then?" Jared laughed, simultaneously tapping his russet leather boots. I felt the corner of his shoe brush against my foot, but he didn't seem to notice.

I was out of my element.

The super-cool, ultra-witty, imaginary Me longed to plonk the medal on his desk with the perfect sharp reply, while the idealistic, compassionate, real Me began concocting scenarios of amusing repartee and the best way to make use of those perfectly toned arms.

Luckily, I didn't have to choose. Mr. Cannon announced that it was time for our group discussion, so I gladly returned to my seat, determined to return the medal to Jared after class.

Thirty minutes later, as the bell signaled the end of the period, Jared walked quickly toward the classroom door. I struggled to move through the line of students exiting, forced to call Jared's name when it looked like he would pass me by. Garnering a few quizzical looks, I squeezed through the crowded doorway to find Jared standing expectantly in the buzzing hallway.

"Were you...*paging me?*" He was amused by the flustered way I'd peeled through the masses. Mentally, I recorded another mark in the "no way" column.

"I found this on the floor. It belongs to you?" I brandished the smooth, bronze medal between us, both a weapon and a shield.

Jared's face paled immediately. "I thought…" His voice caught, laden with emotion. I watched the storm rise again, Jared's face stretched open in rolling waves. He breathed deeply, clearing his throat. "I thought I'd lost it," he whispered, pain etched into the corners of his mouth as he reached a hand toward the medal, lightly grazing my fingertips as he delicately lifted it from my grasp.

Jared's vulnerability was palpable. Muddy and thick.

"It must be very special…" I dropped my words to a whisper, matching the pillow-soft tenor of his brokenness.

Jared ran his thumb across the face of the burnished metal, rubbing the words, transcribing memories along the lines of his skin. "It belonged to my brother."

I heard the past in his words and felt lost. Jared continued haltingly, "Justin loved baseball." Long, soft lashes shaded two cerulean seas. Rubbing the medal one last time, Jared placed it carefully in the front pocket of his dark-wash jeans, pocketing his emotions as well. I could feel the moment tightening, the air stiff.

"I have Biology." Jared's voice was clipped. He pivoted, angling to continue down the hall.

I imagined how terrifying it would be, emotions exposed to a stranger. "Sure," I spoke softly. Jared started to walk away. "And listen…" He paused, cheeks slightly flushed, scuffing the corner of his boot on the carpeting. "If you, uh, have any more questions about Westlake…." I smiled, trying not to sound as awkward as I felt.

The corners of Jared's mouth slid upward just a little, but his eyes remained flat, "I'll remember that."

Thirteen.

In the weeks that followed, I learned more about Jared, but not from Jared himself. The mysterious new student was quickly becoming Westlake elite, due in large part to the Bronson wealth, but made legendary by his athletic prowess. Apparently, Jared was an unbelievable baseball player, having made a name for himself at private leagues along the East Coast. Now that he was finally in high school, the recruiters were buzzing, eager for the spring season, and Westlake administrators were passing his name around at fundraisers like champagne, lubricating the wallets of alumni and prospective parents alike.

Not long after news of Jared's baseball talent surfaced, the hotshots and cold souls fawned, eager to make him one of their own. Girls with cool smiles, boys with quick laughs.

It was *these* elite, the Untouchables, who began the sea of tiny whispers. Who donned fake smiles of empathy as they shared the sordid details of Jared's mother drinking her grief. Who pursed pouty lips, excited to air someone else's dirty laundry. Jared's mother's drinking was made more salacious by the tragedy of its inspiration: the drowning of his youngest brother, Justin, two summers ago. The two boys had been inseparable.

I felt sympathy for him. Even as Jared fraternized with the most careless, most selfish students Westlake had to offer, I understood the social survival rules. Eat or be eaten.

December had arrived, crisp snow icing the river birch, and everyone was buzzing about the Winter Festival, a tribute to the coldest season made warmer by a string of concerts and plays, capped by Westlake's biggest annual fundraiser: the dinner auction. Though the proceeds of the auction were donated to the Lakeside Food Pantry, the greatest benefactors always seemed to be Westlake students and their parents. Competing for the biggest buy or the greatest gift was a serious matter. The winner retained bragging rights until next year's Festival, or in the case of a few particularly legendary moments, forever. Memorable auction items from past years included a weekend trip to Camp David, a songwriting session with John Legend, and tickets to the World Cup, accompanied by David Beckham. Surprisingly, the expensive, exclusive items were not always the most desired. Prestige was most desired. Prestige among your peers was the greatest prize of all.

"Are your parents coming to the auction?" Veronica slowly stirred her passion fruit smoothie, dipping a pinkie finger into the creamy top layer. We were perched atop tall, metallic stools along the wall of windows inside Banana Blend, one of our favorite after-school hangouts.

I dug my spoon into a cup of pomegranate sorbet, "No, they'll be at a conference in Portland that night. Something about post-traumatic stress that my mom's excited about," rolling my eyes, "and my dad's tolerating."

Veronica sticks out her tongue, "Your parents are adorable. Stop ruining it."

I smiled. "You're right. They are pretty cute." Married for twenty-four years, my parents acted as if every day was their anniversary. It could be embarrassing to find evidence of their affection: compliments scribbled on Post-It notes in the kitchen, fresh daisies in the front hallway- my mother's favorite, or steaming cups of espresso delivered for my dad, staying up late on a midnight grading binge. Veronica was good about reminding me how lucky I am to have such a happy home; her own had its regular ups and downs, with more downs than most.

"Well, much as I love Teddy and Jane, it'll be less embarrassing when we bid…" Veronica withdrew a glossy black brochure from her teal Kate Spade knock-off, "…on all this deliciousness."

Wiping a stream of pomegranate juice from my index finger on a bright, yellow, banana-shaped napkin, I pulled the brochure closer. The words "The Date" were scrawled across the front cover in neon pink. "What's this?" I asked, mouth full of sorbet.

Veronica's eyes gleamed. "This is only the most *fun* bidding item yet." She paused, smiling mysteriously, "I *really* had to pull out all the stops to get this. Despite the fact that he's totally smitten with me," Veronica batted her lashes, tucking her chin to her shoulder playfully, "Parker Williams practically had a *panic* attack handing it over." Veronica leaned in, blonde locks swishing against my shoulder. Dropping her voice nearly to a whisper, "What we have, Andie, is an exclusive, front row seat to..."

I scooped the last bite of mini heaven from the yellow paper cup. "All right, V- out with it."

Veronica pretended to pout. "So not fun, Andie. Ok, ok...it's a front row seat to the most desirable guys at Westlake." She pronounced this last bit with a ta-da motion, but I kept waiting for the ta-da revelation.

"Really?" I couldn't keep the disappointment out of my voice. The last thing I cared to do was spend time wondering about the guys who had deemed themselves too wonderful. It's not that I didn't dream of the perfect relationship, or hell, even just a really, hot kiss- no, the reason I had a hard time getting excited about dating at Westlake was because most of the guys I'd encountered so far seemed to only care about money, themselves, money, and oh yeah, themselves. There were definitely exceptions- I'd met plenty of nice guys on *The Howl* newspaper staff- but I was a lowly freshman writer, and the smart, funny guys I fantasized about were all fairly intimidating upperclassmen. Besides, I could guarantee the boys who'd be part of this date auction were *not* going to be any of the cool writers I knew; they were much more likely to be the douchebags who only cared about their own reflection.

Irritated that I was spoiling her good mood, Veronica retorted, "*Some* of us *like* the idea of dating, which I may remind you," light punch to my shoulder, "is practically the most normal thing about high school. Or life." Veronica softened suddenly, voice like whipped cream, "A life without love is no life at all..."

Watching the hopeful face of my best friend, considering the layers of "almost" that clothed her daily, I accepted the fact that not only was I going to peruse the date catalogue she was avidly flipping through, but I was going to attend the auction and support her crazy bidding. For all her daydreaming and harebrained schemes, Veronica was the sweetest, most loyal person I'd ever known and I'd do anything for her.

Fourteen.

The night of the auction was one of those perfect, winter nights: cold enough to bundle into my favorite downy jacket, air so clean I wanted to drink it, snow neatly piled along the streets, glistening in the moonlight. Veronica arrived at my door promptly at seven, gorgeous in a camel-colored wool skirt, one-shoulder sapphire sweater, and loose curls delicately brushing the center of her back. Glancing at my simple grey pencil skirt and red Oxford button-down, I felt underdone.

Veronica bear-hugged me as we walked toward her mother's car, leaving a trail of jasmine in the air. "I'm so glad you're coming with me!" She danced a tiny pattern in the sidewalk snow blanket, winding white swirls across the edges of her knee-high leather boots. "Wouldn't want you to miss a minute of my glorious victory!"

I laughed at her giddiness, "Well don't keep me in suspense- who's the lucky date?"

"Oh, I couldn't possibly decide, so I'm letting Fate handle this one. Fate and a little spiritual guidance, of course." Veronica's face turned serious as she grasped the tiny Earth-shaped orb she wore around her neck each day. Encased in four thin platinum lines, the deep blue and green stone had become a talisman for V since she found it at the See and Séance store last year. What began as a dare- to see who could find the wackiest gift for one another- turned into a regular pilgrimage after Veronica discovered *Mother Voices: Unlocking the Truth inside the Earth*. I know that it sounds crazy, to believe in some sort of pagan intuition, but Veronica was innocent in her passion. Her heart was so incredibly open to the world, to heroes and miscreants alike, it was hard to fault her for such unconditional acceptance. Veronica wasn't stupid- she'd risen to the top ten percent of our class easily- but so many of our peers missed that- choosing only to see her beauty or eccentricity. These were the reasons I hoped a night like tonight would fall in her favor. Whatever "spirits" might exist, I needed them to work their magic.

When we arrived at Westlake, the circular drive was full of quietly humming limousines, whisking guests in and out of the night. Valets in crisp white shirts shivered in the chilled air, tapping their feet to keep warm as they waited for the line of luxury vehicles to diminish. Veronica's mother, Maggie, sighed softly as she pulled into the drive, no doubt noting the excessive display of wealth. She must have been used to that life, once upon a time, with a father who worked for Halliburton and a mother who lobbied in Washington. But Maggie had chosen a different path. Four years in the Peace Corps, followed by a job as a social worker for the Veteran's Affairs Office was incredibly fulfilling, but not nearly lucrative enough to warrant a spot at Birchfield Prep, the feeder school for Westlake. No, it was Maggie's parents who'd insisted on the private schooling, pressing so hard Maggie had little room to protest. It's hard to say no to a gift like that for your child.

"Thanks, Mom. Love ya," Veronica leaned forward, lightly kissing her mother on the cheek, and then we were swirling among the masses, surging toward the front entrance of Keller Hall. Inside, tiny white lights were strung across the ceiling in a web of stars; white orchids lined the soft gray walls, irises flourished in iridescent towers at the center of each table, and the sounds of a single violin floated in the air.

"Wow." I couldn't help myself. "It doesn't even seem like the same place."

Veronica grabbed my hand, "C'mon. Let's find our seats. I want to see who's here."

After checking in at the hostess table, we were ushered to a spot just left of center, prime viewing for the auction items onstage. Veronica's grandparents had purchased the seats, so we were spared the indignity of the tables in the back. At least that's how Veronica explained it. I didn't care where we sat, but I had to admit, the ambiance was beautiful.

"Hey, V, are you thirsty?" I watched her gaze circle the room. "I'm going to see what they've got." Servers in tuxedos were patiently attending to the crowd in the foyer, trays of champagne flutes and smooth, pink cocktail glasses floating in and out my vision like fireflies at dusk.

"Hmmm?" Veronica murmured over her shoulder, lost in thought.

Shaking my head, "Be back, 'kay?" I smoothed my skirt as I stood, suddenly self-conscious. Walking with Veronica, I rarely thought about myself. Now, I could sense the tiny wobble of my feet in unfamiliar heels, the way this skirt hugged my backside, and the slight dampness of the curls along my face, glistening from the warmth in the room. I took a breath, and walked determinedly toward the nearest server, ready to snatch a glass from the tray balanced on his arm. Just as my fingers grazed the edge of the tray, a diamond-laden hand swept in front of me, clutching an empty champagne flute, nearly knocking into me.

She was both beautiful and overdone. Violet eyes overshadowed by thick black lashes. Full lips smeared with lipstick the color of fire. Long, fitted dress, plunging at the neckline. Escorted by Jared Bronson.

He hadn't noticed me yet, every atom of his body attuned to the woman at his side. "Jared, baby, get me another, will you? I've got to find Coach Williams..." The edges of her words sloshed together, pitching fore and aft as the sail of her arm threatened to sink the both of them.

"Mother—"Jared's voice was an iceberg, nearly submerged. With a quick twist of his wrist, he steadied her sail.

"Your off-season training is *not* what we've come to expect and I intend to rectify that." Despite the slur of her words, intensity carried her voice. "Immediately." This was a woman who always got what she wanted. Before Jared could say another word, she was gone, working her way through the crowd, nodding and smiling.

Jared turned his gaze away from his mother and his eyes met mine, pupils wide with embarrassment. I couldn't think of anything to say.

A switch flipped inside Jared's eyes and he was cool again. "Ready to bid?" Jared directed his question to me, but I noticed how his eyes were planted over my shoulder.

I felt more out of place than I had walking the room. "I'm here with Veronica Linwood. She's the one---"

Jared cut me off, "-I know who she is." Then softer, "We have a class together."

"Oh." Clearly, any moment we'd had in the hallway outside English was long gone.

Jared stepped close. So close I could see the quick rise and fall of his chest through the Armani suit jacket that he wore so seductively it could've been a towel for the flight my imagination was taking. "She's not always like this."

"Veronica?"

Surprised annoyance ran wild across his face, "My *mother.*"

"Oh." Apparently my vocabulary had been reduced to single words. *Why was I letting this guy get to me?* Yes, he was attractive, but he wasn't the most gorgeous specimen in the world, and he certainly wasn't the nicest. Something about Jared distracted me in a way I wished I could ignore.

He seemed eager to talk, nervous even. "She wants my life to be perfect. It's her way of trying to make up..." The words he didn't say were blaring in my ears. Jared's eyes fluttered. Was he blinking back *tears?* The icy way he turned his emotions on and off was dizzying. Then, soft as a whisper, "It's exhausting. I'm never going to be..."

Him. If the words Jared didn't say were horns, this was an air raid siren. His face was a kaleidoscope, fragments of emotion pixelating across strong jaw, narrow nose, ocean eyes. Silently, I watched the moment crystallize, not sure how to react.

The ocean stilled as Jared locked his gaze with someone behind me. Turning, I saw Brad Kingsbury, resident asshole, with a legion of his cronies. They were laughing openly, making faces. It wasn't hard to figure out that talking to me was part of their joke. Jared smirked and slid his fingers across his forehead in a mock salute. Turning back to me, he mumbled something that sounded like "Sorry" before grabbing a drink and walking away.

This guy was a head trip. Cold, yet vulnerable. Eyes full of waging battles. He was so messy I couldn't decide if I wanted to pretend we'd never met or save him from the depths.

"Andie!" Veronica materialized out of nowhere, grabbing my arm. "They're going to start. Come back to the table." She was buzzing, making it nearly impossible not to smile.

"All right," I laughed, "But can you release the death grip?" She untangled her fingers, playfully slapping my shoulder in response.

"Well, move it then, *mon ami*. I don't want to miss a thing." Veronica winked, tossing her hair over shoulder as she sashayed across the room. *What a little diva.*

The first dozen auction items were traditionally luxurious, and totally boring. I stifled a yawn and snuck a look at the time on my phone. At least one more hour until dinner- I didn't know if I was going to make it. Looking around the room, I could see that I wasn't the only one getting a little stir-crazy. The emcee must have sensed the antsy mood of the audience, so he tried adding humor with his item descriptions, but no one was biting. Not in this crowd.

Suddenly, Veronica sat up straighter in her chair, clutching the clandestine date brochure beneath the white, linen tablecloth. Ushers were passing out copies of the very same glossy black booklet. "It's time," she whispered gleefully, placing her pocketbook on the table.

"Great," I murmured, wondering how many of my least favorite people would be strutting the stage. I could've looked inside *The Date*, my own copy in hand, but my only intention now was to minimize the damage Veronica might cause if left completely to her own devices. The only saving grace was that she couldn't compete with the wealth in the room.

V leaned in close, squeezing my hand with excitement, "Grandma gave me a delicious wad of cash to spend tonight." I tried to smile, but I could only manage a half-grimace. Veronica frowned instantly, "Andie, live a little. And stop trying to mother me. I'm a big girl." She straightened in her chair, turning her back to me.

"Veronica," I tried whispering, but the lights had been dimmed and the steady beat of bass was now humming in speakers around the room. Brad Kingsbury stepped forward, sauntering across the stage, one hand thumbing the pocket of his black tuxedo pants, the other swinging casually at his side. He paused to flash an arrogant grin at the crowd as the emcee recited a list of his attributes, surprisingly long for someone so vile.

"V," I reached out again, touching her shoulder this time. She half-turned. "Don't be mad." I watched the muscles in her face relax the tiniest bit. As long as we'd been friends, it was impossible for us to stay angry at one another for more than a moment. "You know I love you." This time, she pursed her lips, trying hard to hold in her smile. "And they don't deserve you." She dropped her eyes to her lap, *The Date* staring up at her. "Besides, I thought you were supposed to be *my* one and only." A full-fledged grin was now radiant across her face.

Veronica turned, grabbing my hand. "You'll always be my valentine, candy heart." I knew I was forgiven. Of all the words to rhyme with Andie, *candy* is the one Veronica couldn't get enough of, developing new pet names every year to tease me. She knew how much I hated the sickly sweet monikers, making it the perfect game for someone who couldn't resist a challenge. On cue, I rolled my eyes and she stuck out her tongue.

On stage, the auction was moving quickly now, Westlake girls putting on a show of who could outbid the last. One by one, the "dates" were accounted for and I could sense Veronica's anxiety, worried that no one would be available. But then, Troy Billet took the stage: shy, handsome, and slightly nerdy. His family was incredibly wealthy, but he never seemed to fit their scene. At school, Troy was involved in mostly academic pursuits; his lone extra-curricular activity *The Howlers*, where he seemed to come alive on stage.

Beside me, I could sense new energy in Veronica. "Troy is so nice," she crooned. "He helped me with my Chemistry lab after school when Mr. Nixon was busy last week." Slowly, she opened her wallet, subtly flipping through bills to check her stash.

Relief washed me in waves. Troy was older, a senior, but he was so nice and *harmless*. As Veronica began her bidding, which she handily won, I sat back and began tuning out. Soon dinner would be served and then we could leave. V and I had planned a sleepover at her place; I couldn't wait to kick back, watch movies, and dish about the night. It was time I told her about my weird encounters with Jared Bronson.

Who was now onstage. Standing before a silent room. The emcee coughed, embarrassed by the lack of bidding, and I could hear Jared's mother's voice, starting to get loud. Jared's eyes zeroed in on her, cheeks reddening as she flapped and waved. A wounded peacock: tragically beautiful, impossible to ignore.

"V, what's going on?" She shook her head, clearly as stunned as I was. Looking around the room, I could see the Untouchables, smirking at their tables, arms crossed, clearly not intending to offer a single bid. *Where were all his fans now?* The emcee recovered from his fumbling, joking about how the ladies must be nervous to be alone with such an eligible bachelor. Beginning the list of selling points once again, I could feel the crowd start to murmur. The gossip about Jared was about to get much, much worse.

Jared's mother stood, unsteady, ready to address the room in a sloppy rage, and his face crumbled.

"One thousand dollars." A woman gasped. It was the highest date bid of the night. Even hotshot Brad Kingsbury had only garnered $650.

I was standing. Feeling the scrutiny of every single eye in the room.

"Andie?" Veronica's eyes were wide.

I could feel the bass in the room, sinking into my skin, matching the frenzied pace of my heart. What was I *doing*? The thought, "My parents are going to kill me," flitted briefly through my mind, but it was nothing compared to the panic of becoming the greatest spectacle in the room.

"Sold!" The emcee gleefully thumped his gavel on the podium, beaming at me as if this colossal impulse was for him and not Jared. Jared who talked to me one moment like I had a window to his heart and then pretended I didn't exist the next. A stream of giggles babbled across the now calming room. There they were- the same untouchable crew- jostling one another. Cats in cream satisfied. *What were they up to now?*

Fifteen.

I could hear my mother making small talk downstairs. Two paralyzed feet-mine- were uncomfortably clad in black heels. In my new, emerald silk dress and platinum heart pendant, I hovered on the landing. All I had to do was take a step, walk down the stairs, and meet Jared for our date. Yep, all I had to do was switch the sun for the moon, turn the sky green, and learn to fly. With my ears. There was no way this wasn't going to be terrible. My impromptu bid was a moment of charity and now all I had to look forward to was an embarrassing evening and the snide looks at school that were sure to follow.

What I wasn't expecting was a smile. As soon as I reached the bottom of the stairs, Jared turned his eyes away from my chatty mother and landed them squarely on my face, grinning the whole time. "You look nice." Another surprise. Since I'd known him, compliments seemed to be words in a foreign tongue.

"Thanks?" I shrugged, grabbing my coat, avoiding the "Be nice" expression my mother was avidly darting my way. "Bye, mom" was out of my mouth the same moment I opened the front door. I had bought this night, but that didn't mean I was looking forward to it. Better to just do it already.

I tried to ignore the fact that Jared's car smelled nice, that the color of his sweater matched his eyes, that a tiny bolt of electricity ran up my arm when he brushed it while opening my car door. Trivial details. The important ones were still blaring: Jared was a mess and he had befriended the cruelest kids in school.

When we pulled into the parking lot for Jensen's Ice Rink, I was shocked. Fancy dinner, boring movie- these were expected. Twirling around on the ice together- totally left field. "We're going ice skating?" My eyebrows rose in consternation.

"Something wrong with that?" There was an edge to Jared's voice, grounding me again.

"Just surprised, that's all. Didn't take you for a twirler," I smirked, knowing how much he probably hated to have even one ounce of his masculinity questioned.

Jared smiled. "Maybe you just don't know that much about me." He winked, opening his door, signaling the beginning of our little misadventure.

"Here we go," I mumbled to myself, wishing I'd worn the sweater and jeans I'd originally picked before Veronica had a complete meltdown in my closet. She'd dragged me to every clothing store in town before settling on the dress I was now wearing. I should've trusted my own instincts. Then again, those instincts had led to my impulsive bid in the first place. Maybe Veronica was right. Maybe I did need some intervention.

I hadn't been to Jensen's in years. Walking inside, I was enveloped immediately with the smell of warm pretzels, hot chocolate, and dampness. Red, plaid carpet lined the front entryway, leading to a long white counter for skate rentals on the left, and a bustling concession area on the right. I waited for Jared to say something, to suggest anything really, but he was too busy looking around to notice me at all. He seemed nervous, cool blue eyes no longer cool, shifting his weight methodically back and forth on his heels. Jared's hands were firmly entrenched in the pockets of his jeans, his charcoal button-down casually draped across his wrists as they jiggled anxiously with the keys in his right pocket and wallet in his left.

"Skates?" I looked up at Jared, waiting for him to snap out of his odd mood. Maybe this is how he always was? Flashing back to the night of the auction, I remembered the look on Jared's face as the entire community of Westlake students and parents stirred. How his mother prepared to embarrass the both of them with her drunken defense. My empathy returned.

In response to my question, Jared walked to the counter and returned with two pairs of skates. "Be right back," he called out as I sat down to lace my skates. I watched Jared walk out the door of the rink, curious about what had him so distracted. As I waited for him to return, I turned my attention to the ice. Couples holding hands were stumbling along together, laughing as they took turns skating and falling. An older couple, my grandparents' age, glided smoothly together, lock-step, never once looking down at the ice as they moved in synch. What must it be like to know someone so well you never had to look down? Song ending, the DJ's voice slid across the room, reminding skaters that the time for open skate was finished. The friendly voice encouraged them to return tomorrow, and to have a safe trip home.

Okay...so now what? Exasperated that the evening kept turning out all wrong, I glanced up as Jared walked in, ready to tell him that he needed a Plan B. "The rink is closing."

"I know." Jared bit his lip, looking over my shoulder.

"So..." Raising my eyebrows, I leaned forward just a bit, waiting. Tiny pangs of hunger growled in my stomach. I'd really been counting on dinner, so I hadn't eaten a thing.

"So... that's part of my plan." Jared smiled, but it didn't reach his eyes. They still seemed nervous. Turning to look at me, "I rented it out. C'mon."

Floored, and suddenly nervous myself, I followed Jared toward the edge of the rink. As we passed the DJ booth, a stocky, balding man with a thick gray beard peeked his head outside the doorway. "Need anything before I take off? I set up the playlist you requested."

"No, that's great...would you just take care of the lights on your way out?" Jared shook the man's hand

and then continued to the opening on the frozen surface. As he stepped onto the ice, the lights outside the rink dimmed, leaving a soft glow on the white space before us. "Take my hand," Jared instructed, reaching forward to lead me onto the ice. My skates touched the ice and I stumbled, nearly falling on my face, but Jared's strong arms grabbed me by the waist, pulling me to him. "Are you all right?" His body was so close.

"Fine," I whispered, sliding backward, creating space between us.

Jared let go of my hands, and skated toward the center. "Come out here. If you stay by the wall, you'll never get better." In the background, the opening notes of Etta James's "At Last" filtered across the ice. Was he trying to be romantic?

"Who says I need to get better?" I glided forward, arms stretched like two soft wings, determined not to be embarrassed.

Jared laughed warmly, the sound dying on his lips as soon as he saw the smile on mine. What was *with* this guy? He shook his head, distracted again. For a moment, we skated in silence. Then, the voice of Rick Springfield floated across the rink, opening chords of "Jesse's Girl" bringing up the tempo. Recovered, Jared suddenly extended his hand, "Try something?"

I clasped my two hands together behind my back, gliding forward and away. "I'm fine." It was hard not to enjoy so much space to myself, cool air from the ice playing with the hem of my dress. Occupying a public place alone- well, nearly- was thrilling. Besides, it was easier to ignore Jared and his sour mood than embrace the disappointment. I closed my eyes.

Opening them a moment later, I caught Jared staring. He beckoned again. "Take my hands." He skated toward me, nearly knocking me off balance. Before I could protest, Jared grabbed both my hands and skated backward toward the center of the ice. Slowly, he turned in a circle, gathering momentum until it felt like we were flying. I could feel the warmth of his hands, the rise and fall in the center of my body, the rush of air & light as we spun. It was great.

As the song ended, I felt Jared's body tense. He let go. "I need to take care of something. Be back in a moment." Jared skated toward the edge of the rink, looking back with the most forlorn expression just as he stepped onto the rubber-padded floor.

Shrugging it off, I decided to make the most of my time alone, skating with the rhythm of the music, twirling once with my arms above my head. Whatever weirdness was going on with Jared, at least I had the chance to enjoy a place I'd loved as a child.

And then, mid-song, the rink went dark. So dark I couldn't see my hand in front of my face. The contrast between the bright white of the ice and complete blackness was disorienting. "Jared?" Maybe there'd been a power outage. Maybe the lights were set on some sort of timer. Maybe Jared had accidentally tripped a switch. I tried again, "Jared? Where are you?"

"Jared?" A voice floated across the ice, mocking my own. A whiny, soprano voice that sounded frighteningly familiar. Then, a giggle.

"Where are you?" A second voice echoed. Male. The darkness amplified the rest of my senses. Sweat began to trickle down my forehead as I processed the fact that Jared and I were no longer alone.

"Jared?" A chorus of voices, dozen or more, chanted his name in that same mocking tone. The sound was terrifying. Crawling inside my skin, sending a line of shivers along every inch of my body. I had to get out of here, but without my sight, I didn't know how that was going to happen.

Blinding light shot across the rink, pivoted, and then landed squarely on my face. Someone was shining a spotlight on *me*. Someone was working very hard to make *me* the center of attention. But why? Squinting hard, I could discern an outline of bodies along the edge of the rink, but the light in my face made it difficult to sense...

Pain. Icy pain. Snowball after snowball hurled at my body, drenching the silk of my dress, building angry red welts as my skin absorbed the frozen bullets, again and again. I cried out, arms raised to cover my face, but the only way to escape, the only way out, was to move, exposing my face and body as I tried my best to skate. Stumbling, the light bounced away, and I could finally see the identities of my attackers. In the forefront, Brad Kingsbury, flanked by Hamilton Smith, and Parker Williams. Behind them, lining up bucket after bucket of snowy death, Jensen Bell and Belinda Chase. I could see others, in the shadows, but the one face I saw next eclipsed all others. Leaning against the side of the rink's outer wall, hands in his pockets, Jared Bronson looked away as my world came crashing down.

Sixteen.

*I speak now because experience has
shown me / that my mind will /
never be clear for long*

"Note to Reality"- Tony Hoagland

March. Junior Year.

I woke up in a panic, having ignored the buzzing of my
alarm for a solid thirty minutes. I must have been
sleeping so hard after…Stretching my arms behind my
head, I could feel the knots in my back, the places
where I'd curled up on the bathroom tile, spending
hours reliving the moments with Jared I'd been trying
so hard to forget. Rushing to get dressed and out the
door, I felt anxious about the day ahead. Today was
the election assembly, and I couldn't let Jared do to
Veronica what he'd done to me.

Later that morning, I passed Brad and Hamilton in
the hallway outside the auditorium. I couldn't help
glaring. This should've been Veronica's moment, not
theirs, and let's face it: no one else had a prayer of
winning. Veronica had become their only true
competitor.

I dazed out during the speeches. What was the point? A few weeks ago, I'd laughed at the idea of running for office. I was content to just move along in the crowd. But Veronica, she'd inspired me. She made me want more. Not for the power- really, the Untouchables would always have the power- for what the office stood for. It was symbolic. It meant something to stand up and say, "I have a voice." And now, we didn't. Again. Things would continue on, only worse than before. Because before, we didn't realize the role we could play. We thought it was hopeless.

I sighed, watching Veronica slump down next to me. But then again, maybe it was hopeless. They'd broken her. Whoever 'they' was and whatever 'they' had done. They'd taken my spirited best friend and reduced her to a sullen mess.

Bullshit. Suddenly, all the anger I'd ever had for the jerks at this school and the administration that supported them boiled over inside of me. Maybe Veronica didn't think she had a choice, but I did. I hadn't made promises to anyone, or deals, or whatever. I was completely free and it was eating away at my insides to sit here and let the aristocratic, misogynistic elite at this school tell *me* who my leaders had to be. This wasn't a free election. This was a hoax.

I felt my feet moving before my brain finished processing. Veronica looked up quizzically, mouthing, *where are you going?* as I shoved past the outstretched knees of kids sitting in my row. More than a few people shot me a dirty look as I climbed down the aisle hurriedly. Luckily, my row was near one of the side doors. I slipped out quietly, missing the glazed eyes of teachers and administrators pretending to pay attention to the orations on stage.

Walking down a side hall, I spotted the door to the backstage, and then sidled over to the control room. I thanked my job on *The Howl* staff for giving me endless assignments to cover musical performances. I'd navigated the area many times before, making it easy to find what I needed today. I looked for the soundboard. Spotting it next to the switches for the stage lights, I searched for the feed to the microphones onstage. Two switches looked promising. Crossing my fingers that I had the right one, I flipped it and waited.

Nothing. Then, slowly, a buzzing started building. It was the crowd. I could hear the murmurs as they pounded on the mike, trying to get it to work. Yes! Okay, now all I needed to do was turn on the speakers for the P.A. Cursing the scribbled writing of the sound techs, I struggled to find the right one. Damn. I should have found that first. Now I only had a little time before someone came back here to figure things out. Couldn't let the precious words of Brad Kingsbury be disturbed. (I'd purposely waited until his speech to scoot out of my chair and run backstage.)

I could hear shuffling at the front of the stage. Sounded like they were moving the mike stand.

Probably trying to check for a loose wire. All right. I could figure this out. Think. I strained my memory, searching back to the last time I'd covered the sound tech program. *Oklahoma?* Yeah, I think so. And it was Marvin Deiken who was showing me around. I remember because he had asked me to the spring formal last year. Marvin was trying to impress me with his technological skills- not, I might add, the sexiest thing a guy can prove- and he'd leaned across the board...I closed my eyes, trying to recreate the moment...Aha! Found it. Suddenly, a screech sounded across the stage, prompting a collective groan from the audience.

Okay, Andie. Now's the time to make this happen. Truthfully, I was petrified. I'd used all my nerve sneaking into the control room. Now, all I felt was jittery. I tried to channel my anger again. It was seeing Veronica slumped in her chair. Holding her as she sobbed. Knowing that she'd given up something she really wanted. Just because *they* told her to.

I concentrated on how much I hated the way our lives were ruled by such a small, spineless group of people whose only merit was wealth. Not even earned wealth, but family wealth. These kids who roamed the halls like they owned the place only did so because they had rich, powerful parents. They were just kids, and I was sick of seeing them ruin my friend.

"Students of Westlake," I paused, listening to my voice echo into the auditorium, "As we sit and listen to the words of our potential future student council, think about the speeches we're *not* hearing today. The words of those who've been silenced. Silenced by a community that believes in wealth above all else. By people who believe in power over integrity. I know a candidate who would've been proud to serve as our president, but she wasn't allowed to speak today. Because those who've always been in control of this school felt threatened by her influence. I speak to you today because I can't stand the idea that her voice isn't heard. But she doesn't have to be the only one. Speak up and tell the administration of this school----"

Dean Brauer burst through the door, face red and puffing. "Andrea Mancini, get off that microphone immediately!" I'd never seen Brauer so angry. Steam was literally rising from his forehead. He lunged toward me, grasping at the buttons on the sound system. "You ungrateful little…" Hearing his words echo into the auditorium, he quickly shut his mouth, settling for hateful glares instead.

Realizing how much trouble I was in, I stepped back from the soundboard, hands in the air. Brauer fumbled with the buttons for several minutes and then gave up, shouting at his employees. "Figure this out, dammit. How hard can it be?" He stormed around the stage, overseeing their work.

I stepped back carefully, easing toward the side door, hoping and praying that he wouldn't notice. I'd made it almost all the way across the stage when a loud voice bellowed, "Stop right there, Mancini! I'm not finished with you." I froze in place, cursing the floorboards that had given me away.

But looking back, it wasn't Brauer's menacing face that made my heart pound that afternoon. It was Veronica's face, moments later, when I emerged under the hawk-like eyes of Brauer. She was stunned-with horror. Her face crumpled at the sight of me and she shook her head vigorously. It was then I realized that my attempt at heroism had really just put a nail in the coffin of Veronica Linwood because the secret was more than I had bargained for. The secret was hidden in Jared's studio, captured on a mini-camcorder nestled into the wall. A camcorder with a very revealing tape.

Seventeen.

Things happened fast after that. It's hard to say what happened when because all I knew was that suddenly my world was upside down. When I'd begged Veronica to tell me her secret, to let me in about what had her so rattled, I never expected the consequences. All I could think about was telling the truth. To me, being honest had always been so liberating. I guess I'd never been confronted with a situation where the truth wasn't liberating: it chained her to the wall.

I first saw the tape, along with so many others, as a text. Well, I guess that's not true. I didn't really see the tape via phone, but I discovered the link when someone- probably one of Jared's friends- sent out the blast. It made me sick, to see her like that: so exposed. And it wasn't what was on the tape that got to me. It was the vulnerability. I thought about how I would feel being so utterly vulnerable to everyone I knew. My stomach turned.

But Veronica acted in a way I didn't expect at all. I would've gone into hiding. Considered changing schools. Anything to move away from the constant looks in the hall, the rumors, and the judgment flying around like a bad smell. No one was willing to stand up for her, even after all she'd done to make a stand for us. It was amazing how quickly one event could completely change the way others saw you. Forever.

Veronica seemed to embrace it. The first two days, I didn't see her. She came to school late and left early. By the third day, it was hard to miss her. Everyone knew what she was doing because she proclaimed it loud and clear. First, the outfits. V always liked to dress well- she shopped more than anyone I knew. She made it work on a shoestring budget by haunting thrift stores and babysitting in the rich neighborhoods to make extra cash. So occasionally sexy, yes, but she never walked around in party gear. Sure, a tight sweater here, a short skirt there. But nothing like this. Now it was like some kind of show. I balked at her see-through shirts with dark bras and ultra-short skirts with thigh-high boots. It was like she was trying to embrace these stereotypes. And the saddest thing of all was how untrue that image really was. I knew for a fact that Veronica had dated several guys but only gotten really physical with two. If I hadn't seen the powerful persuasion of Jared Bronson firsthand, I'd have been shocked by Veronica's choice that night. But he was very, very charming. Could have easily lulled her into feeling more comfortable with him than she'd normally be.

It wasn't just her outfits, either. V had changed. Overnight. Suddenly she was the one cracking jokes in class and laughing loudly down the hall. Where was the confident, witty girl I knew? Where was my best friend?

At first, I brushed it off as some reactionary phase. Something temporary. But when she began the protest, I didn't know what to think. It seemed like Veronica, but Veronica on steroids. Everything was excessive, off-kilter. Even our conversations became disjointed.

Walking up to her at the locker, I took a deep breath, making a point not to say anything about the tube top she was wearing over a thin pink tank. "Hey…"

She didn't speak, and then turned suddenly as if she'd only just heard me. "Oh, hey, Andie!" Her eyes were bright and wild. "Wanna help me hang these posters after school?" I looked skeptically at the brightly colored papers in her hand. Each one contained bold statements about female power, using quotes from women as diverse as Gloria Steinem to Courtney Love. At the bottom, she'd scrawled, *Join the Fight* with her phone number in bold.

"I don't know, V. Seems a little…intense." Part of me felt awful for holding her back. Wasn't I the one who'd pushed so hard? But now Brauer was on the prowl and one wrong word was sure to send us both into his office. I'd only missed getting suspended by a hair. My mom had talked Brauer down, speaking earnestly about emotional distress in so much psychological jargon, Brauer was ready to say anything to get her out of there. Normally, I was a big wuss when it came to breaking the rules. I was all for wronging a right, but my methods were *usually* less antagonistic than papering the walls with words meant to incite a riot. The election speech debacle was my one, crazy detour off the straight and narrow.

Veronica popped her gum loudly, standing back to rest her hands on her hips. "Someone's getting cold feet now, huh?" She looked so hard at me, I felt her eyes move right through me. "Look- I can't make you get on board. You're going to do what you want to do...isn't that how it always is?" There was a bite to her words. "So fine. Don't help me. Wouldn't be the first time." She slammed the locker shut and started down the hall, fiercely clicking the heels of her three-inch boots. I waited for her to turn around. She didn't.

I felt like crap. All I'd wanted throughout this whole mess was to help Veronica and now it seemed like she was the one I couldn't stop hurting. What was I supposed to do? Mom thought she needed counseling. She'd offered to refer her to a colleague, but I knew the last thing Veronica wanted to hear right now was that something was wrong with *her*. After all the crap with Jared and the video, the last thing she needed was more input on what *she* could do.

We didn't talk the rest of the day. Or the next. Every time I spotted her at school, Veronica would jump into conversation with someone else or turn and walk away. She was avoiding me, but I didn't know what to say to her either.

It wasn't until the Monday after a big party weekend that I really started to worry. Everyone was buzzing with stories about the party. I only half-listened because I couldn't care less. My one foray into the Westlake party scene had been a disaster. I wasn't about to start getting into it now.

"She was *totally* wasted, and all over everyone." Two girls talked animatedly, strolling into the bathroom. From inside the stall, I recognized Jensen's nasally voice.

"But did you see her outfit? That was the best. God, if she didn't look like such a complete slut, I'd have been jealous of those boots. What were they, like, all the way up her leg?" Liz Nixon's voice went up an octave at the end. Whenever she was excited, she started to sound a little like Mickey Mouse.

"Tell me about it!" I could hear compacts snapping as they fixed their make-up. "But that's not all...the worst part was when she started dancing on the table. I thought Mario was going to have a heart attack with all the excitement. Did you see him try to look under her skirt?"

"I heard that she wasn't wearing any underwear, so it must've been quite a show." They both laughed. "Although, she's such a dirty ho, I don't know who would want her now." They laughed again, and I could feel my blood start to boil.

I pushed open the stall door, planting my feet right in front of Liz. "Maybe if you weren't such a heinous bitch, the guys at this school would give you some attention too." I glared at her, waiting for a response.

For a moment, she didn't say anything. She just stared. Open-mouthed, her pale pink lipstick pressed to her bottom lip. Then, smacking her lips together, she arched an eyebrow, looking me up and down. "And what do I care what *you* think, Mancini. You're just the pathetic sidekick."

I laughed, glancing between her and Jensen. "You're one to talk." She coughed at the implication, face reddening. "But that's not what this is about and you know it. This is about you drooling over Jared for the last year and a half." I stepped closer to her. "Any girl who caught his eye would be a slut to you."

Liz turned even redder, pursing her lips together. "What do you know about it anyway, prude?" She hammered back through gritted teeth.

I froze. *Did she know?* Jared had made it painfully clear that he didn't want any news about that night to make its way into the open. *Would he have broken his own promise? After everything?* The idea made me dizzy. I didn't care if people knew I'd turned him down. Talk of being prudish didn't faze me. I'd never given much attention to the guys here because they didn't care about the things I did. I had big plans. Ivy League university. Then law school. Or maybe journalism...but regardless, I didn't have time for the petty problems of a high school relationship. So calling me names like that…who cares? What I really cared about was what Veronica would think. I'd kept that from her, the information about Jared that night. And looking back now, maybe that was careless. I'd thought I was protecting her, giving Jared the chance to let her down easy. But really, maybe I was just protecting myself from the difficult conversations telling her would bring.

Pushing the doubts from my mind, I turned back to Liz. "I guess I've got better things to do than wasting my time with the jerkoffs who paw your skanky ass." I said casually, rinsing my hands in the white porcelain sink. Grabbing a paper towel, I called over my shoulder to Jensen, "Next time you decide to talk shit about someone's party behavior, check your own track record. It took days to wash the drunken slobber off my clothes from when you fell on me at Jared's."

With that, I walked out the door, hearing Jensen furiously screeching behind me. "What a bitch! Did you hear her? *Ugh!*" Water ran in the sink as they continued talking, scrambling to get their things together. Not wanting to face another scene, I turned down the next hallway, trying to calm down. It felt great to tell those two brats how I felt, but it didn't change the fact that people were really talking about Veronica.

I had to find her. If Veronica didn't know the things people were saying, I certainly didn't want girls like Liz and Jensen to be the ones to tell her first. The bell rang, bringing me back to reality. Where would she be right now? I racked my brain for her schedule, trying to remember. Physics? Sounded right.

I bolted down the science hallway, avoiding Dean Gruber's roving eye as I snuck past the T-intersection near the office. Stopping at Ms. Winters's door, I peeked through the window. I could just see the top of Veronica's head through the long, rectangular window. But how could I get her attention without alerting Ms. Winters? She was a real stickler for any disturbances. Her classrooms were like tombs.

Carefully, I perched up on my tiptoes, leaning forward to press my body against the door. I stared at Veronica, willing her to look my way. *This was never going to work. It's not like we had some kind of...Wait.* She looked. I waved, signaling her to come outside. She nodded the tiniest nod and then stared back at the board.

A minute later, the door opened and Veronica stepped out. "Hey," I whispered to her from the alcove nearby, "right here." She walked over, a puzzled look on her face.

"What's wrong?" She glanced up and down the hall, keeping her voice low. "You never skip class...are you okay?" Veronica really looked concerned, which gave me such a sense of relief. We'd formed a tentative peace, but things had still been strained.

"No, I'm fine. I mean…I guess I'm not fine at all. I'm upset…but it's not about that…it's not about me." I was rambling. She looked at me, waiting. "It's you. I'm here because of things I've heard about you." I looked up.

She raised her eyebrows. "Me?" Veronica stiffened her shoulders, waiting for my criticism, I guess.

I softened my voice. "Not about you, like I'm upset with you. About you, like things I've been hearing today." I stopped to look at her, twisting my mouth a little to the side in a half-grimace. "When I was in the bathroom just now, Jensen Bell and Liz Nixon were there. And they were talking about some party."

A look flashed across her face. I couldn't quite place it. Discomfort? Regret? Whatever it was, it wasn't pleasant. "Yeah…" she waited for the rest.

"They were saying things about you," I squirmed, playing with a piece of my hair, avoiding having to actually say the words. "Things I didn't like."

Veronica smiled wanly. "I was at a party this weekend. It may have gotten a little crazy, but nothing I regret. Not really…" She looked at me cautiously. I could tell she was trying to gauge my reaction to the things I'd heard. She was trying to figure out if I would look down on her or if I would support her. Veronica was one of the people I hated to disappoint the most in life. When she gave me that look, the one that said *I didn't expect that from you*, I always melted into a puddle. And so I got it. As much as I felt that way about her, she probably felt that way about me.

"No, V. It was the *way* they talked about you that had me worried. I don't care what you do…I mean, that's not really true: Of course I care about what you do…But I care when people at this school, people *anywhere* are calling my best friend a slut. That's not who you are. And I can't stand that they think that." I grabbed her arm earnestly. "You're so much more than that."

"More than a slut? Ha!" She laughed bitterly. "Not to these people. Ever since that video, everyone sees me how they want to see me. Guys want to party with me because they think I'm easy. Girls won't talk to me because they think I'm a slut. And the people I love, the ones who know me, well…they see me as a new person…right?" Her eyes were wet as she looked at me, daring me to prove her wrong.

But I couldn't. All the things I'd do to protect her, to support her. The one thing I'd never do was lie. I couldn't lie to her. Keeping my secret with Jared was one thing; lying to my best friend's face was another. I wouldn't do it. Not then. Not today.

"V- I love you. You've been my best friend for the past seven years. Ever since Miss Hartgen's third grade class…remember the glue wars?"

She laughed. "You glued a pencil to Jimmy Lorkin's head." Veronica's eyes twinkled with the memory.

"Well he deserved it! He ruined your Wonder Woman lunchbox. I couldn't let him get away with that." I smiled, cocking my head to the side to look at her closely.

"Always protecting me. Even now?" Veronica had quieted again. She was asking me to make it all okay. To tell her that I believed in this new version of her. But I just couldn't do that.

"I'm here for you, but that doesn't mean I don't believe that things could be better. Different-"I began.

"---That's what I'm looking for, Andie. Different!" she interrupted.

"Not different then. Different now." Veronica looked puzzled by my words. "The last few weeks, you've been so different. When everything broke with the video, it was awful. I half expected you to be gone for awhile, get out of Dodge, ya know?" I smiled at her. "But you didn't. You came back...And then it's like somebody turned up the volume. Like someone reached over and turned up your dial to eleven... it's just a lot to take in. It's not the Veronica I've known." She put up her hand to stop me, but I just barreled ahead. "I don't want to get used to that girl, because that girl isn't really you." I paused, feeling the tears start to well in my eyes. "Where did you go?" I asked softly.

"Andie..." Veronica breathed in deeply, looking for a moment like my best friend again. I watched her stare at the wall behind me, glancing at the rows of classrooms, the empty hall. Then something hardened in her eyes, and she leaned toward me, "Around here," waving her arms, "I didn't get any respect before. All of that, the party invitations, the waves in the hall, the conversations with cute boys. None of that was real. It wasn't real because when push came to shove, those people completely turned on me. As soon as I had something they wanted, they came after me. Any reputation I had, any relationships I'd made didn't matter any more. It didn't matter because the people who make the rules *say* it doesn't matter." She leaned against the wall heavily, looking up at me with hands outstretched, palms up. "So, what am I supposed to do?"

"You're supposed to fight! Show them they're wrong. Call their bluff." I paced angrily. "Don't play into their stereotypes with sexy clothes and this outrageous protest." I waved my arms toward the neon posters on the wall.

"What do you think this is, Andie?" She stepped away from the wall, arms open, circling the hall, "This *is* my fight. The fight for the right to say what I want to say, wear what I want to wear. The right to not be penalized for being sexy. For kissing a boy at a party. Or even having sex with him." Veronica hugged her arms to her chest. "What would it be like, I imagined, to be the 'it' girl in school? To have everyone waiting to hear what *I* would say, to have the gorgeous guy with the hot car next to *me* at the football game? I wanted those things, Andie. I just didn't realize what kind of price they had…"

"This isn't your fault, V. Jared seduced you. You couldn't help that he did that. It's not your fault," I argued vehemently.

Veronica laughed softly. "Andie…Jared didn't seduce me. He didn't manipulate me." She paused. "I found him."

I was stunned. All this time, I'd believed Jared was the evil mastermind behind their sexual encounter. That he'd lulled her into his studio, plying her with drinks and charm. The idea that Veronica was actually the initiator didn't compute in my mind.

"Really?" I let my mouth fall open a little, still recovering from the surprise.

"Yeah." She looked sad all of a sudden. There was the regret I'd been searching for these last few weeks. "I saw him that night…from his kitchen…and I just decided to approach him. To make my move." Her eyes were glued to my face.

The kitchen…My mind reeled. I was back in that moment on the terrace. Jared's hands roving my body. Pushing him away. Falling to my knees on the stone path. I don't know how long I was there, but the next thing I did was go to look for Veronica. "The kitchen?" An idea was forming.

"Yeah. The kitchen." Still, she stared at me. Eyes locked onto mine.

"The kitchen…" We were in the kitchen, Jared and I, just before we went onto the terrace. Getting a glass of lemonade. Right before he…

The kitchen. "When?" I demanded, voice rising a little. "When were you in the kitchen?"

Veronica ran her toe along the floor. Looking down now. "I was looking for you."

"When?" My heart was racing. This couldn't be. Not this. "When were you looking for me?"

She looked up again. "Not long after we got there. You'd…disappeared." She licked her lip. I noticed how pale her skin seemed. Just now.

"Before you and Jared…." I couldn't finish the question. I was sweating now.

"Before me and Jared…" She nodded.

I swallowed. The next words were going to be the hardest I'd ever spoken to her. The question I had to ask but dreaded asking more than anything I'd ever asked before. The question that would change everything between us. "You saw us?"

She didn't move. The air was frozen between us. I could hardly breathe, waiting for her response. I prayed she'd say 'no'. She had to say 'no' because if she didn't…if she'd been there…

"Yes." The word was hoarse, like a whisper. I felt my vision start to tingle. This couldn't be happening. Not her. She wouldn't have left me there. She would've come out to help me. She wouldn't have…she couldn't have…with him then.

I had to continue. Even as my head began to float above my body, I had to keep going. Digging. Poking at this wound. Meticulously exposing the raw flesh, terrified of how deep this wound might be.

"You saw him? What he did?" I was crying now. Tears I couldn't feel but found on my hands. My face was numb. She was staring at the floor. Unable to meet my face.

"Yes." This second affirmation was quieter but more explosive in my mind. She was there. She saw him, the way he'd forced himself on me. The way I'd fought him off.

"You saw me?" The space around my eyes was starting to blur. From my tears or my fading body, I didn't know. Just that I was shutting down. I was drowning and the person who usually held my life vest was the one pushing me under.

"And then..." I choked on the words, "you followed him?" I didn't know how to process this all. I needed to sit down but we were in an alcove. Near a dozen classrooms. Nowhere to rest. Nowhere to hide.

"Yes." She'd found her voice again. Maybe the reality of what she was saying or the relief of finally letting it out was a way to find strength. Either way, I could sense her coming toward me, but now I was the one who didn't want her to be close.

"You said," I knew this was the most important part, "that it was your idea." I swallowed at the implication of my words. "That you *wanted* him." I felt my stomach lurch at the idea.

Veronica started crying. "Yes. Yes, I wanted him. I was jealous that he'd picked you and not me." She wiped her nose on the back of her hand, stemming the flow of tears only a little. "I resented the fact that he'd never kissed me like that." She looked into my eyes, crunching her brow, "*I* wanted to be his choice. *I* wanted to be the one in the spotlight."

"Spotlight?" Disgusted, I felt my arms drop to my sides. Pretty soon now, I'd lose all control. I was only holding it together by the thinnest of threads. "Is that what you think I felt when he forced his body on top of mine? Special?"

"Andie…" A new round of tears rushed from her eyes.

"I felt…I felt…" I couldn't find the words. "Helpless. Helpless and manipulated. He used me to feel better about himself." I paused, letting the situation sink in. "And then you used what happened to me…as an opportunity…" I shook my head, numbly. "To sleep with the guy who forced himself on me…" It was all too awful. That night at Veronica's house, when I tried to force the secret out of her, I'd never imagined anything so terrible as this.

"Attack you…Andie, I saw you kissing him too…was it really like that?" Her eyes pleaded with me to absolve her. To play down what happened between Jared and I so that she wouldn't be some kind of monster. But I couldn't do that. I couldn't do that to myself.

I looked at her sharply. "I said 'No'. More than once. And he kept going. He…" I shuddered at the memory of my bare skin exposed. How vulnerable I felt. How cheap. But I didn't want to be in that night. I was here. Now. Trying to put the pieces together. And I still had questions left to be answered. "What did he really threaten you with? Before the election?"

Veronica's face changed. She tried to evade my gaze, but it was locked on her now. Every ounce of my fading strength was focused on her face, on her words. "He said," she paused, pursing her lips together and blowing air slowly between them, "he said that he'd tell you." She glanced up once, quickly. "He'd tell you about that night."

"What about that night?" I pressed, "Be specific."

"He'd tell you that I knew. That I saw." I flashed back to my conversation with Jared in the door of his studio. That whole time, he was playing with me. Just a game to make me the fool. This whole time, he has probably been laughing, knowing that I'm standing by my best friend, knowing that she betrayed me even though I had no clue. How much fun he must've had watching me keep this secret, all the while oblivious to the way Veronica had chosen him over me on the night of the party.

"You didn't care about the video?" If Veronica had really been afraid of Jared talking to me, did that mean she didn't care that a video of her and Jared was floating around school?

"I didn't know about the video...not then, anyway. Jared told me that he'd taped us, but it was dark in his studio, so I didn't think it could be much of anything. I didn't know he'd set it to some night vision setting. I figured it was an idle threat because he'd be exposing himself too." She paused, picking at a fingernail. "It was stupid. I should've figured he'd have it rigged to keep himself out of the shots. I guess that's where he takes all the girls." She looked up at me hollowly, "And I'm just one of them now...some kind of lame trophy." She looked so sad. It was hard not to be empathic, my go-to, but that meant letting go of some of my own pain, and I wasn't nearly ready to do anything like that.

"Sounds like that's what you wanted. Some stupid place in his world." The words fell out of my mouth harshly. Bitter and bruised. Truthfully, all I wanted to do was leave. I needed to decompress. To sit down and let myself completely zone out. I didn't have the energy to be angry. Veronica's confession had drained my emotional tank. I was empty. Just waiting to feel again. I started to walk away, turning at the sound of her voice.

"Please...Andie, don't walk away." Veronica's voice was strained with emotion.

I just looked at her.

"Andie!" she cried desperately. "I know it was a mistake." She walked toward me, grabbing my listless arms, pulling my hands toward her heart. "I know it was. If I could go back..."

And that was it. Something in her face felt off. I knew and she knew too that if she could go back, she'd do it again. Maybe not the election. Maybe not this stupid campaign now. But that moment. The chance to be part of their world, to be *special* to someone like Jared Bronson...she'd do it again.

That's when I walked away. For good.

Eighteen.

By April, she was gone. After our moment in the hallway, Veronica's escapades accelerated. Posters graduated to impromptu speeches on the front lawn. Speeches became rallies. But it was never enough. Even as Dean Brauer consented to talk about making a change to the election process next year, Veronica still pushed. She was propellant, fueling a single fire, grown large and out of control. Watching her speak, seeing the wild look in her eyes and the vacant smiles, I knew that this wasn't really about the issues. It was about how she saw herself. How she wanted to be seen.

I'm not going to say I didn't miss her. It was impossible not to miss her when she'd been the center of my world. Veronica was my sounding board, my cheerleader, my reason to laugh. Losing her was devastating. But I couldn't go back. Going back meant losing myself.

For the first two weeks, she called every day. The messages still reverberate in my head. Her voice: pleading with me to see her side. To forgive.

"Andie...I miss you so much. You mean everything to me. Please...please call me. Hate me, okay, but don't give up on me."

"Andie, listen. I don't expect you to understand. I just want to talk to you. Everything's a mess and you're the only one who gets me. Please call."

"Andie. I know you're listening to these messages. I guess that means you don't want to talk, something I never thought would happen to us... I really hope you call."

But I never did. I never called. And somehow, time hurtled forward. Every day was slow, but every week was fast. So here I was. Five months later. September of my senior year. Picking up the pieces. Thinking of our friendship, I know it'll never feel right until we talk again, but I don't know how I can face her. And yet, something has to give. Someone has to heal.

Nineteen.

Contemplating the strange, I'm comforted
By this narcotic thought: I know my soul.

-Claude McKay, "I Know My Soul"

September. Senior Year.

Monday morning. Standing at my locker, the dial
moved slowly in my hand. Fourteen. Twenty-six.
One…One…Of course it was one. The metal creaked
as I lifted the navy blue handle and felt the force of
Anatomy, Advanced Writing, and Modern History
straining against the rusted metal door. Time to do it
all over again. Sounds came back into focus. Laughter
rang by in peals, beating to the cadence of bobbing
ponytails and crisply ironed collars. Whispered
conversations about this weekend's activities. Clicking
heels and worn tennis shoe shrugs. These were the
sounds of life going by, just as it always had, just as it
always would. I picked up the Modern History
textbook and placed it in my red leather backpack.

Notebooks and folders found their way into the
bag. And then, I could sense a familiar figure hovering
just outside the horizon of my vision. Ethan Jameson.

Memories of our double date flooded back- the way I'd assumed I'd hate him; how hard I tried not to laugh at his jokes or recognize his irresistible smile. Now here he was: the new kid, standing next to his cousin, one of the people I hated most in this world. I couldn't look at either of them without seeing Veronica. Without reliving the Whole Messy Awful.

I could hear Ethan laughing at something Jared said, punching him lightly on the arm in response like some devil-may-care tableau I couldn't tear my eyes away from. Watching them broke the spell of any flirtation I might've been entertaining. I processed the inevitable: Ethan Jameson was Jared Bronson. Their connection meant everything. It shouldn't really matter, though, because dating was the last thing on my mind. Dating involved trust and trust wasn't in my repertoire these days: too expensive. Dad always used to tease me about being gullible. "You'd invite the devil himself over for dinner if he asked you nicely," he'd joked. Guess Dad had been right. But the rumors about my dating life weren't true. Kids said I was a prude, or when that grew too boring, they called me a dyke. Neither one was anything to be excited about. Neither one was true.

In reality, these days I was saving myself for...college. And until then, I had novels with romantic heroes and grand, sweeping gestures. Landscapes where one could be rescued by the smart, witty philanthropist with sexy eyes and a sense of adventure. As much as Veronica and I used to talk about breaking down the door to the boys' club, I was a sucker for a good fairy tale. Everybody wants to be rescued from something.

I'd become something of a social hermit after everything that happened last year, but this was kind of okay with me. I had so many plans. This was my year to make waves as a writer on *The Howl*, get accepted to Brown, and maybe, just maybe leave behind some kind of legacy at Westlake. Something to say, 'I was here'.

Later that day, I'd noticed Ethan in the hallway again, this time checking out his locker while my locker neighbor Belinda Chase fell all over herself checking *him* out. Any guy that Belinda was juicy over was a guy unlikely to catch my attention. She was pep squad queen, preppie, a bubble-gum blonde. But out of the corner of my eye, I noticed that Ethan was ignoring *her*, which surprised me. Belinda was just the kind of eye candy who usually had the Untouchables salivating. They'd never take her to their family luncheons, of course, but they'd definitely invite her over for a party. Ethan didn't even look her way.

I didn't think more about Ethan that day until he caught me off guard before Phys. Ed. I was just heading into the bright blue locker room- some alumnus had donated money to have the walls painted with the color she felt would best ward off our hunger in some crazy holistic fitness plan- when he called out to me.

"Hi, Andie." He paused for a moment, waiting for me to acknowledge him. I looked up and nodded, hoping that he'd interpret my silence for aloofness. "Where's your sidekick?" His voice was slightly husky, low, but not too low- just enough to be curiously appealing. I stared up into green eyes flecked with golden brown. They drew me in with their swirling colors. He blinked and they warmed, turning more golden as he looked at me.

I stood still for a moment. It'd been a long time since anybody'd asked me that.

Ethan cleared his throat. "Did I..." He looked uncertain. "It *is* Andie, right?" As he scrunched his brows, I noticed how open his expression was. How he didn't seem to be thinking about anything else. How he didn't seem to care that we were standing in the middle of the hallway, or that I was wearing a faded Redskins sweatshirt I'd borrowed from my dad along with baggy cotton shorts I'd had in my closet forever.

Nodding slightly, I replied, "She doesn't go here anymore." My voice felt small.

Thankfully, Ethan didn't press. He nodded, casually placing one hand in the pocket of his dark wash jeans. "Ok, well, regardless...it's nice to see at least one familiar face." He smiled, dusting sunshine in the spaces between us.

"Sure." I wiggled my foot, one of those nervous gestures I'd perpetuated, well, forever. Silently, I prayed that my crazy hair wasn't too out of place. Then checked myself: why did I care?

"I'm on my way to..." he shuffled his notebooks a moment, finding his class schedule, "Philosophy." He leaned closer to show me the creased paper, pointing to the course title and teacher's name. I could smell the lightest scent of soap, something crisp and summery. It was delicious.

"Boulanger, huh? He's an institution around here," I smiled, finding my voice. "A little cranky sometimes, but funny. You'll like him."

I wanted to freeze this moment, for Ethan to talk with me for just a few more minutes. Something about him made me feel relaxed, a feeling I rarely experienced these days, but I couldn't think of anything else to talk about- which was maddening. Watching Ethan fold his class schedule and place it back in his pocket, I had the sudden urge to run a hand through his hair. Ethan straightened, adjusting the strap of his backpack, smiling at me once again.

"Thanks, and see you around, okay?" He murmured in that low, sexy voice. As he turned and began casually walking away, I observed his lean body moving down the hall, admiring the way his jeans hugged...

Ethan suddenly turned back, once, to wink in my direction, sending my stomach into flip-flop mode. *Had he seen me staring?* I felt my face redden.

By the end of the day, all the girls were buzzing with talk of Ethan. Westlake Academy was a small school- under 500 kids- so any new blood was bound to make social headlines. I couldn't help feel a little deja-vu. Wasn't this exactly the situation when Jared started freshmen year? Mysterious new guy with the ability to flip my stomach? I better be careful.

According to Lonzi, even though he was Jared's cousin, Ethan was just as much a mystery to the Untouchables as he was to me. Lonzi was my secret insider and on-call gossip queen. He skated the line between Untouchable and, well, the rest of us. Lonzi's dad was the mayor's chief of staff, rightfully earning him a place among the Richie Rich ranks.

Unfortunately for Lonzi, but fortunately for me, his flamboyant fashion sense and infatuation with the boy bands placed him just outside the social circle his family status deserved. But Lonzi could care less. There had been some hairy moments in middle school- my mind flashed back to chocolate chip cookie bombs in the cafeteria and some song about swirlies- but by now, Lonzi was as confident as could be. A couple summers in New York with his sister, Chance, the fashion designer, and he tuned a deaf ear to obnoxious teasing. That confidence earned him the ticket back into their world. Lonzi had no qualms about telling it like it is, and he'd sent more than a few girls into tears for making an ignorant comment in class. Thankfully, he and I had long passed our time to butt heads. Once, freshman year, Lonzi'd made fun of my idea notebook in front of our entire Algebra class and I'd responded by not talking to him for a week. That pretty much ended that. Now, all I had to do was give him the death stare and he knew to back off. Still- he always had the scoop, so when he brought back the stats on Ethan, I decided to tune in.

Ethan's parents had just moved here from Boston. Ethan's dad (Jared's dad's brother) was an orthopedic surgeon who'd just remarried for the second time to a twenty-something blond runway model. Apparently, she'd caused quite a stir in the office when she came to register Ethan- strutting in with black leather mini, thigh-high matching leather boots (four inch heels) and an ultra-tight fire engine red cashmere sweater. With legs a mile long, she'd drawn the attention of every male, and a few females. Dean Brauer had literally vaulted out of his office to help her. According to Lonzi, Ethan played it cool, unbothered by his new stepmom's distracting nature.

On the gossip front, Lonzi had tried his best to score more info about Ethan, but the guy was pretty secretive. Everything about Ethan's family was common knowledge because the student aides in the office shamelessly eavesdropped about every little thing. Forget about keeping a low profile if you were sick or in trouble. Suzie Griffin was the worst, sticking her giant frizzy head into everybody's business. Once, she'd told everyone that Lonzi had herpes, just because she heard him talking to the nurse about his "condition." The rash turned out to be a nasty case of poison oak, exactly in the places you *never* wanted to scratch in public. But still! It took Lonzi weeks to live down the talk, all because Suzie decided to run her mouth. So it was no secret that Ethan had arrived. I wished I knew more about him than that he had a rich daddy and supermodel stepmom. What I knew didn't place him in my social circle, and yet, there was something about Ethan that seemed different than the rest of that crowd.

Over the next week, I ran into Ethan, or at least near him, a few times. Normally, I wouldn't pay so much attention to someone else's schedule, but each time our paths crossed, Ethan made a point to wave hello or smile, reminding me that I was the only person besides Jared he already knew at Westlake. Still, I figured it was only a matter of time before Ethan stopped making the effort. It'd taken Jared, like, eight seconds to fall into the Untouchable crowd, and since Ethan was already blood-related, I figured that had to be some kind of legacy bid. Besides, I was super busy these days. I didn't have the time or energy to be distracted. College applications had me crazy stressed every night and, *finally*, my role on the paper had increased. Cressida and Jon- the editors I was most desperate to impress- had taken me under their wing. Ideally, I could write a few headliners this year and secure my spot in a writing program next fall. This was the moment to leave the trials of Westlake behind and begin some kind of *real* adventure.

Twenty.

I was searching for a book. Working at the Covington Branch Library was an awesome part-time job, one that I especially loved because whenever we were slow, I could sneak into the stacks and bury myself in a novel. It wasn't *exactly* okay- Suzannah Forsythe, the wild-haired, scatterbrained librarian- chastised me constantly for not filing or reorganizing or some other menial, boring task. But mostly, I loved my job. And this particular night I'd finally found the book I'd been searching for, one I'd been trying to track down since I'd heard it mentioned on a History channel special that my dad made me watch. My dad watched documentaries like they were going out of style. This time, though, he'd actually stumbled on something I liked.

Immediately after the show, of course, I'd forgotten the title and the author, making it nearly impossible to find until I'd racked Suzannah's brain for women's history and feminism, bribing her with lemon cheesecake when she started to lose interest in my search. Today, when Suzannah, who never finished a sentence and wandered off on tangents that could last a full five minutes or more, gave me the call slip, I tried hard to make my way upstairs three separate times. Waving the paper in my hand urgently, I finally escaped to the third floor wing atop the winding metal staircase. Dark wood and musty green fabric adorned the walls. A few vanilla globes hung delicately from the rose-painted ceiling. Many years ago, Suzannah's late husband, Jeremy, had painted beautiful gardens on the ceilings of the library. Often, I caught Suzannah staring at the ceilings with a moony expression on her face. It was the only time she ever seemed focused, actually.

Suzannah had taken forever to hone in on this particular book. Forever included stories about her great-aunt Winnie, who used to be a suffragist; the Presidency of Woodrow Wilson; life before the microwave; and of course, a mini-lecture on the best fabric for knitting a sweater. Personally, I'd never be caught dead in one of Suzannah's crazy sweater fashions- for which she has deemed all weather and seasons fair game- but I've long learned that to get what I want from her requires hunkering down for the conversation long haul.

So I'd finally wrestled the information out of her, stumbled up the long, winding staircase, and settled into the velvet divan for a moment's breath, when I was surprised to hear a familiar voice. I could swear it was Ethan Jameson. Not that I could pinpoint every Westlaker, just by hearing them speak, but Ethan's voice was so distinctive, so appealingly masculine. It sounded like he was walking around just below me-three flights to be exact - but in the alcove of the staircase, his voice carried straight upward. I sunk deeper into the plush crunch of the velvety divan. Half-annoyed. The library was *my* place. A place to always feel at home. I never felt that way at Westlake and I didn't want Ethan bringing that insecurity to me here.

"Third floor…Okay, thank you…. No, I hadn't thought of that…." I could hear Ethan trying to end his conversation with Suzannah. *Ha! Good luck!* I took a deep breath, smoothing the frenetic waves of my hair, pacing the aisle between Science and Philosophy. I could feel my heart pounding and it startled me. I glanced around the wing I was sitting in. *Damn.* I really didn't want to talk to him right now - I still hadn't decided whether or not it was even worth getting to know him if he'd only end up in the same place Jared had been reigning for years.

"Well, I should probably take a look at this…Yeah, thanks." Ethan's voice amplified. His footsteps tread closer to the first rung of the staircase. I heard the mumbling under his breath as he moved farther and farther away from Suzannah. "Crazy lady." Steps grew louder, the distinctive walk of a heavy boot, climbing rapidly at a determined pace.

I sucked in my breath. *What could I say now?* Clearly, there was no place to hide in this tiny vestibule. My only saving grace was the fact that I had a purpose for being here and a purpose for leaving. But the thought of talking about *The Feminine Mystique* made me groan. It'd be just another excuse for the stupid guys at Westlake to joke about my sexuality again. I could hear them. "Andie's reading about women and their mystique? I can show her *all* about mystique. Just give me five minutes in the back of my car." "Andie wants to know more about women? Must be getting ready for her big lesbian date tonight." No, the idea of sharing my reading list with any guy, especially one of my peers, was totally out of the question.

"Hi, Andie." While I was imagining sinister gossip scenarios, Ethan had snuck up on me: chocolate brown fitted pants, light blue tee, brown leather cord & silver pendant dangling just below his collar. Sweeping a hand through the layers of his chin-length, caramel hair, Ethan looked like he could simultaneously hike the Appalachians while penning poetry about the sunset that changed his universe.

"Hi." My voice cracked a little as I raised my eyes to meet his. His richly colored, chameleon eyes. Despite my charge to ignore him, it was hard not to notice the changing palette of his eyes: green, blue, hazel, and grey.

"So- what's your poison?" He cocked an eyebrow, slowly smiling down at me. My breath caught as he gently licked the bottom corner of his lip, waiting for my reply.

"Poison?" I racked my brain for the connection. Though a little hemlock might come in handy someday... Jared's face flashed into my mind.

Ethan laughed easily, tucking a lock of hair behind his ear. "I was just wondering what you were doing up here." He leaned in gently, dropping his voice to a conspiratorial whisper. "What are you searching for?"

You. The soundtrack in my head was suddenly queuing the aching chords of every great love song I'd ever heard, hurtling off a cliff like a runaway train. Startled by my emotions, I pulled the brake. Hard.

"Well, actually..." Blindly reaching for the nearest book and channeling my most intellectual tone, "I've really been interested in this lately." I swung the book off the shelf, twisting the worn fabric in my hands to brandish the front cover.

"*The Anatomy of a Frog?*" Ethan drew both eyebrows together in scrutiny, then quickly shifted to a smirk. "Really, now? I had no idea..."

Oh my God. Could I have picked anything weirder? My attempt to ignore Ethan, to play it cool, was completely thwarted by my own awkward randomness. Great. Now I'd really have to feign confidence. "Yeah, you know, just a little light reading." I spun him a devilish grin of my own, and then turned quickly back toward the bookshelf. *Calm down.* "What about you? Anything scintillating in the stacks today?"

Ethan processed my words carefully, stepping back toward his tan knapsack. For a moment, I wondered if he was going to respond. Then, he cleared his throat gently and looked down at his hands. "Just needed to get out of the house tonight." Embarrassed by how much he'd shared, Ethan quickly switched tones, "Gotta get started on my History project. I, uh, missed the research days before I moved in." Ethan adjusted his bag on his shoulder, running the strap absentmindedly through his fingers as he talked.

"Oh." I stalled a moment, gathering my thoughts. I was curious, but clearly, he didn't want to talk about this. Made me question how perfect Ethan's life really was. "Well, I should really get back downstairs. Suzannah only gave me a short break, so…" I let my words trail softly as I took three steps toward the wrought iron railing.

"Sure." He threw the reply over his left shoulder, turning away from me. "See ya later." The words were barely out of his mouth when I lost sight of him, rounding the corner to the dusty shelves in the back.

"Andie!" Suzannah's sharp voice drew me out of my reverie. Frantic about being caught snooping, I launched myself toward the railing and vaulted down the first three steps.

"Coming! Just looking for something." I let my heels clank on the metal steps, signaling to Suzannah that I was indeed on my way. "Impatient!" I muttered to myself, annoyed by Suzannah's demanding nature.

Lately, Suzannah had grown more and more intolerant of other people. She used to be so laidback, breezing through the library with smiles, armed with cranberry oatmeal muffins or orange blossom scones. It was always such a pleasure to work with her, but since her husband had been gone, some days, I worked my shift and then left as quickly as I could. I hated thinking of Suzannah this way, especially since she's been like an older sister to me ever since I started working at the library three years earlier. Honestly, it was only a matter of time before they hired me. I'd been claiming the sofa in the reading room as my own since the day I received my library card. Books have always transported me. No matter what my life was like, what crazy scheme mom had cooked up or friendship drama had unfolded, the characters I met in the pages of a crisp new novel or a worn classic- they all became friends.

Slam! Startled, I turned away from the circulation desk, broken from my thoughts. Cressida Maas had just entered the library, pulling the door aggressively behind her. It's how she often entered a room- loud, bold, and with a surety that turned heads. Cressida was undeniably beautiful- long, raven locks fell like a silken cascade down her pale white shoulders. Deep blue eyes were framed by dark eyebrows, arched to give her a perpetually haughty look. But the most striking thing about Cressida was her height. Long, toned legs were always carelessly crossed at the knee.

Completely oblivious to her observers, she stretched and flexed en pointe, drawing a dozen eyes. When Cressida moved, everyone watched.

"Andie, thank God!" Cressida moved across the library foyer in one sweeping motion. "This is an emergency. I need all of you, right now, for *at least* the rest of the night. You're not busy, right?" I cringed. It was moments like these that I was painfully aware of my lagging social status. How could she assume that I'd be at her beck and call? Oh that's right, because my social life these days consisted of sharing crazy stories with Suzannah, daydreaming about romantic encounters unlikely to be, and hanging out with Kermit, my faithful Golden Retriever.

Taking a deep breath, I moved closer to Cressida as she searched furiously for something in her leather satchel. "Hey- it'll be fine, I'm sure." I willed my words to be true. "What's wrong?"

"Everything. Just everything. Dean Brauer has decided that our editorial piece on the decision to exempt athletes from Community Service requirements is antagonistic and now he's trying to pull it. Ms. Sheraton's working on it, but if it doesn't go through, we need a whole new piece by tomorrow morning for our final layout. Tomorrow! He's doing this on purpose, I just know. That bourgeoisie douche bag!" Cressida had the delicious habit of using fifty-one cent insults: high brow vocab mixed with common lingo. It always made me smile- though I'd learned not to smile in front of Cressida when she was angry. It was usually guaranteed to set off a fresh rant.

"I thought he approved that two weeks ago?" Ms. Sheraton usually presented each issue's layout to Dean Brauer in advance. We'd learned this was best to avoid "surprise" cuts- namely when one of the wealthy alumni or influential community members complained about us taking a "negative slant." Negative slant, my ass. All they really cared about was distorting the truth until it smelled pretty.

Cressida raised her ebony eyebrows to the line of her diagonally- swept bangs. "She did! Ugh!" Freshly angered, Cressida banged her fist on the small oak table next to the new books display. Out of the corner of my eye, I watched the new John Grisham novel shift on its frame. I willed it to stay put, knowing how loudly Suzannah would yell if she saw a novel out of place. "And then he just changes his mind," Cressida swiped her bangs furiously from one side of her forehead to the other, "because Miranda Bronson feels *offended* by the fact that her *son* might be *targeted* as one of these privileged athletes!" Cressida gritted her teeth as she spoke, punctuating every few words with a rise in her pitch. It would only be a matter of time before Suzannah whisked into the room to remind us- not so subtly- that libraries were for "quiet expression."

At the mention of Jared's name, I felt my anger surge. I shoved those thoughts away quickly. That was then. This was now.

Trying to remain logical, I worked to soothe Cressida's bitterness. "You know there's nothing to be done about that now. Once he's decided, he's decided. The only thing we can focus on is the next piece. But we'll think of something." I smiled reassuringly at her, "We always do."

"So you're in, then? To write the next piece?" Cressida looked pointedly at me, waiting impatiently for my response.

"Of course." My heart skipped a little, knowing how much work I had ahead of me. It was rare that I got to write the editorial, so when it was offered, I always took my shot. "I'm done here at nine. Should I meet you at the *Bean?*" *Bean There, Done That* was our favorite coffee shop in town. Many of us on staff had made it our unofficial home mainly due to the hippie owners, Marvin & Rain, who offered free refills to their favorite rabble rousers. Last year, we earned M & R's rabble rousing status when we published an editorial about the many ways that corporate America was sucking the souls out of today's youth. Dean Brauer had been on a brief sabbatical for that one, and Dean Stander never quite lived down the wrath of the upper-crust alumni.

"Mmmm…I've gotta check in with Jon first." Cressida dug through her satchel, pulling out a thin tube of vanilla-flavored lip gloss. "Can you get started on your own and I'll come by before closing?" She opened and closed her large eyes, batting her lashes at me with a smile on her face.

I felt a sudden surge of pride. This was a chance to do it on my own, to really make a statement. "No problem," I breezed, outwardly minimizing my feelings of excitement. "I'll get things rolling and then we can talk when you come by." I shrugged my shoulders lightly.

Cressida lifted one eyebrow at my nonchalance. "Really? It's not too much?" Warily, she slung the burgundy satchel over her shoulder and adjusted the silver buckle on its front pocket.

"Cressida- I've got it." Staring her directly in the eye, I smiled and presented my most capable look, smoothing a crease in my dark purple Oxford shirt. I'd paired the shirt with an indigo and gray wool skirt, gray tights and short black boots. It was one of my few "dress-up" outfits for school. Usually, I preferred faded jeans and plain V-neck tees. Comfort over fashion any day of the week. But today was Laundry Day at the Mancini household. So Westlake got its rare glimpse of me in a skirt.

Instantly, she relaxed, looking me up and down. "Of course you do. You're the best." Smiling broadly, Cressida threw her arm around my shoulder and pulled me to her, miming a kiss near my right ear. "Mwah! Fabuloso!" Straightening up, she tucked a runaway strand of hair behind her delicate ear. "All right, then, I'm off!" Cressida strode purposefully across the creaking oak floor, pausing only a moment to fling open the three paneled door before grabbing her cell and furiously punching the keys. This is how she always was, though, so I never felt offended anymore by the way her interest moved and probed like a giant laser beam.

Walking back to the circulation desk, I pondered the topic of the editorial. I wanted something provocative, but not too outrageous- no point in stoking the administrative fires by creating a new controversy. My mind raced with a thousand possibilities- most of them either too boring or too inflammatory. Social issues were good, but since the recent election, everyone was kind of burnt out on the whole political thing. Rich vs. poor. Elite vs. social reject. I needed something new, something that would get me noticed, really taken seriously as a writer.

Mid- thought, I heard steps behind me. I turned and saw Ethan walking down the stairs, a small stack of books in his hand. Suzannah was right behind him, talking up a storm. "It's just a little bit of lemon juice and cilantro to finish. Doesn't that sound enticing?"

Ethan smiled patiently at her, and then winked when he caught my eye. I felt my stomach drop, watching his easy walk, the way every muscle moved in synch: fluid. He walked with rhythm, easily carrying himself toward the desk. I breathed in, catching a whiff of soap and cologne. He smelled like summer just after a rain. It was wonderful.

Suzannah was still carrying on a stream of conversation with Ethan. I had to hand it to him - he was being a good sport. Usually, patrons' eyes were completely glazed over by the time Suzannah let them go, but Ethan actually seemed to be listening. Suzannah gently lifted the books from Ethan's hands, placing them one by one atop the counter, scanning the bar codes while she talked.

Suzannah's eyes never left the books. She chattered on, "...and I remembered the name of that delicious treat, honey—"

Ethan interrupted her, smiling, "The cookie's called 'Honey'?"

Suzannah blushed furiously, "Oh, you little devil, you know I was 'honey-ing' you." She swatted his hand playfully, taken aback. "Noooo, *dear*. The name is some kind of war cry, some kind of military term, Enemy...or Rebel...yes, it's Rebel...Rebel Yell?"

"Rebel Bell?" I was really hoping Suzannah wasn't talking about Bean.

"Yes! That's it," Suzannah grinned at me. "And darling," turning back to Ethan, "it's a bell-shaped, shortbread with the lightest lemon frosting..." Glancing up, "You know, Andie, from that coffeehouse you love—what is it called again? *I've Been There Before?*"

"*Bean There, Done That,*" I mumbled, hoping Ethan wouldn't be able to catch the name. I *really* needed to concentrate on this editorial after my shift, something that might become impossible if Ethan was around.

"Sounds cool," Ethan caught my eye. "Guess I'll have to check it out." He grinned and my stomach plummeted. Guess there was no way I was getting away from distractions tonight. Now I just had to keep my fantasies in check- keep remembering what blind trust had gotten me in the past: heartbreak.

"Andie? Hello?" Feeling her impatient gaze on my face, I realized Suzannah had been calling my name.

"Mmmhmm?" I looked up from the pile of papers I'd been absentmindedly shuffling.

"I asked if you had already brought in the books from the repository." Suzannah puffed at the curls falling in her face. "I'm ready to close up here soon." She was clearly annoyed by my pace. Truthfully, I hadn't done much work the last hour. With both Cressida and Ethan distracting my attention, my normal habits were seriously lacking.

I reached for the key ring hanging beneath the ancient metal cashbox- kept around for the occasional paid fine or change for the soda machine and squeezed Suzannah lightly on the arm. "Be right back, 'kay?" Before she could add any other tasks to the list, I skipped across the foyer and pushed my body against the dark wooden door. It creaked slightly as I moved through, the hinges long needing oil. But I loved this door. It was one of my favorite parts of the library- old and full of character, nicked and scratched over time.

The weight of the door made walking through it an event, which is how I always felt moving into the library. The hush of the foyer when I entered was a respite from the busy street outside. Now, as I walked out onto the concrete stoop, I stopped to observe the street traffic. It was surreal- how much my whole world changed everyday just by walking through a door. This was my home, my sanctuary. Outside- well- the outside had never fully accepted me, I guess the same way I'd never fully accepted them. But here, in a world of captured thought, of engraved ideas, of idealists and thinkers and philosophers, here I felt safe.

Here, I felt home.

Grabbing the faded red wagon next to the entrance, I wheeled it close to the back side of the repository. The door opened easily as I slid the key into the lock. I sent my body on autopilot, reflecting on the whirling emotions this evening. First, seeing Ethan here- feeling embarrassed, yet excited, during our conversation; then Cressida with the editorial. So much to think about. All I wanted was to make a mark, to pick up where Veronica left off and really stand for something at Westlake. Saying the words to myself, I felt this courage brewing. We could be so much better if we just had a direction that didn't involve catering to the rich and powerful in this community. We needed to shake things up…if only I could think of a way to do that…

"Must be an exciting book, to capture your attention like that," Ethan's voice floated over my right shoulder, sending a warm flush across my face. The low, husky tone of his words was both soothing and exciting.

I looked down at the book I was clutching tightly in my hand, realizing that in the midst of my thoughts, I'd just been standing there, staring at the title. "It's one of my favorites actually." I turned to show him the cover of Ayn Rand's *The Fountainhead*. "Have you read it?"

Ethan studied the cover a moment, reaching out to pull the title closer to him. His arm gently brushed mine, leaving a trace of soft cotton along my skin. "Sure. A must read for any modern rebel, right? Is this where you get your revolutionary spirit?" he teased.

I bristled. Had Ethan heard about Veronica, about the campaign, and assumed I was out of control too? I thought about all the lies Jared could have told him, plus all the time V and I'd spent last year trying to get people to sit up and take notice. *Was that what he meant?* The idea that Ethan could be mocking me was unsettling. "I've gotta finish this up before we close," I turned away, gathering the rest of the books into the wagon at a faster pace.

I heard the shuffle of his feet. "Guess I hit a nerve," Ethan mumbled beneath his breath. "Goodbye, Andie," he replied in a louder voice, footsteps trailing toward the parking lot.

I sighed. This was not the way I really wanted to end our conversation- honestly, I *did* like talking to him at dinner last year- but his assumptions annoyed me. Too many people had underestimated me in the past, and after the last year, I had built a wall of protection. Just because I was quiet did not make me a pushover, or a follower either. Suddenly, I had my idea. An idea that went far beyond the editorial to Veronica-like proportions. That's what we needed- a real shake-up. And I could be just the woman to do it.

Twenty-one.

An hour later, I walked in the door of *Bean*, breathing in the pungency of espresso and caramel. I paused at the giant bronze coat tree to hang up my cocoa suede jacket, and then sauntered toward the counter, glancing at the drink board as I walked. A delicious scent wafted my way- cinnamon, I think- and so I ran my hand along the glass bakery case, searching for the tasty culprit.

"Snickerdoodles. That's what you're smellin', love," Rain noted. She must have noticed me breathing in with that wanton look on my face. "On the house, if you buy an extra large latte," she grinned at me, knowing that she'd already made the sale. I've never been one to resist a sweet treat, especially when Rain's the one doing the cooking. She studied for two years at the Culinary Institute, before leaving D.C. behind to settle in Westlake. I've no doubt she could have been a master chef at a fancy restaurant if she didn't have such a big distaste for anything large-scale or high-brow.

"Sounds great!" I breathed in the warm air, unable to resist the sweet smells. "How 'bout a shot of caramel too, please?" With my order ready to go, I searched the small café for the perfect working table. Passing over the two mahogany tables and overstuffed navy loveseat, I settled on the small pine table in the corner by the fire. Just enough space to focus and not enough space for anyone else to set up camp. I'd been here too many times on crowded nights, stuffed between noisy college students feigning study time and first dates who ignored the fact that anyone else was in the room.

Sitting down, I could barely contain my excitement. The idea had been brewing since that moment outside the library and, by now, I'd had an hour to mull things over. The words flew from my fingertips and for a solid forty minutes the only sounds anyone could hear were keys clacking and the occasional sip from my latte. Reading it over, I felt good about where the idea was headed. It started with the announcement last week for the Mr. Westlake competition. Every year, male students competed for the top prize: a $10,000 scholarship from the alumni association. It was a ridiculous prize, considering all the contestants were part of the Westlake elite: money was the last thing they needed. The contest was really just a chance for Westlake families to show up one another and the scholarship was an excuse to make it a school function. What had me thinking, though, was how limited the contest had always been. Frankly, I'd never paid much attention. V and I used to laugh about the speeches the contestants would give, but we never invested much more time than that. But now...the more I thought about Jared and his cronies ruling this school, the more I saw this contest as one giant symbol of everything that was wrong at Westlake. It was time to pose that question to the student body.

Buzz. Curious, I paused from my work to check my vibrating cell. It was Cressida. She was probably got caught up in some romantic interlude with Jon, hoping I'd finish writing on my own. Reading her text, I couldn't help laughing. So typical. *Can't make it by there tonight. Work hard & email me the finished copy ASAP. You're the best. C.*

If I hadn't been waiting for an opportunity like this forever, I might be frustrated that she was blowing me off. Cressida had a tendency to dramatize life to epic proportions and then expect the rest of the world to come to the rescue. Luckily, people always seemed to be waiting in line to help her. She was so used to it, the way everyone fell at her feet, that she never considered another way. If only. *What must it be like to be that dynamic?*

For the past ten minutes, I'd really just been waiting for Cressida. The editorial was done, ready for polish and then on to press. I scrolled through my address book, finding Cressida's email, and then attached my file to a very brief message. *Here it is. A.*

Ding. The bell above the door clanged lightly, so I looked up to check out who'd walked in. From my angle, I could only see a pair of brown pant legs, then the line of a back, and finally, a chiseled jaw. *You've got to be kidding me*! It was Ethan; he'd actually shown up. Damn Suzannah and her blathering about recipes.

I watched as Ethan ordered a drink, and then picked out a fudge brownie from the glass case. He strummed his fingers lightly on the glass while he waited. Rain smiled shyly at him as they talked. I could see how she was taken in by his voice. He laughed lightly at something she said and I swear I saw her blush.

In my mind, a miniature battle was waging. I could leave now and avoid any more awkward moments. But the thought of talking with Ethan was terrifyingly exciting.

"Is this seat taken?" In my reverie, I hadn't noticed him cross the room. Suddenly, Ethan was standing before me, waiting patiently for my response.

I hesitated.

Ethan scrunched his brows in confusion. "Have I done something to bother you?" I couldn't believe he was being so direct. *Who says what they really mean to the person they really mean to say it to? What was I supposed to say?* That I was worried he was a total jackass like his cousin, or that I didn't trust my own instincts because I'd been so horrifically wrong about who I let down my guard with in the past? Neither answer was appealing.

Instead, I looked down at my coffee cup, "I just don't make a habit of sitting with people I don't know…" *Know whether you're capable of ripping my heart*

in two. Know whether I'll regret talking to you. Know
whether you're as diabolical as the cousin you walk the halls
with, the one you laugh with in the cafeteria. Know whether
the sight of your face and sound of your voice will revile me
one day, just like his does. I couldn't look at Ethan's face.
If I looked into Ethan's face, I might lose this sense of
caution. In my head, I counted the seconds instead.

"Andie..." Ethan slid into the seat opposite mine,
waiting until I met his gaze. I could barely breathe with
him so near. Every nerve in my body was on fire under
the scrutiny of his beautiful, complicated eyes. In my
imagination, Ethan's low voice whispered in my ear,
Ethan's fingers pulled my face toward his soft,
sensuous lips. Aware that I was probably awkwardly
staring, I shook my head, trying to clear the spell he
was casting. Ethan smiled charmingly, "I don't bite..."
raising one eyebrow in question, "well..." he winked,
eyes twinkling, "unless you're *into* that."

"Shit." Standing quickly, trying to escape the
visions of Ethan biting my lip now running rampant in
my mind, I banged my knee solidly on the pine wood
table, "I mean...oww, dammit," I rubbed the spot on
my now throbbing knee. "It's just that I'm in a rush."

"Clearly," Ethan smiled out of the corner of his
mouth. He pointed to my purple, paisley oversized
bag, stuffed to the brim with candy wrappers, fringed
notebook paper, and of course, my laptop. The laptop
I'd nearly left behind.

Ok, so apparently there was no dignified way out of this situation. Better just to exit now before I made an even bigger ass of myself. I grabbed the handles of my bag, hurriedly pulling them toward me, knocking over the wooden chair in the process. Mortified, I crouched down to lift the fallen chair, banging my head on the edge of the table. *Really?* I paused, taking a breath. *Get a grip, Andie.*

Ethan leaned across the table, holding back a wider grin. "I guess you were right- sitting with me *does* seem to be dangerous for you." He looked so smug, basking in the realization that he made me nervous, just like I'm sure he turned dozens of other girls into fawning idiots. I *really* didn't want to be another fawning idiot.

I raised one eyebrow, staring him down. "I'm not looking for a bad boy." Gathering the rest of my things, I turned to walk away. "'Night," I managed to keep my demeanor impassive as I moved out onto Baker Street, knowing that he might be watching me through the window. At least I was able to walk away.

Twenty-two.

The next morning before school, Cressida texted me: *Love it. Love it. Love it. See you at layout.* My heart filled with pride. I was about to launch my writer's voice into the Westlake World, and it was both terrifying and thrilling. I'd written plenty of articles for the paper but never something designed to stir the social world of our school in quite this way. I thought of Veronica, then, and what she'd say if we could talk about it.

Pulling into the parking lot, I saw Hamilton Smythe and Brad Kingsbury leaning casually against the side of Brad's BMW. As usual, a small harem of cheerleaders flocked nearby, preening to get their attention. Right on cue, Jared Bronson walked up and looped his arm around Miranda Peters, head cheerleader and shoe-in for this year's Homecoming Queen. She gazed adoringly up at him in a way that made me feel ill. Couldn't she see how little he really cared about her? It was common knowledge that Jared preyed on underclassmen at any party where Miranda couldn't attend. Her parents were super strict, so Miranda rarely made it to an after-game party. But she was also built like a Barbie-doll, attaining head cheerleader with her perfectly exccuted triple handspring. So, in the tradition of all top Westlake families, the star athlete- Jared- was dating the head cheerleader- Miranda. I couldn't help feeling a little sorry for her, though. This editorial was going to royally piss off Jared and his cronies, reason for anyone caught in the crossfire- like Miranda- to suddenly find herself in the path of a madman. But I couldn't worry too much about that- I guess we all made our choices.

All day, my focus wandered. Usually, paying attention in class was a breeze. With a Sociology professor father and Psychiatrist mother, academic success was just as mandatory as breathing. Anything less than an 'A' was completely beneath me, as my mother would say, careful to express in the very next line that this was not a judgment, of course, but merely congruent with my worldview, which has been conveniently shaped by she and my dad these past seventeen years. But today- today was a struggle to maintain my concentration. As hard as Mr. Jacobsen tried to engage me in the discussion of the factors leading up to the Cuban Missile Crisis, well, there was no way that I could think about anything except my new mission. Anything, that is, until fifth period.

Normally, fifth period was my sanctuary- Sculpture: the one class I took that had nothing to do with my college aspirations and everything to do with a passion I longed to explore. Though I had absolutely no experience at all, Ms. Firelli had made a special exception for my entrance to the class. I had never taken Art Foundations or even a Ceramics course - two of the prerequisites. But I loved sculpture. Two years in a row, I'd volunteered at the Westlake Art Musuem, learning all about art history and artistic technique so that I could be a docent next summer. Ms. Firelli visited the art museum weekly, so I'd had many chances to talk to her about my passion. She bent every rule in the book to get me a coveted spot in her Sculpture class this fall - and I adored every minute of it. To tell the truth, I was terrible. Every ounce of creativity I had was in my writing. The art of molding beauty with my hands, of creating three-dimensional emotion - completely surpassed my lowly abilities. But that didn't stop me from loving it. I couldn't get enough of these moments: sitting with my IPod - gentle tones of *Cream* strumming through the earbuds, fueling my thoughts into my hands. It was the sense of abandon that I loved. The moment to be in the world and out of my head simultaneously, to just feel something and let it flow through my fingers into something real. Tangible emotion.

Today, I was really in the zone. Our assignment was to sculpt an emotion and I'd finally found a direction to take the piece. Feeling the clay in my palms, I began to move, forming the base of a triangle with my hands. Satisfied with the initial shape, I grabbed a wire end modeling tool to begin the crags and peaks to form part of the mountain. Delicately scraping and cutting, I didn't hear the classroom door open, but I could sense something- enough to look up.

Ethan Jameson was standing a few feet behind my station, talking to Ms. Firelli. She looked perturbed by their conversation, but with the sounds of *The Cure* now buzzing in my ear, I couldn't make out anything they were saying. Frustrated by the distraction, I turned back to my piece. I was trying so hard to just let go right now, to ignore the mounting pressures of college applications and school projects, not to mention, this editorial I'd now launched myself into. Fifth period was supposed to be a Worry-Free Zone and now the irresistible force of Ethan Jameson was sidetracking me once again. Unfortunately, I couldn't just get up and walk away from this one. Anxiously, I brushed the hair from my forehead, pulling long, auburn strands away from my face. Wrapping sections of hair between my index and middle finger, I stared again at the mound of clay resting on the large, wooden board. Willing something magical to happen. Wishing I could figure out what I wanted.

I sensed Ethan's footsteps in the next row. Crossing my fingers that he wouldn't sit next to me, that he wouldn't completely throw my life out of orbit, I continued working, trying desperately to re-enter The Zone. I concentrated on the movements of my fingers, watching them from outside myself. Who *was* I anymore? It'd been so easy to know that when I was with Veronica. She'd known me better than anyone, and until the moment she shattered my trust, well... now it felt like I had to discover everything all over again.

Absorbing the warmth of the clay, I focused on the filmy feeling of drying clay across my palms, the reality of tiny bits of clay caught beneath my nails. This was the most difficult part- not getting so overzealous with shaping that I completely lost the piece I had begun. Lately, I'd felt this force, this *need* to create more powerfully than ever. All I wanted was to leave a piece of myself in this world.

Creak. The table across from me groaned and I looked up, startled. It was Ethan. Of the two stations left in the classroom, he'd chosen the one on my side of the room, to the great disappointment, I noticed, of Belinda Chase. I'd been the unfortunate witness to her obsession for the past week because my locker was two down from Belinda's. She'd waited for him to walk through the side door every morning, "accidentally" bumping into him, spouting one lame excuse after another to hold him hostage in conversation. The number of times she "forgot" some vital piece of information that Ethan had to explain to her was pathetic. It was amazing that she had the self-respect to continue greeting him each day after the ridiculously lame conversation they'd had the day before. But she kept at it, especially with the unabashed encouragement of her fellow pep squadettes.

Belinda shot me the evil eye, flipping her long, blond hair away from her face in disgust. She'd seen Ethan talking to me that first day, and I'd read her jealousy loud and clear. I might not be a tall, willowy blond, but I had more fuel in my daily conversation vehicle than she'd be able to salvage in a month's time. I smiled demurely across the room, just enough to provoke a heavy sigh and grimace from Belinda's lips. Good. Let her sulk. I was doing my best to avoid Ethan Jameson anyway.

As if in defiance of my declaration, Ethan looked my way and smiled. Damn him. I was trying to ignore the way he sent my stomach into tail spins. Pasting on my best passive look, I focused all my concentration on the mold in front of me. Today was about other things.

Twenty-three.

Later, when the final bell of the school day rang, I rushed out of Anatomy class, pushing my way against the throng of foot traffic surging toward the parking lot entrance doors. *The Howl*'s office was a corner classroom on the third floor- not the most coveted location- in accordance with our place in Westlake social standing. Writing for the paper ranked somewhere between performing onstage with the thespian Howlers and waxing poetic with You Kant Take It with You, resident philosophy club. We hadn't achieved Chess Team status, but the road to Student Council was far, far away.

Walking in the door, I saw Ms. Sheraton talking animatedly to Jesse Millen, Sports Editor. Jesse was the sole cross-over member of the staff: popular with the Westlake elite for his athletic prowess- Jesse had been captain of the basketball team two years in a row- and loved for his witty sports column each month for the *The Howl*. Jesse fought each week for more space in the paper- Sports was only allotted a two-page spread- but Cressida had stated quite clearly on more than one occasion where Jesse could stick his ideas when he questioned the size of the Features section- three pages. In reality, Jesse had a point. There was no reason not to alternate section sizes from issue to issue, especially when Sports had more to do with Westlake students directly than the Features section. However, I would never mention this to Cressida- not without risking my personal safety.

Assuming this was the usual battle, I turned my attention away from Jesse and Ms. Sheraton, looking for a place to set up camp. Sitting atop a student desk in the back row of the room, I tapped my pencil impatiently, waiting for Cressida and Jon to walk in the door. Seven agonizing minutes later, I heard Jon's booming laugh echo down the hallway. Cressida flew through the door, banging the bronze doorknob loudly against the wall.

"Cressida, please!" Ms. Sheraton glanced up from her desk, now disengaged from the battle with Jesse. She shoved a stray strand of chestnut hair from her face with a nude-colored pencil, leaving the pencil behind her ear while she gave Cressida a look of distracted frustration. Mumbling to herself, she refocused her attentions on the ledger before her. Uh oh. That could only indicate budget issues, which most likely meant that Dean Brauer had once again slashed the paper's budget in favor of some much less worthy cause, like paper cups for the latte machine.

Ready to fire a sharp retort, Cressida's eyes flew wide open, but before she could speak, Jon clamped his hand over her mouth and drew her across the room. Jon was much more perceptive than Cressida

would ever be. When she was fiery, he was cool.
When she was emotional, he was logical. For a
moment, I thought I was about to witness World War
III. The look she gave Jon could have skewered even
the toughest soldier, but one whisper in Cressida's ear
and a conciliatory look came over her face.

"Fine," she hissed at Jon, pushing him away, but
already she had softened and I could see she didn't
really mean it. Spotting me in the back of the room,
she strode over in typical Cressida-demanding-
attention-fashion. "Andie! Ready to do this?"

I nodded, sliding off the top of the desk to meet
Cressida and Jon at the row of computers along the
back wall. "I've been thinking about a headline all day,
but I can't quite get the right wording." I grabbed a
chair next to Jon, sitting backwards with my chin on
my left arm.

"How about 'No Girls Allowed?'" Jon queried,
leaning back in the faded brocade chair to stretch his
long legs. He meticulously cracked the knuckles on
each finger of his right hand, waiting for my response.

"I don't know…doesn't that sound too much like a
'club'? This is about more than just the contest.
It's…it's…." I struggled to find the words that would
match my emotion. My blood pumped fast just
thinking about the pattern of self-righteousness I'd
lived through year after year. "No!" Both Cressida and
Jon looked startled by my outburst.

"Chill out, okay? We can work on something else…" Jon looked wounded by my more than obvious lack of enthusiasm for his suggestion.

"It's not the title," I began softly; "it's this issue for me. I guess I didn't realize how strongly I felt. We just have no voice, you know- we come here day after day and they always get everything. They make the decisions that determine what goes on here and they're not even…they just don't care the way…" I felt the words coming out of my mouth and I was surprised to realize how much I meant them, "the way I do."

Cressida sat quietly, unusual for her, but I could see she was taking it all in. "Hmmm…" A slow smile began to slide across her face as she put it all together. "You know, when this hits the press, there's really only one logical next step." Her grin was full wide by now. Cressida snapped her gum loudly, winked at me, and then leaned so close I could smell the peppermint chill of her breath. "We've got to have a female contestant. And I'm looking right at her, kiddo." Extremely satisfied with herself, Cressida kicked back in her chair, planting her cream suede boots along the length of Jon's lap.

"What?" My mind spun wildly. I wanted things to change, yes, but I was *not* comfortable being the center of attention. It was one thing to paste my name on an editorial, but to truly be in our school's public eye, in person, was completely unacceptable. No. Way. "No, this is *not* what this is about, Cressida. And besides, someone like you is a much better option…" I pleaded with her to see another way.

"Someone like me?" Cressida looked so amused with herself I wanted to slap the grin right off her face. "What exactly is that supposed to mean?" She waited patiently for my response with full knowledge that this was just the kind of conversation I absolutely hated.

"You *know* what I mean! These things are just popularity contests. They're about the pretty people and we all know that that's not my strongest area…" I gave Cressida my best death ray stare for making me say what aloud what she knew I'd been thinking from the moment she pointed me out.

"I KNEW IT!" Cressida clapped her hands together, swinging her legs to the ground to plant herself directly in front of me. "When are you going to get your head out of your ass about yourself, Andie? You're deliciously sexy, *chica*, and articulate as hell when you're not petrified that every tiny little thought in your brain might not be the most insightful thing anyone's every heard. All right? You. Are. Perfect for this. 'Kay?" Cressida began rummaging through her satchel, clearly done with this topic. I suddenly realized that it was decided. Once Cressida got something in her mind, heaven help the person who tried to stop her. She was worse than a dog with a bone. At least the dog might be distracted by some other bone—oh no, Cressida was indefatigable. I was most definitely screwed on this one.

"Look- it's not really important right now to even talk about that. All we need to do is get this to print. Who knows? Some other girl may read this and just, you know, get all over it." I felt better just saying it aloud. "Can we just let it go?" I picked at my burgundy-painted fingernails, chipping away at the peeling paint on my right index finger.

Cressida grunted in my direction, demonstrating how little she thought of my idea. But she knew me too. It was better not to press the issue right away. She'd let me sit on this more and more and then I'd be so wrapped up in the idea, I'd actually be on board. Damn her. Cressida was completely maddening- how much she knew just the right way to get me to see her side of things. But I knew her too. It didn't take much to get her anger boiling and then all I had to do was sit back and watch. I knew she'd always have my back and as much as she drove me crazy half the time, I really loved being her friend. Really, the only predictable thing about Cressida was her intense loyalty. And THAT was definitely worth the headache.

An hour and a half later, we wrapped up the layout and electronically sent the pages to our printer in town. I felt great. In just three days, the issue would be ready to distribute and all of Westlake would see the gauntlet we'd thrown. I hugged my knees together, content with the way things turned out, eager to see where this could go.

Later that night, I plopped onto my bed, stretching out across the plush down comforter. I let myself relax each muscle at a time, a trick my Aunt Nina- massage therapist at large- had taught me just before the ACT test last spring. I'd been a nervous wreck about the test, swearing it would be the death of me, the end of my future career as a successful...something...when my aunt found me in the kitchen, hunched over a prep book, hyperventilating into my third consecutive espresso. She'd triaged the situation--- addressing my serious caffeine high first--- and then gave me a variety of muscle relaxing techniques to rely on the next time my anxiety totally ran away from me.

Taking deep breaths, I tensed and released muscle after muscle, feeling myself slowly dissolve into a state of relative normalcy. Regardless of how I might feel tomorrow, the paper would be out, and so really, the situation was completely out of my hands. Part of me felt good about that- knowing that there wasn't a decision to be made. Right now, I could only think about what might be next...how angry would people be when they realized that I wanted to mess with their traditions? Counting the number of evil glances I was sure to see in the halls, I felt myself drifting off to sleep. *Tomorrow was another day.*

Twenty-four.

The halls were eerily quiet before third period. Copies of *The Howl* were open everywhere. In the library, in the locker hallways, in the senior café, students milled in groups, pages open to the Opinions page of our latest issue. I grabbed a stray copy from a table in the library, and then flipped to page two, checking out the final design.

"Holy shit." The librarian shot me a pointed look as soon as the whispered words were out of my mouth. "Sorry…" I gave her my best sheepish expression and then resumed my panic. I was going to kill Cressida. Not only had she plastered my picture above the headline, she'd paired it with an editorial about knowing when to fight the system, essentially painting me as some sort of rebel. She'd changed my editorial from a statement on behalf of the entire paper into a personal commentary. To make it worse, she'd all but guaranteed that this was only the beginning---billing me as the next column writer for *The Howl*, dubbing it as "Andie, the A-Kicker". How did she get this by Ms. Sheraton? Our sponsor was much more liberal than the average Westlake teacher, but she'd never go for something as blatant as that.

I didn't know what to think. My head was spinning and I had to reach out to steady myself on the smooth, oak library chair. All I wanted was to upset the system a little, to get people talking, but I didn't want to be at the center of the conversation. I should've known she'd take it too far. Yesterday, when I saw Cressida's impish smile, I should've been warier. It's just... It's just a little too much.

Gathering my books together, I snapped the red leather bag across my shoulder and took a deep breath. Those looks I'd prepared for last night. How would they compare to the looks I'd get now? I bit the inside of my lip, hesitant to make my way out into the halls again. But I had no choice. This was my school - I couldn't just run away when things became difficult, even if Cressida had completely taken liberties with my work.

As soon as I pushed open the library door, I came face to face with Ethan. Of course. He didn't smile, and at first, I thought this would be number one of many cold greetings today. I started walking past him, when he lightly grabbed my arm. He smelled amazing. Clean, citrus soap and the faintest hint of Calvin Klein. He wore a fitted, navy blue button-down shirt with the sleeves rolled up to reveal strong, tan forearms. A slate gray tee peeked out beneath the open collar of his shirt, offset by a brown corded necklace with a silver, circular charm. The same necklace I'd seen him wearing in the library the other day. I could just make out a word engraved on the charm, but it was too small for me to read. At least not without leaning in very, very close. I shook the idea from my head.

"You okay?" Ethan asked, concern written on his face.

I paused, thinking about how to answer. I didn't want anyone to know that I wasn't on board with Cressida's full-blown campaign until I'd had a chance to decimate her myself. Fireworks blew in my head as I imagined the very serious words we were about to have. Whenever I was really mad, my vision blurred, like a tunnel, until all I could see was the cause of that anger. It's a good thing I didn't get mad that often, because when I did, it was an all-out explosive mess—anyone in a thirty-foot radius was in serious danger.

"It's just been an interesting morning…" I sighed, looking up into his face, admiring the green hue his eyes had taken on this morning. I could get lost in those eyes…

"Yeah, I could see that." I waited for him to make some smartass comment about the articles this morning, but he just looked back at me with kindness. *Why did he have to be so great?* "Must be something in the air…been a pretty weird couple days for me too."

I was instantly curious. Every time I'd seen Ethan, he acted like nothing could *ever* bother him, so confident and cool in his skin. "Oh yeah?" I focused on the corners of his mouth, trying to read the half-smile settling across the right side of his face.

"Yeah," Ethan ran a hand through his hair. "I-uh-left some friends behind, back home…" He paused in thought, pulling on the edge of his sleeve. "Let's just say it's been a little hard to say goodbye…which is why I've been spending time with my cousin."

At the mention of Jared, I stiffened. *How much did Ethan know about Jared's past?*

Ethan continued, "And my cousin is…" He sighed, rolling his eyes, "Jared is…"

An asshole. A pig. An alien from Planet Dickwad. The list of names rolled on and on in my head.

"Different." Ethan seemed relieved to have finished his thought. He straightened his shoulders. "But maybe there are *other* people I can hang with too…" Ethan smiled broadly.

Blushing, I feigned ignorance. "Like who?" My heart was pounding, waiting for affirmation, waiting for Ethan to say something I could replay in my head, words that would melt like chocolate inside the heat of my imagination.

Ethan leaned forward, catching my eye. "I don't know, Andie…who could that be?" Light danced in his eyes as he stepped closer to me.

In the background, the minute bell rang. *Shit. I was going to be late and the last thing I wanted today was to draw extra attention to myself.* Head spinning, I tried to make my exit. "I, uh…should get to Advanced Writing. Mr. Cannon is ridiculous about tardies." I adjusted the strap of my shoulder bag and turned to the right, ready to book it down the hall.

"Is that really true?" Ethan's voice hung in the air, just above my left shoulder. "Or are you trying to run away from me again?" The timbre of those low, husky tones sent an electric tingle from the small of my back all the way up the left side of my body. I could feel my breath still a moment with his nearness. All around us, students pushed by in a cacophony of sound. Clacking heels, loud laughter, shouted names across the hallways. I heard them and I didn't hear them all at once.

I couldn't respond. Part of me ached to give in, to trust again. But I was terrified about what I might lose. There was a reason I loved falling into the storylines my books had to offer. I was safe there. I could fall in love with the dark, handsome, brooding lead and I'd never be hurt when he left. I'd never have to be rejected or manipulated or lost. I'd never have to really give anything away.

I felt overwhelmed by Ethan's question. If I was really honest with him, I'd be vulnerable. The thought of that, of vulnerability, was completely terrifying. There was no way around it. So I did the only thing I could do in that moment: I lied.

"Running away?" I swallowed the truth. "I'm not running away." The truth was that I didn't trust myself anymore. What kind of girl is charmed by Jared Bronson twice? What kind of girl is betrayed by her best friend? My heart had been so cruelly stomped upon I didn't know how to begin again. Looking into Ethan's warm face, I wanted so badly to be fearless. He waited for me to go on, eyes widening with the invitation to be truly honest. Something about Ethan made me want to share every tiny thought that had ever tiptoed across my consciousness.

Shyly, I smiled, tilting my head to the side, "Actually..." My heart fluttered with the possibility that something might really be happening between us. And then, a hand squeezed my shoulder. I turned, curious, and stopped cold. It was Jared's hand on my shoulder, Jared's fingers intrusively kneading the muscles in my neck. I jerked away from his touch, heart pounding furiously as I struggled to keep it together.

"Hello, Andie...it's been a long time," Jared winked and I could feel bile rising in my throat. I took a few steps farther backward, feeling dizzy. Jared stared pointedly at Ethan next, jaw tightening a little as he spoke, "Need to talk to you... *cousin.*" Ethan glanced back and forth between the two us, reading the tension.

I twisted, racing down the hall, feet awkwardly catching every few steps as I tried to place as much distance as I could between my body and what had just happened. A painful realization crystallized: Ethan and I could never be *anything*, not as long as Jared was Jared. Not as long as we were still here at Westlake.

As much as I longed to cast away the weight of the last few years, it would never *really* go away until I didn't have to walk these halls, until I could guarantee that the devil himself wouldn't smile at me ever again.

Twenty-five.

The sprint to fourth period felt like miles. Willing my breaths to slow down, I pleaded with the gods of fate to give me a respite from drama this next period. The morning had already been a roller coaster- I just needed to slow down a second. Advanced Writing was usually a great class for me. But stepping through the door of the classroom, I knew immediately that today would not be one of those days.

Twenty-three heads swiveled in my direction, many of them stopping mid-conversation to look up. Their expressions were mixed. I saw more than a few proud smiles from the girls in class, though Jensen Bell and Liz Nixon- two varsity cheerleaders- shot me a nasty glare instead. The guys' reactions ranged from curiosity to disgruntlement. Trenton Styx and Anthony Montano, wide receiver and tight end for the Westlake football team, seemed annoyed but not angry. Really, the only angry face in the crowd was Hamilton Smith, but that was no great surprise. I'd pretty much undermined his whole presidency in front of the entire student body.

This wasn't the point, by the way. The point was that Westlake Academy had not only created an elitist environment, it had also designed a Boys' Club. How could we host a Mr. Westlake competition- with a prize of college scholarship money- and only offer it to male students? It was the most blatantly sexist thing Westlake promoted and it didn't even have to be. It would be so easy, really, to open up the competition to Westlake women- to make it a gender-free contest. And yes, I may have mentioned that we've never had a female student council president or a female administrator or girls' soccer team or girls' volleyball team or girls' track team- the only sports available to Westlake girls were tennis and softball. So yeah. Hell, yeah. It was a manifesto of sorts. A diatribe against the dominant male voice at Westlake. A chance for Westlake women to really say something about how they're treated here. At least, that's what I was going for, but judging by the cold shoulder I felt from a good third of the room, I began to question my decisions. *Had I just made myself a social pariah?*

Catching my eye, Hamilton mouthed, "Bitch" and then deliberately sneered as I began to move through the room. One by one, I felt my steps melt into the forest green carpet. I willed my feet not to stumble as I made my way to a seat by the back window.

Liz Nixon clucked as I walked past her to my seat. She leaned across the aisle to whisper loudly in Jensen Bell's ear. "*Somebody* doesn't get enough attention at home." They both giggled and looked my way.

I thought about telling them exactly where they could shove their assumptions.

Jensen leaned back in her chair and twirled a strand of her long, blonde hair around a red, manicured fingernail. "Whatever. It's not like anyone else would actually run…who wants to campaign against a bunch of guys?" She rolled her eyes toward the ceiling.

Liz laughed, short and harsh. "As if someone like that is even *into* men. Only a real dyke tries to enter a male competition." She snapped her gum against her teeth and glanced boldly over her shoulder in my direction.

"If you ask me," Jensen leaned toward Liz with a wicked grin, "I'd much rather be *under* a bunch of guys than up against them." She raised one eyebrow seductively, "Unless…" Jensen swiveled dramatically in her seat, stretching her torso across the desk, hands flattening against the cool, wooden surface, chest pressed to the writing handbook sitting atop the desktop. "I could be up *against* a wall…"

Liz reached across the aisle, swatting at Jensen's outstretched arms in mock disapproval, smiling as she settled back in her chair. "You're so bad, Jense."

Jensen straightened her body, arching her back to stretch her arms behind her back. "Bad, maybe…" She giggled, "Disgusting and pathetic…" Jensen's voice rang loudly as she stared pointedly in my direction, "never."

My stomach churned, listening to their cruel talk. I was angry about the way they tried to pick apart my life, but mostly, just defeated. *Was this how students would see me?* Liz and Jensen painted me as attention-hungry: desperate to be the center of conversation. Someone who couldn't go out with the boys, so she wanted to *be* the boys. Inside, I knew that they were wrong. That they were ignorant bitches who didn't know a thing about me. But that was just it. For all those at Westlake who didn't know me, would they see things with the same oblivious eyes?

Luckily, I didn't have long to ponder because Mr. Cannon passed out a selection of Modernist poems for us to analyze in no fewer than three paragraphs apiece. Normally, I'd feel a little anxious, trying to select the perfect words for my essays, but now, I was so grateful for the distraction, I hardly even minded. The period passed by in a blur. As I threw myself into the world of Ezra Pound and T.S. Eliot, the dismal day faded a little. Ironically, the dark pictures painted by the poetry actually made me feel better. What was a little gossip compared to the demise of human society?

As the bell rang, signaling the end of the class, I gathered my purple Mead spiral notebook, favorite silver pen, and completed essay in my hands. Standing up, I stretched lightly and sighed, preparing to walk through the masses once again. On my trek toward the front of the room, I felt a set of eyes watching me. I turned to look across my left shoulder, noticing Miranda Peters standing with her baby pink Gucci bag perched carefully atop one bare shoulder. Charcoal-colored cashmere cut across her chest in soft angles, opening up to reveal her left shoulder. A black lace camisole peeked through the top of her sweater. It wasn't surprising to see her so fashionably put together; what was surprising was the expression on her face.

"Can I just tell you," she began hesitantly, frowning with each successive word, "you're right, you know." Miranda paused, having trouble with her next thought. "I can't really say that, in front of people…I know what that makes me…" Miranda bit her lip and shook her head in disgust. "…a coward. It's just…" She ran her hand through her curled, honey-blonde hair, pushing a breath hard out of her lungs at the same time. "It's just so hard to be honest sometimes." Miranda widened her eyes. Alarmed by the vulnerability of her words, she gasped softly, and then pushed her way toward the exit. Pausing in the doorway, she spoke one last time. "No matter how much they push- just don't give up, okay?" Miranda managed a crooked smile and then she was gone.

I was stunned. I'd never guessed Miranda Peters felt anything but, well, belonging with the "in" at Westlake. To hear her talk about feeling trapped, about fighting against the people she spent day and night trying to please, was shocking. I felt a sudden wave of sympathy for Miranda. I knew what it was like to feel trapped, but I never felt that way about my friends. Sure, Cressida drove me insane sometimes, and Lonzi was one big ball of drama pretty much 24-7, but they accepted me for who I am and vice versa. Even my acquaintances on *The Howl* staff all made me feel welcome as Andie, the individual. I never had to change for them to accept me. I couldn't imagine that- having to mold myself to someone else's expectations all the time. Just thinking about it was exhausting.

Miranda's words stayed with me as I walked out into the bustling hallway. Thankfully, I was just another face in the crowd out there. The daily business of personal gossip, weekend plans, and five minute PDAs temporarily drowned out any controversy inspired by this morning's edition of *The Howl*. Grateful for lunch, I wound my way down the Foreign Language wing toward the atrium. A few moments alone with my book and Cobb salad sounded perfect.

The atrium was empty when I arrived. This was, hands down, my favorite spot at Westlake. Betrand Skyview was an open-air space filled with native trees and wildflowers. Smooth wooden benches were hidden among the trees, little mini-havens from the polished mahogany wood and thick, green brocade that adorned most of Westlake. I could breathe out here. It was amazing in the winter too. When snow lined the branches of the white pines and frosted the lilac bushes, a sense of serenity fell across the space. For its beauty- but mostly the seclusion- the atrium was also a popular make-out spot, and so I was relieved to find it empty.

Opening the lid on my salad, I sat down on a bench surrounded by lilacs and irises to think about my next move. If the administration opened up this contest, Cressida was right. We needed a candidate. And judging from the harsh reactions of some of my peers, finding that person might not be so easy. Cressida believed I was the best choice, but I wavered. Even with the gender-rule broken down, this was still a popularity contest. More than ever, it was vital to have a winner on our side, or we'd make a mockery of the contest and be laughed at any time we tried something like this again. I had to make Cressida see it my way. I could be convincing too. Resolved to persuade her during our meeting after school, I sat back to enjoy the last few minutes of my lunch.

The door to the atrium creaked open slowly. Heels clicked on the wooden walkway. Click, click. Pause. "Hello?" a female voice called out, muffled by the breeze on the maple trees nearby.

Was she talking to me? "Yes?" I replied warily.

"I'm looking for…" I heard a paper rustling during the pause, "Andrea Mancini". There was a question in her voice.

"Oh- yeah, that's me," I answered, standing up and moving toward the voice. As I rounded the corner, I saw that it was Miss Carroll, Dean Brauer's new secretary. Every two years, Dean Brauer found some reason to change secretaries, citing budget cuts, educational level, and even dress code as cause to hire someone new. Miraculously, the "best hire" each year was younger and prettier than the last. If he kept this up, Dean Brauer would only be able to hire twenty-two-year-old supermodels.

"Andrea?" She waited for me to nod, though I'd answered her already. "The dean needs to see you right away." She paused expectantly.

"Can I finish my lunch first?" I felt annoyed by this intrusion. Just when I was finally feeling relaxed, I had to visit one of my least favorite Westlakers.

"Um…" Miss Carroll looked uncomfortable. "He said to find you immediately." She furrowed her brow and crossed her feet awkwardly. I could see that she wasn't going away, so I might as well just accept my fate.

"All right," I sighed, "let me just get my things." Great. Not even a moment to myself today. Sluggishly, I gathered my bag, shoving the half-eaten salad inside. I looked longingly at the untouched Snapple Raspberry Tea. So much for my haven.

Walking into Dean Brauer's office a moment later, I was surprised to find Ms. Sheraton sitting uncomfortably in one of his giant, mauve leather armchairs with the carved cherry wood detail. The dean's office was full of stuffy, ornate furniture and dark, Gothic paintings. Everything screamed, "Look at me. I think I'm important." All show and no substance. Dean Brauer to a tee.

"Andrea Mancini." The dean walked toward me, placing one hand on my right shoulder. "Come in." He motioned for me to sit in the matching armchair next to Ms. Sheraton. I scoured her face for information as Miss Carroll closed the door behind us, but she gave nothing away. This unnerved me in a way that being summoned to the dean's office hadn't. If Ms. Sheraton wasn't on my side, I didn't know what to think.

"Andrea..." Dean Brauer began, settling himself behind the curved cherry desk.

"It's Andie," I interrupted. If I had to miss my lunch hour for this, I definitely wasn't going to spend it listening to my grandmother's name. Mom only called me Andrea when I had really upset her.

Dean Brauer looked startled for a moment, "Okay, Andie then." He smiled in what seemed to be his attempt to reassure me but only resulted in a creepy arrangement of his shiny, capped teeth. "I had the *pleasure*," he paused on this word, leaning forward while raising one eyebrow, "of reading your editorial this morning and I just wanted to chat with you about it." He smiled again, one of those pasty, game-show host grins that might blind a person if she looked at it too long. Dean Brauer crossed his hands together, extending each elbow across the desk to lean forward even farther. My stomach churned a little. Was this his approach with the endless stream of female secretaries? Overpower them with waves of Stetson cologne and television grins? I suddenly felt a lot less annoyed with

Miss Carroll. Remember to bring her a box of candy on Secretaries' Day- God knows she had to put up with a lot.

He seemed to be waiting for me to respond. Okay. Don't know what I'm supposed to say exactly. Thanks? He can hardly be excited that I've questioned the gender equity of Westlake under his reign. Who would? Maybe the best approach was ignorance. Let him sweat it a little. "I'm glad you liked it," I flashed him my own pasty smile, wondering if he'd notice that I thought he was a real douche.

"Yes, well...ahem." He cleared his throat. "We," looking at Ms. Sheraton, who did not, by the way, seem to be giving any affirmation to his words, "just wanted to see how serious you were about the Mr. Westlake competition, considering that it's already underway and..." He was getting on a roll now, leaning back and raising his voice with each line, "it's really too late, then, for any other candidates this year." He shuffled a stack a papers vigorously. "So in regard to next year, we can certainly take your ideas into consideration..." Stopping to look at me. "If you'd like to speak at the Spring board meeting when we talk about next fall, well, that'd be just fine. 'Course, you won't be here next fall, being one of our fine seniors, but your words may inspire the Board of Directors to consider additional opportunities for our fine Westlake ladies in the years to come. In the meantime, of course, it's important that we clarify that with our current study body so there isn't any confusion about this year's fundraiser. You do want to support Westlake, don't you?" He nodded once at me, taking a pad of paper from the corner of his desk to write me a hall pass. This was my dismissal. Just like that.

"No." Dean Brauer looked up sharply as I spoke. Halfheartedly, I tried to soften my expression. On top of everything else today, I didn't want to get in trouble too.

"You don't want to help your school?" I could see his nostrils begin to flare. He stopped writing the pass to point the pen toward my face. "How can you ask for change when you don't even support Westlake Academy?" His eyes flashed dangerously.

"That's not what I'm saying 'no' to, sir." I knew how important it would be to tread carefully here. Glancing sideways at Ms. Sheraton, I could swear I saw a tiny smile at the corner of her mouth. "I'm saying 'no' to retracting my comments because it's not too late for this year's competition." I leaned forward with excitement, placing one hand on the edge of the smooth, cherry wood desk. "The deadline to enter is Friday. We still have the rest of this week."

Dean Brauer sighed and bit back a frown. I give the guy credit for trying. He was definitely working to keep his cool. "Friday is when the candidates are announced to the school. The deadline's actually Wednesday afternoon. Your administrators need time to...prepare for the contest. This is why we ask for all candidates to present themselves by Wednesday." He sat back in his chair, smug.

"But...you never advertised it that way. All of the announcements talked about Friday. Today's Wednesday. How..." I felt duped. Of course he'd change things to work his way. Using the ploy of insider info. Of proper notification. It was bull. He knew it and now I knew it.

"I see how confusing this can be, *Andrea*. It looks like there's some sort of miscommunication about the dates, but I assure you, our student council is very aware of the correct deadlines and would be happy to explain it to you if you just asked." He smiled in that sickeningly sweet way that only the perfectly smug know how to do. "But if you have any questions about that clarification for *The Howl*, please see me. I do want us to be able to communicate *clearly* with the student body on this issue." He looked at me very pointedly. Oh I get it, Dean, I hear ya loud and clear. Too bad I'm not going to play your game.

"Don't worry, Dean Brauer. I'll have the issue clarified this afternoon." I smiled in my best "up, yours" fashion, held my head high, and walked out of the room. I could hear Ms. Sheraton talking to Dean Brauer the moment I left. The farther away I got, the less I could hear, but I knew from Ms. Sheraton's tone that she was fighting the retraction valiantly for me. No worries, Ms. Sheraton, because the only "clarification" Dean Brauer was getting was the name of a candidate by this afternoon. I didn't care if I had to bribe our ancient guidance secretary, Mrs. Harrison, to enter the contest. A Westlake woman would submit her name this afternoon for the Mr. Westlake competition.

Charging down the hall, I nearly ran headfirst into Hamilton Smyth. Bracing myself for the torrent of insults I'd endured from some of his cronies this morning, I was surprised to find him smiling at me as I brushed past. Huh. Not what I expected at all. Maybe he wasn't such a jerk after all. Unless...

I glanced over my shoulder to see Hamilton joining Jared and Brad for a round of high-fives. The trio looked my way a few times before continuing their love fest. They must've already talked to Brauer. And he promised them that he'd make it all go away. I'm sure of it. Flashing the boys my most winning smile, I saluted once. Tarnishing the shine on their good graces was definitely going to be fun, way more fun than I'd expected.

Hugging my books to my chest, I felt great. Who knew that a showdown with Brauer would leave me with such a high? Maybe this rebellion thing was easier than I thought. Earlier today, I'd felt so uncertain. Veronica's campaign last year and the embarrassing way it ended...getting involved at school had negative connotations for me. But if I felt the way I did now, maybe I'd be okay. Maybe what happened last year could be buried, could be forgotten.

The end of the day came quickly enough, scrunching the time I had to find the perfect Mr. Westlake candidate. But I knew who I'd ask. All she needed was a little ego-massaging, and Cressida would bite. She loved attention and she loved irritating the UTs. What better way to get under their skin than to make a mockery of their precious competition?

I slid easily into a student desk near the door of *The Howl* office, eager to catch Cressida as soon as she walked in. Esther and Amelia popped in a moment later, giggling to each other.

"Andie! Kick-ass editorial. I'd give a million bucks to watch Brauer's face when he saw that one this morning!" Esther grinned, displaying a row of neon green rubber bands, neatly stretched around each of the braces on her bottom teeth. The neon green matched the Teenage Mutant Ninja Turtles baby tee she wore atop a black 'n white striped long-sleeved shirt. Esther finished her look with a black skirt adorned in giant safety pins. I swear she changed those rubber bands at least three times a week to match her crazy ensembles. It was fun to walk down the hall with her, just to see kids' reactions. No outfit would be complete without a crazy coif to match. Today, Esther had wound her long, raven hair into Princess Lea style buns, threading a neon-green ribbon through each one.

Amelia laughed. "No way. I'd rather see Hamilton Smyth's face. You know he was counting on winning this year. Now you've taken the shine out of his stupid crown." Amelia popped a giant wad of purple gum between her teeth. Her tortoise-shell glasses shifted on her face as she scrunched her brow, concentrating hard on the giant bubble in progress.

"Gross, M." Esther swatted Amelia away as the bubble grew larger. "How long have you been chewing that gum anyway? I swear I saw you with that same piece in Pre-Cal this morning." Esther mimed vomiting.

Amelia rolled her eyes. "I have a whole pack, 'kay? 'Sides, you know I'm going for the record." She wiggled her eyebrows and raised her hands in mock trophy celebration. "It's only a matter of time before Guinness discovers my incredible talent." Amelia took an exaggerated bow, but I felt my attention drawn away. I could hear Cressida coming down the hall. She did always manage to enter a room like a hurricane.

"Finally! The end of this freaking day! My God- I thought Mrs. Jensen was going to talk about the two-party system until the end of time. Like it's *ever* going to make a difference. Ugh!" Cressida slung her bag off her shoulder, nearly knocking over a freshman staffer in the process. Some of our new underclassmen hadn't yet learned to steer clear of Cressida when she was in tornado mode. It usually took a few accidental shoves or less-accidental glares for new staffers to find their best path.

Spotting me, Cressida suddenly flew to my side. "My girl." She hugged me fiercely, so close I couldn't smell anything but her Victoria Secret body lotion. "You. Are. Dynamite. Absolute dynamite." She pulled away to look me full in the face. "So, you ready for the spotlight? We've got lots of work to do, let me just say." Cressida began looking me up and down. "That untamable hair, for one. But, it's gonna be great. I know it."

As she began rambling on about task lists and sponsors, I suddenly realized where she was going. And that was just not happening. No way. No how. My job was done. Well, okay, only half-done. Because what I needed now was a candidate for this whole deal. And that was clearly Cressida. Or anyone else, for that matter. I didn't care who it was. I only cared that there was someone. But this…this would just not work.

"Ohhhh, no," I began. Pulling Cressida's fingers away from face, which she'd been examining with Janika Green, our Health & Beauty editor. "This is NOT happening. NO. NO. NO." I stood up and backed away from the group, which had grown considerably since this whole thing dawned on me. "You guys have got the wrong idea." I shook my head vigorously.

"Andie, baby," Janika crooned, "you'll be fabulous. Trust me." She deftly plucked a stray hair from my sweater, as she sized me up from head to toe. Janika was striking with her 5'11" frame, accentuated by a pair of dark denim skinny jeans, fitted white collared shirt, and cropped black vest. Knee-high jet black spiked-heel boots fit like a glove, extending her height an additional two inches. Janika's hair was always changing- with a mother who owned the swankiest salon in town, she had her pick of the top stylists any day- but today she had her ebony locks cropped just above her shoulders with a messy bang and tiny electric blue highlights peeking through every time she brushed a strand behind her ear. Janika looked like a supermodel every day and could, therefore, not be trusted to give me any real, sound compliments about my look. I mean, really?

I felt frantic. They weren't backing off and I felt my high slowly fading. My role was here on staff, writing away and occasionally fighting epic battles with Brauer. But not on stage. I was tongue-tied and petrified of the spotlight. Not exactly your best candidate. Every time I stood up on stage, all coherent thoughts escaped my brain. I became mush. I flashed back to the sixth grade spelling bee when I'd frozen on stage with the word "minutiae". Okay, so that's a hard word, right? But the problem wasn't my spelling, it was the fact that I stood in front of my *entire* class and choked. When the announcer called out my word, all I could manage to get out was "M…uh" over and over. Oh yeah, it was just me and the mike, and a suddenly accumulated stutter the like of which earned me the nickname "Mandy" for a full school year. Kids would walk down the hall saying "Hi, Mmm…uh- andy" over and over, sending me to the girls' bathroom in tears.

So it was easy to see why this competition was a problem. I would campaign my heart out for whoever we chose. It just couldn't be me. So I did what any self-respecting girl would do- I begged and pleaded. "Remember sixth grade, guys- the spelling bee debacle? This is a terrible idea. Don't make me do it. Please! Somebody. Anybody? There HAS to be another girl who's a better choice. I know it…Cressida? C'mon. This is your thing." I sent my most pitiful eyes in her direction, even resorting to pouting my lip, just a little.

"Andie- don't you see? That's just what everyone expects. They won't see you coming- which is EXACTLY why you'll be just fabulous." She turned back toward the throng of staffers surrounding her, barking out orders. "Esther- we need espionage. I want to know exactly what those brainiacs in Smyth's corner are thinking. Scope it out." Turning to Jon, she turned her tone to honey, "Sweetheart, would you please draft up a platform for us. Something liberal, but not too liberal, feminist, but not too feminist."

For a moment, I though Jon was going to growl at Cressida's demand, but he seemed to think better of it, leaning toward me to confirm, "Cressida's right, Andie. You're the best. And we'll help you with everything. This is our chance to show the UTs there are other people in this school." He smiled to himself, turning away to begin writing the campaign speech of all campaign speeches.

My insides groaned. This was quickly spiraling out of my control. What kind of monster had I created? I felt my resolve waning. It *did* seem like I'd have a lot of help, and maybe I had a responsibility to the cause I'd incited. If I wasn't willing to stand up for my words, how could I expect someone else to?

I sighed. This was going to suck. When I'd marched out of Dean Brauer's office, I had every intention of marching *back* into his office this afternoon, application in hand. I'd just never expected my own name to be on that form. Oh well. Roller coaster, here we come.

By the time we wrapped our meeting at 3:30, I had just enough time to make it down to the administration office before they began their afternoon closing. Dean Brauer liked to leave exactly at 4:00, so he expected the secretarial staff to have every last inch of the office shut down and prepped for the next morning at 3:59. When I walked in at 3:41, Miss Carroll was already frantically filing away the day's work. Brauer absolutely hated any clutter, openly chastising his staff for papers left out on a desk from day to day. How he expected them to actually accomplish anything with such obsessive cleaning standards in place is anybody's guess. True to form, Brauer only *really* cared about appearances.

Miss Carroll looked startled when I approached her desk. "Hi. I'm here with the clarification that Dean Brauer asked for." I smiled sweetly at her, trying my best to get past her desk to the dean's office.

"Oh!" Her eyes widened a moment, giving away the fact that she'd probably been eavesdropping on the conversations before. Why else would she suddenly look so tense?

"Um…okay. You can just leave them with me," her eyes pleaded with me to follow along, hoping to avoid any potential scenes at such a late moment in the day.

"Dean Brauer asked for me to deliver these personally," I lied easily, "so he can make sure that this thing's all wrapped up today." Her eyes narrowed. Miss Carroll and I both knew that she couldn't dispute me without giving herself away.

"All right, then. Let me buzz him for you." Turning away to speak in low tones into the phone receiver, Miss Carroll alerted Brauer that I was here. A moment later, she placed the phone back in its cradle and straightened her blouse expectantly. Hmmm. Maybe she actually likes the dean's attention.

"Andie!" Suddenly Brauer appeared in the doorway, arms open as if to suggest that he was glad to see me. If only he knew. I hid a smile and walked with him toward his office. "So glad you were able to rectify things so quickly." He paused to hold the door of his office open for me. "It looks like we were able to see eye to eye after all, eh?" He leaned in close to cuff my chin, prompting a nauseous rise in my stomach. Ich. Who did this guy think he is, anyway? Oh right- a chauvinist pig.

"Definitely." I gave him a luminous smile, handing over the application packet simultaneously. "It was so good of you to clarify the deadline for me so I'd have time to get this in. I imagine this solves things a bit?" I batted my eyes in the most innocent look in my repertoire, and then turned toward the door, not waiting for a reply. "Thank you, so much, Dean Brauer. The women of Westlake are really looking forward to this."

Feeling the heat of his gaze on my back, I made it halfway through the doorway before he replied. "This is…" he sputtered helplessly, 'this is NOT what we talked about, Andrea Mancini. And furthermore, it doesn't comply with the rules…" I felt his voice lower a few notches, a sense of calm entering his words. "So really, it's just too bad, but it won't work out this year." He reached out to hand back the application materials.

I turned to face him. "Well, that's just it, Dean Brauer. We looked very carefully at the rules and not a single one states that the contestants have to be male. So…I guess we're good. Thanks for thinking of us, though." I winked, smiled, and stepped quickly out of the room. Better run now while he's still in stunted meltdown mode.

I breezed past Miss Carroll's desk, leaning down to whisper, "Sorry! I think I just woke the beast," then marched out the door toward the student parking lot.

Breathing in the cold, crisp air, I felt amazing. *Who cares if I'm the one in the spotlight?* The point isn't to win- it's to show the Untouchables that they're not the only voice at Westlake. If that means feeling a little, *or a lot*, silly onstage, I guess that's just the price to pay. Besides, the image of Dean Brauer fuming would stay with me for a long, long time. That was definitely worth the price of admission.

I was in a haze. A delicious, I-just-got-one-over-on-our-ass-for-a-dean high. So high, in fact, that as I squeezed between two sleek trucks in the parking lot, I walked smack into a tall, lanky figure cutting across the aisle. Now here we were, tangled up on the asphalt. I caught a whiff of summer rain and instantly groaned. *Are you kidding me?*

"Of course it's you," I mumbled, trying unsuccessfully to untangle my leg from the strap of Ethan's satchel. He smelled amazing.

"What was that?" Ethan grinned, inches away, sitting on the ground with his hands resting casually behind him as I continued trying to extricate myself from the pile that had become both of our bags and now, my ankle.

"I can't…" I closed my eyes a moment, wishing that when I opened them next, Ethan would've disappeared. He didn't. Left knee hugged to my chest, I set my chin on my forearm and sighed, gesturing to the knot I had now made. "It's a mess."

Gently, Ethan lifted my right ankle, slowly unwinding the strap of his satchel. The sensation of his strong hand on my calf, lifting my leg, bending my knee until it brushed against my chest…I let go of my left knee, stretching my arm backward to rest my palm on the asphalt. The tiny chips on the rocky surface were sharp- a contrast to the tingly warmth rising in response to Ethan's hands on my body. I bit back a sigh as his fingers brushed bare skin on my ankle while he unraveled the canvas strap, nearly unraveling me along with it.

"Better?" Ethan's eyes were two swirling palettes.

Seconds passed. *Stop looking at him like a dumbass.* "Mmmhmmm." *You can't say anything more intelligent?* I chastised myself, waiting for words to catch up with my body. My fairly immobile body, languishing in the nearness of Ethan. He smiled and my resolve wavered. *Would it really be so terrible to get to know him?* Ethan held out his hand.

Nearby, a car door slammed. Voices carried across the lot. I could hear a small parade of footsteps, punctuated by laughter. I took Ethan's outstretched hand, finally finding my feet. "Thanks." Ethan smiled again, looking adorably sexy in his fleece-lined leather jacket, mussed hair falling across his right eye. He shook his head a little, running one hand through chestnut silk, glancing my way before he dusted his faded blue jeans.

"Hey, Jameson…" Ethan turned toward the voice filtering outside the tinted window of a black Audi now idling behind us.

This was my chance to leave. Picking up my bag, I searched for my car keys, digging through zippered pockets filled with paper gum wrappers, lip gloss, Papermate pens in blue ink, hurried notes scribbled on *Bean* receipts, and Hershey's chocolate kisses. "Dammit." I knew they had to be somewhere, but right now, I couldn't find them anywhere. Behind me, I could hear the Audi driving away.

"Seems like you're in a hurry again." Ethan walked toward me. "Saving the world must be busy business." He looked directly into my eyes, not teasing, just looking. And with the weight of this day settling, I was suddenly so tired. All I wanted was to let down my guard after this incredibly long, frustrating, exhilarating, anxiety-ridden, crazy day. No one had really listened to me at all.

Thinking about it was even more exhausting. I'd had a thrilling moment with Dean Brauer, but even that was a fight. Come to think of it--- all day I'd been fighting. Fighting to hold back fire in front of Liz &

Jensen in Advanced Writing. Fighting with Brauer. Fighting NOT to be the one onstage with Cressida and all her cronies on *The Howl*. Fighting closeness with Ethan. Fighting myself. As it dawned on me how much I was closing myself off from the world by pushing Ethan away, I started to feel sad.

"Maybe too busy…and-I'm sorry about this morning…I had to…." As I struggled to find the best way to explain why I'd run away outside the library, Ethan cut me off.

"Hey- no big deal." His voice was soft.

Nervous, I tried my best to make small talk. "So…where were you headed before I crash-landed on top of you?" I blushed, remembering the pleasant warmth of his strong body across from mine.

Ethan raised an eyebrow, no doubt noticing the slow blush creeping along my cheeks. "Guitar lessons."

I glanced behind him, looking for an instrument case. "Without a guitar?"

Ethan laughed, "Yeah, that'd be pretty stupid, huh?" I waited for an explanation, but he didn't offer one. Instead, he changed the subject. "Do you like foreign films?"

Okay, a little left field. "Umm…yeah?" Dad liked bringing me to these obscure films at a tiny, hole-in-the-wall theater across town. Mom hated anything with subtitles or open endings, so watching movies at Reel Life had become a strictly father/daughter event in my household. We hadn't seen anything in awhile, but it was fun geeking out with my dad.

"*Really* convincing." Ethan murmured, shaking his head with a wry smile. "Nevermind." He turned away for a moment, disconnecting, and I cursed my hesitation. If I didn't say or do something right away, he'd never know that I *did* like talking with him, that as much as I felt conflicted about whether or not WE were a good idea, there was one thing I didn't question: how much he intrigued me.

I grabbed Ethan's arm. "No, really, I do...you just surprised me." Letting go of the soft leather of his jacket, I bit my lip, waiting.

Ethan's eyes brightened, "Good, because one of my favorites is playing at the Magnolia next week and I thought you might want to go...with me." The intensity of Ethan's gaze sent me spinning. Considering his offer, I tossed around a few others in my head. *Run away with you? Sure. Hitchhike across the country? I'm there. Fly to a deserted island, warm breezes kissing our skin as you kiss me desperately? Absolutely.*

"Looooooser," The whiny voice carried across the lot long before I saw her face, but I'd recognize that off-key-creepy-ghost-girl-horror-film voice anywhere. Jensen Bell leaned outside the passenger window of Liz's blood-red Jeep, Diet Coke poised precariously in her hands, ready to launch in my direction, until she spotted Ethan. Disgust and incredulity written simultaneously across her face, Jensen pulled back.

Suddenly remembering herself, she smiled sweetly at
Ethan, "Lookin' GOOD today, Ethan." Jensen ran her
fingers through her hair, not-so-subtly brushing blonde
locks back and forth across the top of her billowing
chest as she crooned. "You should come over *really*
soon." Jensen leaned farther outside the window,
bending forward to give Ethan a full view of her ample
cleavage. "Really like to spend some *time* with you.

I coughed, embarrassed by how unabashedly Jensen
was serving herself up to Ethan. I mean, yeah, he was
hot as hell and I'd spent many moments fantasizing
about being close to him, but there's no way I'd ever
just blatantly throw my body at him, or anyone.

Ethan blushed and I wanted to hurl. *So that's all it
takes? Slut Central arrives and Ethan's ready to board? No,
thank you.*

"Yeah, okay," I jiggled my keys in my right hand,
annoyed that this was actually happening. That *Jensen
Bell*, of all people, was someone Ethan would give the
time of day. Not bothering to wait around for Ethan's
attention to return, I started walking away. Suddenly,
I couldn't *wait* to get in my car, blast the radio, and
just yell. It was that kind of day. Considering and then
dismissing whether I should wave goodbye, I began my
trek to the "The Barge"- Veronica's nickname for my
boat-sized vehicle, a '71 Cutlass my dad insisted I drive
because it was the only way to "keep me safe". Dad
was overly anxious about my driving abilities- just
because I've had a fender bender or two...well, okay

five actually…he was sick of imagining my crumpled body, limbs flying every which way in one of those modern, compact vehicles. "Oh no…give her the boat", he'd said. But actually, I'd fallen in love with my golden behemoth of a car. It was nice to drive something with a little character.

"Andie," I heard Ethan calling after me as Liz and Jensen drove away. He jogged to catch up with me, lightly grabbing my arm when he reached my side. "I hope you have a good night." Ethan's gaze was warm. He didn't smile, but I could feel his concern radiating up my hair, tingling at his touch. Then, just as suddenly, he let go, and started walking across the lot.

Yep, it was definitely time to go home.

Twenty-six.

Pulling into my driveway, I sat for a moment, staring at the robin's egg blue shutters, at the empty flower boxes- plucked clean for the coming winter- at the wizard weather vane my dad bought at a flea market one summer, his joke to us about the science of meteorology. This house was full of memories- summers spent poring through paperbacks in the fading yellow hammock we sagged between two, too-close together birch trees. Autumn evenings around the fire pit, listening to the absence of sound, when the kids who used to spend hours touring the summer streets have gone to bed for school and the symphony of insects no longer sings. This is my home, just like Westlake has become my home. As much as I complained about it, it was still mine. As scary as this next week would be, I was also a little excited.

I walked into the house, surprised to hear my mom making an inordinate amount of noise in the kitchen. Glancing into the doorway of our cozy breakfast nook, across the aisle to the larger space we used for both eating and prepping meals- well, at least my dad and I did- I watched my mom brush flour from her face, forehead glistening with sweat, Betty Crocker in one hand, spatula in the other. The table was a mess of egg shells, butter wrappers, piles of flour- in varying sizes-, measuring spoons tossed inside measuring cups.

"Mom?" I tried not to seem too nervous about the chaotic scene spread ominously across every inch of countertop, center island, and kitchen table.

"Andie pandie!" She beamed at me, dredging up one of the more embarrassing nicknames she'd created- something I'd foolishly hoped would die with elementary school. "I'm making something new- just had to try it- salmon quiche- doesn't that sound *amazing?*" As she talked, she wandered from table to island to counter, absentmindedly picking up bowls and spoons, stirring and mixing in a seemingly random series of steps. No, wait. This was my mother's cooking. It was *definitely* random because she had *no idea* what she was doing. I loved my mother dearly, but her cooking was terrifying.

"Um...where's Dad?" This was definitely an emergency-pizza night. I needed Dad, stat.

Mom stopped her frenetic wandering to walk toward me, brushing the hair from my forehead, leaving a streak of flour along my left eyebrow. "Just you and me tonight, kiddo. Dad's got a meeting with the Dynamic Duo." Fred and Amelia Rabowski- dubbed the Duo- were Dad's two crazy department chairs. Actually, Amelia was truly the chair, but her husband, Fred- also a History professor- was so intrusively involved, he might as well be the co-chair. They were crazy because you could never guess what they were thinking *and* because they liked to host these intense weekend retreats- complete with weirdo seminars like Eye Listening, Mindset Cleanse, and Letting Go of your Inner 'No'. I had to hand it to Dad, he had a great sense of humor about it- nothing was better than the detailed stories he recalled after a Rabowski Retreat.

"Ohhh...man," I laughed. "Hope Dad can keep a straight face." Suddenly realizing Dad's absence meant I'd have to actually eat whatever my mom was making, I began laying the groundwork for tonight's hunger strike. "But, yeah, Mom, I'm not really that hungry...maybe we shouldn't do much, anyway, if Dad's not even going to be home."

Mom beamed, "That's the best part, Andie: I can just keep it the oven for Dad to eat when he gets home." She started whistling, turning to the stove to stir a sauce that was already bubbling out of control. "And you- missy," looking over her shoulder at me, "need to eat if you're going to be ready for the big day."

"Big day?" I honestly had no idea what she was talking about.

"Isn't tomorrow your Physics test?" *Physics test? Physics test?* Suddenly, my eyes widened. *Crap.* I'd been so wrapped up in the article and prepping for the competition, I'd completely forgotten about schoolwork. This test was going to kill me if I didn't study tonight.

"Right!" I grabbed a bottle of water from the fridge, racing into action. "Mom, I'm going upstairs to start studying, 'kay?" No matter what, I couldn't let anything distract me from my classes, my grades. College was too important to me. Even *The Howl* didn't compare to that- though I was really hoping that writing the big articles this year would great for getting into a cool writing program.

"Just come back down for dinner…" She called after me, as I flew up the stairs to my room. *Time to focus.* Stretching out across the bed, I groaned, lugging the Physics textbook out of my bag. I pored through the chapters for this unit: time and space swimming circles in my brain. The more theories I studied, the more questions I had. Mostly because my life felt like its own series of questions- ones I desperately wanted to answer but wasn't sure how. My eyes grew heavy. Maybe everything would be clearer in the morning.

Twenty-seven.

The next morning at school was a blur. Classes passed
by easily enough, mostly because news of my entrance
in the competition hadn't yet reached the Westlake
masses. Yesterday, we'd decided to capitalize on the
novelty factor with a surprise attack. We'd wait until
Friday's announcement to "launch me," as Cressida
lovingly referred to my contestant status. I felt like a
debutante before her first cotillion, only I was
Cinderella sans Fairy Godmother, a fish out of
water...If this was one of those cheesy teen movies, I
was the plain Jane before the fabulous makeover. And I
was doing my damnedest to keep Janika and her beauty
kit away from my closet and, most especially, my face.

I also hadn't thought about Ethan at all until I saw
him fifth period, which was a miracle, really,
considering how I'd dreamed about him last night.
Apparently my subconscious was not cooperating with
the whole No-Distractions plan.

In the dream, he was standing next to Devil's Hike,
a narrow path that wound along the edge of a cliff on
Mount Sage. When I spotted him, I was so far away,
hiking through a tangled forest, sticky mud clinging to
the bottom of my boots, sun beating down on my head
in that way that's almost too-hot, skin stinging along

my pre-sunburnt hairline. I couldn't see Ethan's face, just the lean lines of his body, hands casually resting inside the pockets of his navy blue shorts, one foot angled toward the rocky edge, one foot anchored slightly behind his torso. He looked so strong, so peaceful. As I brushed past the final tree, stepping into the clearing, I breathed in the clean, thin air and acknowledged what I'd been trying so hard to stifle: I wanted to be close to him.

Just as I was about to speak, to call Ethan's name, I heard a new sound: heavy boots barreling through the tree line to my right. I turned, startled to witness Brad Kingsbury bursting through the trees. Disappointed, I paused, but only for a moment. It was the look on Brad's face that spurred me forward. Anger creased the lines of his forehead, dark eyes were narrowed, and the smile on his lips was grotesque. Immediately, I tensed. Every ounce of negative energy in Brad's body seemed to be trained on Ethan, but Ethan had no idea. Without thinking, I started running, screaming Ethan's name. I tripped over rocks along the worn, grassy path, momentarily dropping to my hands and knees as my feet stumbled beneath me. Ethan remained still, transfixed by the horizon, ignoring my shouts. Terrified, I watched Brad close the distance to a handful of feet, arms pumping as he raced toward Ethan. I pushed myself off the ground, sprinting as fast as I could toward the edge of the cliff. The cliff Ethan was standing so close to. The cliff where so many summer hikers had fallen, some who never made it back. It was this moment Ethan finally heard me, turning to look over his left shoulder, toward my voice, giving Brad the perfect moment of distraction-to shove Ethan. Screams reverberated in the air, my voice gasping as I watched Ethan's body flailing, losing his footing. I launched myself the final feet, desperately reaching for his hand, fingertips connecting just as he began tumbling. I locked onto him, pulling with all my might, dropping to my knees to save myself from tumbling along with him. Yanking hard, I could feel him grasp the ledge with his other hand, pulling his body upward. I leaned down farther, gripping my hand along his arm, pulling his elbow, his bicep, now his shoulder. Heaving one last time, I ground my elbows into the rocky surface for leverage, closing my eyes to block out the image of Ethan's face, terrified and desperate. Sensing the nearness of his body as he edged closer to me, closer to safety, I breathed a little easier, finally willing open my eyes to stare into the icy blue pools of his eyes. Gasping, I loosened my grip, inching backward in shock. Shock because the one I was trying to save was not Ethan.

"Andie!" Jared's voice pleaded. "Help me." The layers of vulnerability I'd once seen were now carefully carved into his chiseled jaw, terror replacing the sharp blue of his typically cold eyes. I couldn't move.

"Andie," Jared whimpered. "Don't let me…" He couldn't say the words, but they reverberated in my head. *Die. Jared would die.* I waited to feel…something. Remorse? Regret? The giant hole of emotion swirling in the pit of my stomach was startling. I looked away, studying the cliffs along the opposite edge of Mount Sage, listening to the quiet calls of birds in the distance, their songs echoing in the canyon.

He was crying now, fingers slipping from my grip. *I could just let go.* The thought, faint at first, sharpened as I considered how much easier my life would be, not to see his face, not to hear his voice, not to remember how much he had taken from me.

So, I let go.

Sweating, I woke up in a panic, reeling from the magnitude of what I'd done. Jared was dead, and it was my fault. How could I? I shivered, startled by how little regret I'd felt in that moment. The fact that it was only a dream paled in comparison to the reality of my feelings. Was I really capable of this? These were the thoughts now barreling into my brain when I saw Ethan. Ethan, the one I'd really been trying to save, the one I felt so desperate to hold onto and the depth of hatred I seemed to be carrying for his cousin, his *family*. It was hard not to think about their connection when my mind was interchanging the two.

I broke from my thoughts as Ms. Firelli walked to the front of the class to talk about a new project. She wanted us to use one another as models for a sculpture. Instantly, my radar was attuned. *Models?* There was no way I wanted anyone else at this school to study my body; honestly, I didn't want anybody, period, scrutinizing me that close.

My hand shot up, "Ms Firelli? Do we *have* to be the models? Can't we just use a picture or something?" I pleaded with my eyes, darting my most intense SOS messages across the room toward my favorite teacher.

She laughed, "The idea, Andie, is to lock in on what's real. If we use two-dimensional prompts, it'll be harder to get that perspective." She smiled reassuringly, "Don't worry- I'm sure you'll be great."

I slumped in my seat, mortified. It was now clear to everyone in my class that I was feeling self-conscious. Knowing that Ms. Firelli just meant to make me feel more at ease, I tried not to feel too upset, but now everyone in class was snickering.

I heard Belinda whisper to her table partner, "Andie was hoping to get another chance in the spotlight. She can't get enough guys to notice her unless she's making a scene." I shot her a dirty look, but it was too late. Half the class had overheard.

Ethan glanced my way, but I purposely stared at the front board. Let them laugh. I wouldn't care. I tuned back in just in time to hear Ms. Firelli doling out our partner assignments. *Please not Belinda. Please not Belinda.* I chanted the mantra in my head.

"Belinda and Angie." *Phew.* I held my breath through the *A...n...* and breathed a sigh of relief when she didn't call my name. "Marcos and Irene... Jeff and Scott..." She flipped through her pages. "Andie and Ethan."

I saw Ethan's shoulders tense at the mention of our names. Maybe he was put off by my ever-changing attitude. I suppose the whole "kiss me desperately" but "stay as far away as possible or I might combust" approach could be a little confusing or...annoying, really. And now that I was having dreams about him, I'm sure it wouldn't be awkward *at all* to work side by side on a class project. Ethan raised his hand, signaling Ms. Firelli. *Was he trying to switch?* Curious, I watched their interaction, holding my breath. She leaned down to hear his question, but Ms. Firelli's eyes never flickered in my direction. *God, I was paranoid.*

Stretching his arms in front of him, Ethan gathered his books and stood up. I breathed a sigh of relief as he walked toward my table. At least he was approaching me. All I needed was another embarrassing moment in class.

"Hey," Ethan's voice was low and husky.

I looked up. "Hi." He sat down across from me, laying his right arm on the table. I could see the outline of a tattoo peeking out beneath his fitted black tee.

"So, I guess I'm your subject, huh?" I managed a weak smile, trying to keep a light tone to my voice. I had to find *some* way around this awkwardness. "I mean, my body, not me, exactly..." I was blushing already. "Well, of course it's me, right? And you too."

What the hell was I babbling about? Get to the point, Andie!
"So, what part of our…I mean, what do you want me
to show you?" As soon as the words were out of my
mouth, I sensed the double innuendo. Freud would
have a field day with my little slip-ups.

Ethan tried to mask a grin, unsuccessfully. He
placed one hand to his mouth, covering his lips as they
stretched into a large smile. And then he just quit
trying. Trying to hide, that is. "You just can't help it,
can you?" Ethan leaned forward, tousled hair falling
across his forehead.

I furrowed my brow. "Can't help what?"
Defensiveness sharpened the tone of my voice.

"Putting your foot in your mouth…" He cocked his
head to the side, waiting for my response. There it was
again. That knowing tone, as if he could really *see* me.

"I don't have any trouble with my mouth…" I
started, realizing how easily I was making it worse. "I
mean…look." Finger pointing in Ethan's face. "I do *not*
have trouble saying what I want to say. That's my
whole deal, okay? I'm a writer. I," raising my chin
proudly, "am a great communicator. It's just the way
you walk around here that's distracting me." I
retorted.

"So I distract you, do I?" He grinned wider. I
panicked, mortified by how much I sounded like a
complete idiot. An infatuated idiot. If I didn't stop
talking---right now---I was going to let slip how much
I'd been fantasizing about Ethan. Clearly, he wasn't as

interested in me if he hadn't mentioned the movie invite again, so I needed to just stop thinking about him.

"Forget it. Let's just do the project, okay? I don't have time for games." I rolled my eyes, waiting for the next smartass comment.

Ethan looked straight at me, silent. For a brief moment, we just stared at each other, not making a move. Then, he spoke. "Sure…Whatever you want, Andie."

Luckily, the bell rang a short time later, breaking the tension. Frustrated by how little we accomplished on the project, I left the art room hurriedly. I had so much to do now that Cressida had crowned me the Mr. Westlake competitor. I certainly didn't have time for more awkward moments with Ethan. Grateful for the distraction, I headed toward Stats.

By the time the school day ended, I was ready for the campaign front. Walking into The *Howl* office, Cressida assaulted me instantly. "Andie! Oh- I've got a million ideas for you, lady. This is going to be awesome," she beamed. "Tomorrow everyone's going to know. Right now, Jonathan's getting us PA time. You know how much Mrs. Harrison loves him? Well…he sweet-talked us a few moments at the end of announcements tomorrow. Thank God she could care less about protocol here…Brauer's going to have a fit when he finds out."

She barely paused for a moment to let me catch up. "What's he going to say on the intercom? I haven't even talked to Jon about my ideas." I felt a little miffed that she was moving ahead so fast without me.

"Ideas? Please, Andie. Leave this for the pros, 'kay? I love ya, but this is chance we've been wanting for years. Can't just start saying anything..." She walked away, distracted by several new staffers who'd walked in the door.

Can't start saying anything? Who did she think she was talking to anyway? I felt my face heat up as I grew more and more angry. This was *my* idea, *my* editorial, *my* stand in front of Brauer. Let's face it- since V left, no one had the guts to make any kind of statement and now they were trying to just walk in and take over?

This was not okay, but I didn't know how to handle it. I *did* need them...There was no way to do this by myself and I didn't want to ostracize myself from any more people at this school. Right now, I had no idea how many Westlakers were really behind me. Maybe it was just this small crowd. Taking my ball and going home was not going to win any new friends. Plus, it just might alienate the ones I already had...

There had to be a way to finagle around this. I just had to work Cressida. Ease back into the game without letting her see that I was actually taking over. If only V was here, she'd know exactly what to do. She'd tell Cressida just how it is, but in that sweet, charming way that no one could ever resist. *Why did she have to betray me?* My heart ached, thinking how much she'd love to see what we were doing. Because really...I'd never think about doing any of this if it wasn't for Veronica.

I shook my head. *Get it together.* I resolved to worry about Cressida's attitude later. For now, she was right. We needed to get this thing rolling. Tomorrow was the day of the announcement and I wanted to be ready. This was my chance to get Westlake to open its eyes and the first step toward rectifying what Veronica had started. It was time to get serious.

"All right, all right. I'm ready to talk strategy, Cress. Enough managing things without me, okay?" I yelled across the room to Cressida, surprising her mid-sentence. She actually looked a little proud for a moment. Maybe she never expected me to really take this on, or to stand up to her about anything, for that matter.

"Glad to hear it, Andie. That's the attitude I'm lookin' for. Steinem's got nothing on Mancini," she winked and punched me lightly on the shoulder.

"Whatever..." I smiled out of the corner of my mouth, acknowledging her teasing. "Hey- remind me again: what are the categories for this ridiculous competition?" I tried to keep my voice casual, but inside, I was freaking out a bit. I'd never entered anything like this my entire life. Okay, yeah, there was the Little Miss Westlake pageant that my Aunt Susan tried to enter me and my cousin Cheryl in when we were eight and nine…Mom had had a field day with that one. Try convincing a therapist to get her daughter to fake-smile and parade around in dresses while telling her at the same time that self-worth isn't about appearances. Oh yeah. That was a fun Christmas when mom and Aunt Susan got into it about the state of girls' self-confidence. Having a mother who read *Reviving Ophelia* as pleasure reading pretty much guaranteed a more thoughtful upbringing than the show-off mentality of my slightly shallow aunt. But anyway…that pageant, in which my talent was baton-twirling, by the way, was my only foray into anything remotely like this. And considering my second-to-last place finish, which ironically enough, seemed to disappoint my disapproving mother, was certainly not encouraging. So yeah, I definitely felt nervous about the process.

Esther walked over to my chair and plopped on top of a desk facing me. She swung her combat-booted legs onto a nearby chair and cracked opened a pink polka-dot notebook. Chewing on a giant feather pen, she recited from a list. "Oral argument, talent bit, and…" She coughed, spitting the pen halfway out of her mouth, "Fashion walk," Esther grimaced at these words, darting me a skeptical look.

"Hey!" I swatted the black lace-up boot nearest my arm. "I can do that." I stuck out my chin defiantly. *No one thought I had any fashion sense.*

Esther was quick to defend herself. "No, Andie. I didn't mean that...it's just that I know you hate that stuff...Right?" She stared at me questioningly, hoping that this was the case and that she hadn't just hurt my feelings once more.

"Okay, it's not my favorite. But I *do* go shopping," I tried to think about the last time I had actually chosen to go shopping and it was a struggle to procure any memory. Sure, Mom had dragged me out to *Serena's* this week, but I did that for her, not me. Maybe Esther was right, but admitting that now would just be another bruise to the ego.

"Of course you do." Esther's words tumbled out in a rush. "It'll be great, Andie. Now back to the talent segment...what can you do?" Realizing that she'd stuck her foot in her mouth, Esther focused on her notebook, creating an imaginary list to avoid meeting my eyes.

Talent? I don't think my work at the art museum counts as a talent I can perform. And reading books is not exactly something you do on stage. *Magic?* I didn't know any tricks and there wasn't time to learn how. Baton twirling was far in my past, and besides, it sounded way too cheerleader-esque to be impressive. Musically, I was okay, but not great. Singing in the church choir didn't exactly qualify me for a solo. There had to be something I could do on stage...Unless...okay, I had an idea but it needed some work...time to think about it.

"Let me get back to ya on that. I've got some things in the works, but...it's a surprise," I winked at Esther reassuringly. No sense sending panic through the troops yet. I just needed to see if my idea would work...

To her credit, Esther didn't look totally convinced. *Damn, I've gotta work on my game face.* But I just kept smiling and motioned for her to go on.

"Okay, Andie. Now for the speech, we figured you'd just talk about the things in the editorial, yeah?" Esther wasn't really paying attention now, scribbling in her notebook, glasses sliding down her face.

"Mmmhmm." Inside, butterflies jumped. *Was I really ready to stand up in front of my entire school and share the thoughts that had kids calling me "bitch" and "dyke"?* Just imagining that scene sent my stomach into flip-flop mode.

"The only thing left then," Esther broke into my thoughts, "is the fashion walk." She seemed decidedly nervous now. Esther leaned in close to me and whispered, "Janika has claimed full access to you in this department. She's kinda commandeered the whole thing, so I'm just warning you."

As if she had radar for her name, Janika burst through the door at that moment and headed right for me. "Andie! I've been looking for you all day. Where do you go, anyway?"

Inside, I laughed. Janika and I never shared any classes, because her motto in school was "Why struggle in a hard class when you can breeze by in an easy one?" While I toiled away in Anatomy and Advanced Writing, she had mastered the art of taking the introductory course in every single department Westlake offered. Janika could win an award for the most varied course schedule at Westlake. But in reality, she was way smarter than that. Janika just wanted to spend her time on more important things than homework. Like fashion. And beauty. And apparently, now me.

"Janika, I've been here all day. If you'd take an Honors class once in awhile, maybe we'd actually see one another," I looked pointedly at her. Janika was way too smart for her own good. During SATs last year, I overheard her telling Cressida that she was disappointed with her 1400. Uh huh. Janika could kick butt if she really wanted to...

"Oh Andie, you know how much I hate most of the kids in those classes- no offense," leaning forward to tap me on the knee, "I can't stand the UTs climbing all over each other for the best grade in class. I'd probably have to carry a barf bag with me everyday and, well that would never go with my outfit." She grinned, running her hands through the air surrounding her body. Today's outfit was chic once again: oversized charcoal cashmere sweater with a chunky black belt slung across her waist matched to a pair of tall leather boots. She'd swept her hair into a loose chignon, a few stray strands of hair falling to frame her face. If I'd let anyone near me for a fashion consultation, it was definitely Janika.

"So what's the damage, huh? Go ahead- give me your ideas about this stupid fashion walk..." I rolled my eyes, sighing as I leaned back on one elbow.

"Stupid? Andie, Andie, Andie. Fashion is everything." She waved her arm dramatically, twirled once, and then sat down with her notebook. "And you...my little pet project, are going to be a vision when I'm through with you." She placed the pen tip to her tongue while she pondered, staring for a moment at sketches she'd drawn there.

Was I really that unfortunate-looking? Everyone kept talking about me as if I was some kind of fashion leper. Lonzi rarely gave me a hard time about my outfits, but maybe he was just being kind?

But still. "Janika!" Startled, she looked up. "I'm sick of everyone telling me I need to change my look for this stupid competition. The only reason I'm entering is to prove to the jerks in student council that they don't run this school. That they can't control everything and everyone." Picturing Veronica in my mind. "So please! Stop trying to turn me into something I'm not. If you do...well, then we're no better than them!" I jumped off the chair and walked out the door. This was supposed to be some kind of empowering thing, not another chance to feel less...

I heard heels clicking on the tile behind me. A hand reached for my right shoulder. "Andie," Janika's soft voice sounded concerned. "No one's trying to change you. We love you." She turned me toward her. Large eyes stared into mine. "I'm sorry that we pushed so hard. See…we all," waving her hand toward the Howl office, "already know how amazing you are. And stunning," she smiled. "The hardest part of my job is going to be getting you to see what the rest of us already do." She paused a moment, taking in a small breath, "Ever since Veronica left…you've been different. Closed off. Quieter." Large eyes searched my face again. "Remember when you guys used to pull off all those crazy pranks?" She laughed. "We used to take bets to see how far you two would go. It was great!" She sobered. "But then, when she left, you just kinda fell into a funk. A long funk. It's time to wake up and be that brave girl again."

I was shocked. Janika put me in line with Veronica? She thought of us as a crazy duo? I'd always felt behind the scenes to V. The back-up dancer. Thinking about the night we papered the alumni statue with posters of sheep being led to slaughter, I began to wonder. *Was I really more involved than I thought?*

"Look, I know it's gotta be hard. She was your best friend. If Cressa went off the map like that, I'd kill her," she put on a mean face, "but then I'd be crushed. But you stayed, Andie. That was the hard part. Not running away after what happened. You're still here. And that takes real guts." She put her arm around my shoulders, pulling me in. "So let's show off that badass attitude, 'kay?" Janika pulled me closer for a hug. It felt good to let down my guard a little. I hugged her back.

"All right, Janika. Your wish is my command," I laid out my arms straight in front of me to hold the imaginary handcuffs.

"Stop being so dramatic, you nut job." She slapped my hands away, laughing. We walked back into the *Howl* office to brainstorm. After all, tomorrow was the first day of my campaign to be the very first Ms. Westlake.

Twenty-seven.

A crack of light peeped through my bedroom window. This was it. Friday. D-Day. Well, I guess D-Day 1. The *actual* D-Day would be the day of the competition- two weeks away. Not much time to plan, when you thought about it. But this was the first D-Day and so I had to be ready. Ready for my classmates' reactions. Whatever those would be. I looked at the clock. 6:52. Okay, eight more minutes of snooze time and then that was it. Time to get up and face this day.

Only, the eight minutes crawled. Looking at the clock every thirty seconds, thinking about the day, sleeping was pointless. I might as well get up. I could already hear Mom downstairs, humming show tunes while she concocted some sort of breakfast-resembling food. Maybe if I got ready quickly enough, I could avoid having to eat it. That possibility sent me into overdrive. The last thing I needed this morning was a queasy stomach after runny eggs with chives or butternut squash & chocolate chip muffins. My mother was the craziest cook on Earth!

Shuddering at the memory of last night's dinner, I raced to my closet, searching for the first acceptable outfit I could find in five minutes. Settling on my favorite pair of dark denim jeans and a jade-green sweater, I raced into the bathroom. One of the best things about this house was my very own bathroom. My bedroom was kinda small- and the worst room in the house for temperature- but it had a bathroom, and that was a Godsend. Thankful I'd taken the time to wash my hair last night- the hours it took to wash and dry my crazy mop of hair was ridiculously long- I piled it into a ball on top of my head and jumped in to take a quick shower.

Hurry. Hurry. I repeated to myself, making record time. I was also avoiding my mom because she'd heard about the competition from Amelia's mother- they both went to the same gym- and had begun peppering me with questions about it last night. I only escaped by claiming I had massive amounts of homework, but I knew there'd be no escaping my mom's probing questions if I had to sit down and eat breakfast with her. I couldn't lie to my mom- *I mean, c'mon, she's a professional listener*, so it's kinda impossible to get things past her crazy probing eyes. So I really had no choice. I HAD to make it out of the house in record time or I was doomed to a questionable breakfast and a long conversation with my mom about "this thing at school."

Ready to go, I cracked open the door slowly. My best bet was a surprise entrance. Just have everything together, and then mention on my way out that I wanted to stop by the Howl office for an early meeting, and go. Mom never questioned those because she was so proud of my work on the paper. She was always encouraging me to "get more involved", so the paper was a perfect way to do something I loved AND get mom off my back about "building my professional demeanor" or whatever other crazy, article-inspired idea she'd think of next.

I crept down the stairs. *One. Two.* Foot all the way to the right for the creak on the third stair. *Four. Five.*

"Andie? What are you doing?" *Crap.* I heard my dad's voice behind me at the top of the stairs. Turning, I saw his puzzled expression. Coffee cup in hand, he seemed rumpled in striped blue pajamas and a terry cloth robe. What was HE doing up this early? Dad had the perfect schedule- only afternoon classes to teach- so I never saw him before school.

"Oh!" I racked my brain for an acceptable excuse. "I'm just practicing my balance. You know, posture is one of the most important attributes for any young woman." I bowed and batted my eyes in mock compliance.

He chuckled. "All right, ham, now get downstairs and eat so your mother can stop banging those pots and pans. I'm trying to focus on grading papers, but all I can think about is what she's puttin' together down there." He grinned at me conspiratorially. More than once, dad and I had *accidentally* ruined some of mom's dishes to avoid having to eat them. We had *Antonio's*, the local pizza joint, on speed dial.

"Okay. Will do." I grinned at dad, exaggerating my stealth walk down the stairs to keep up the ruse. Looking back over my shoulder, I winked at him, thankful that he'd already started walking back to his room. Phew. All I want to do is get out of here, quick.

Reaching the last stair, I cocked my ear toward the kitchen, listening for mom. She was humming *Les Miserables* full steam now, furiously whisking something at the same time. I could hear Kermit's nails scratching on the cabinets, probably trying to convince my mom to give some scraps. In this household- with the crazy combinations- Kermit earned A LOT of table food, mostly when mom's back was turned. Sometimes Dad and I had to walk him three times a day just to keep off the extra weight.

Grabbing my purse from the table in the hall, I cracked open the front door. "Bye, Mom. See you after school." One foot out. And...

"Andie! Wait, honey..." Mom came skidding down the hall from the kitchen, sliding in her pink, furry slippers. I loved Mom's look in the morning. Sharp business suit. Three large Velcro curlers piled on top of her head. Mickey Mouse apron. And of course, furry pink slippers Dad and I had been trying to throw away forever now. They just kept coming back.

Mom shoved a warm paper bag in my hand. "Here's something for the road, okay?" *How did she know I'd be sneaking out the door?* I looked at my mom, confusion written all over my face. "Don't look so surprised. You need to work on your stealth mode a little more, darling." She winked at me. "And I want to hear ALL about your campaign when you come home tonight, okay?" Kissing me once on the cheek, she checked for smudged lipstick and then, shoved me gently out the door. "Git now."

When I arrived at school, the halls were quiet. It was nice. A chance for some peace before what might be a very stressful day. I told myself that I didn't care what people said about me running. That I was doing this for myself, recreating the spirit of something that died last year. Something I missed dearly.

But it wasn't just for me. When Veronica started her campaign last year for student council president, the response from so many of the girls at school had been incredible. They'd been waiting. Waiting for someone to remind the administration and the Untouchables that Westlake lacked another voice.

But it'd been a disaster. First, the blackmail. Jared holding the secret over Veronica's head. Then, the sex tape tarnishing Veronica's reputation. But the cout de gras had been the fiery response Veronica had unleashed after the scandal. Her approach had been two-fold: launch an intense feminist campaign to stop the misogynistic ways of our administration and prove that sexy was powerful. The dance-party protest riot in the cafeteria was apparently the last straw. The campaign had ended with Veronica's expulsion.

So I knew how much Brauer and his team hated the idea of me running for Mr. Westlake. I'm sure he thought that I would follow in Veronica's footsteps. That my goal was to cause a scene, to make a mockery of Westlake traditions. But that wasn't it at all. I just wanted to get back to where we started. Because in the beginning, V and I had a good idea. Her motives for the campaign were so vastly different from mine today, but it didn't have to take away from what I was trying to do. Just because Veronica and I didn't talk anymore...

The announcement came at the end of first period. Every day we stopped before second period to hear the day's notices and, of course, any inane words from Dean Brauer. This time, though, he'd made Mrs. Harrison take the mike. Her voice was so scratchy and hoarse; it was hard to decipher anything. There's no way Brauer could say my name and save face, I guess, so he was making us all suffer through the long and painstaking reading of the names under Mrs. Harrison's direction. I tuned back in to hear her read the third name, "Jared Bronson." *Great.* Not that I was surprised, but I was hoping to avoid seeing him backstage during any of these activities. I was curious about how he was going to run against his best buds, Brad Kingsbury and Hamilton Smith. Would they flip a coin to see who gets the votes of their cronies? "Anthony Montano." Not a surprise. Being a star on the football team practically guaranteed you Big Man

on Campus following at Westlake. "Andie Mancini." I
heard Mrs. Harrison stumble a little, then continue on
as if she'd misunderstood that Andie was not a guy,
but Andrea, the girl who'd been following her around
in the guidance office all semester. Knowing Mrs.
Harrison and the scatterbrained way she carried
herself, she probably thought I had a twin brother
named Andy. "And Ethan Jameson."

Okay. Not bad. Looking around the room, I saw a
few raised eyebrows, but no one was throwing
stones…yet. Suddenly, I started in my chair. *Wait. Did
I hear the last name correctly?* I'd been so busy looking
around the room when Mrs. Harrison called my own
name, I'd hardly paid attention to the end. *Is Ethan
really running too? Running against me?* I swallowed,
hard. The likelihood that he'd ever view me as some
sort of amazing, sexy, brilliant, independent woman
shrank in my mind as I imagined us pitted against each
other for the title of *Mr.* Westlake. He's going to think
I'm some kind of freak.

I was disappointed. During the fashion walk
portion of the contest, the tradition was to be escorted
by a young woman, or in my case, young *man*. Part of
me had been hoping that I'd have enough courage to
ask Ethan to be my escort. That when it came time to
walk down the runway in whatever get-up Janika had
put together, he would be on my arm. But not if he
was running against me.

Guess Lonzi would have to step in again. One more chance to be labeled as the girl who couldn't 'get any' by her peers. Good thing I supposedly didn't care…In the middle of that thought, the bell rang, temporarily interrupting any worries.

When I made it to fifth period, there was a stranger sitting at Ms. Firelli's desk: a substitute. On the way to my seat, I glanced at the front board. The substitute had written a very brief, but very clear task list with only two items: (1) Find partner; (2) Work on projects.

I felt the butterflies surge in my stomach, imagining spending a whole period with Ethan at my side. It'd be the longest we'd ever talked to each other. The longest we'd ever been near each other. Silently, I cursed Ms. Firelli for her absence. If she were here, I knew we'd start with our daily exercises first, sculpture project second.

Ethan walked in the door and my stomach flip-flopped. Damn. Was he *ever* going to stop having that effect on me? He walked toward his desk, paused to look at the board, and then sauntered toward me. I watched the line of his lean body moving so fluidly, so confidently in my direction. I held my breath just as he stopped at my table. Placing his books on the smooth, wooden surface, his hand slid across the seat opposite mine. *Good. He'll sit over there.* Ethan ran a hand along the edge of the chair, watching my face. His fingers paused and I swear I noticed a tiny smile. Then he kept moving, walking slowly around my chair to slide into the seat next to me. *Was he messing with me?*

"Hey," Ethan nodded, stretching his legs.

"Guess I was hoping you'd be sick today," I smirked, resolved, for *once*, not to be a blathering idiot in front of him.

He laughed easily. "Oh...and here I thought you didn't like me or something." His grin stretched wide across his face.

"Whatever..." I mumbled, shuffling papers on my desk. Truthfully, I was just stalling. I knew the parameters of this project backwards and forwards. Pretending to be engrossed in the assignment prompt, I waited for the bell to ring. The start of the time when I wouldn't be able to avoid Ethan and his smoldering grin.

Buzz. The substitute teacher stood, pointed at the board, and then sat back down. He unfolded a copy of *The New York Times*, procured a pair of tiny, brown speckled eyeglasses from his shirt pocket and began to read. *Okay. I guess that was that.*

I could feel Ethan's eyes trained on me. When I didn't turn my head, he coughed. "Andie? Were you planning on paying attention to me at all today or do I have to sculpt myself?" Playfully, he waved a hand across the length of his body, reminding me again why I was so nervous.

"I guess I could pay a *little* attention to you," I smiled, tucking a section of auburn locks behind my ear, "but don't let it go to your head- this is strictly business."

Ethan grinned, lightly bumping my shoulder with his own. "Good- I mean, I *do* think you're pretty horrible, so..."

I glared in mock-offense at him, shoving his hand away, "Jerk."

Ethan sat back, raising his palms in a gesture of surrender. "All right, you got me. I'm the terrible one. But in all seriousness..." Ethan moved his chair a little closer. "Do you have any ideas about the project...besides that it's about you," grimacing, "and me", puffing his well-defined chest in pride. My face reddened, so I ducked my head to hide it.

"No, actually..." *Focus. Focus. Focus.* "I hadn't thought about it much." *Lie. Lie. Lie.* All I *could* think about- besides this harebrained competition scheme- was Ethan.

"Fine. Then you'll let me pick?" *Sure...pick whatever you want, Ethan. All I want is to crawl under this table to hide my face.*

"Mmmhmm," I mumbled.

"Good. Now give me your hand." My heart stopped. *What was he talking about?*

I fumbled for my voice. "I don't...I mean, here?" I looked up into his hazel eyes, locked into their green hue today.

He smiled, mischief highlighting the forest in his eyes. "For the project? I'd like to sculpt your hand."

He paused. "What did you think I meant?" His eyes sparkled a little as they searched mine and I knew then that he *did* know.

"Nevermind." I uncurled my hand and reached across the short space between us. I didn't know what to do with it. First, I lay it palm down, fingers outstretched. But that didn't look right. So I twisted my wrist, turning it upward instead. Slowly, I clenched and unclenched my hand, staring at my long, slender fingers, at the chipped magenta paint on my right ring finger, at the tiny scar zigzagging between my left middle and pointer fingers.

Ethan stared at me. "So…done with the finger calisthenics or were you planning an aerobic workout next?" I blanked, suddenly aware of how spastic I must seem. I pulled myself out of the awkward funk with a moment of honesty.

"I just don't know what you want." Well, that was certainly true in more ways than one.

Ethan stared back, eyes softening. "Just relax, okay?" He picked up my hand, laying it palm up inside his own. His hand was soothingly warm. Firm, but not too rough. It was a strong hand; one I'd like to hold. I shook the runaway thoughts from my mind. This was just a project. Ethan was Jared's cousin. I repeated the words like a mantra in my head.

But when Ethan ran his finger along the edges of my hand, the sensation was so *good* I just wanted to melt into the table. So much for staying focused. Ethan stared at my hand thoughtfully, tracing the grooves and lines, then the spaces between my fingers. I bit my lip. Electric surges feathered up and down my arm, but I wouldn't lose it. I *couldn't* lose it. Not in school. Not sitting right next to him.

And then Ethan stopped, placing my hand gently back on the table. "Okay," he replied with confidence, "I've got it."

"Oh," I croaked, finding my voice. "Ummm…"

Ethan leaned forward, casually resting his right forearm on the table, hand sunk into his hair, "I think it'd be cool to blend our sculptures together…unless…" He paused, raising one eyebrow, "… you have a different idea?" Ethan looked at me patiently, evidently waiting for my artistic brainchild. Desperately, I willed myself to—on the spot--invent the most original, mind-blowing concept known to Man, but with all my creative energies lately poured into *The Howl* and this competition, I couldn't think of a single mediocre idea, let alone a brilliant one.

"Not really. I was, uh, still thinking about it," I answered in my most pensive tone. I hope Ethan didn't think I was boring, that I couldn't design some kind of art project because I was creatively stunted.

"Good, because I think I've got something." Ethan laid his hands out on the table excitedly. "What do you think about sculpting one another's hands and then placing them together on one stand…almost touching. You know…like that scene in the Sistine Chapel?" I nodded, listening. "And then between them, between the two fingers, we could put this barrier. Showing the great disconnect between human beings, the way we're so close, but so far away." He looked adorable, face lit up by the idea. I could see how much he loved art. And for me it was the same, only my skill level was woefully deficient. Poor Ethan didn't know that I was a "special" edition to Ms. Firelli's class. The last project had nearly killed me, but, thankfully, Ms. Firelli took liberties with her grading scale, adjusting it so I didn't fail miserably. (It would've been a shock to my 3.98 GPA. I couldn't afford to have any class, let alone an elective, tank my pre-Ivy application surge.)

I had to admit, Ethan's idea sounded really cool. Plus, I was incredibly relieved to have Ethan choose what we'd be sculpting. Hands, I could do. Anything else: I might lose my mind.

Decision made, we started working, first picking out materials for the model. After confessing that I didn't have many art classes under my belt- which necessitated an explanation of my work as an art docent- hopefully not too geeky- Ethan suggested that we start with my hand first. Fine with me. I needed to get over these jitters before I started shaping his hand. That's all I needed: sweating and shaking to mess up the mold.

I closed my eyes, focusing on the way Ethan's fingers expertly traced every inch of my hand. He measured, moved, measured, and traced- all with a thoughtful expression on his face. As I watched Ethan concentrate, the way he bit his lip, barely sticking his tongue out next to his teeth, scrunching his brow, I knew I was going to need one hell of a distraction to avoid thinking about how I'd like to grab his shirt collar and melt my tongue into his.

I tried my best to think of something horrible. *Ebola. Flesh-eating viruses. Meal worms. (I know, meal worms are not disgusting, but after spending a month tracking the little critters for a seventh grade science project, I couldn't think about them without cringing.) Ok, good. This was working.*

This was not working. It was so *not-working*. Eventually, I just stopped trying, letting my mind run amok instead. I mean, why not? My thoughts wandered back to my dream the other night. What if we'd met at Mount Sage, but not at Devil's Hike? There was another place, down near the base, a beautiful stretch of grass right next to a lake.

We meet there—accidentally- both looking for a place to escape. I'm sitting in the grass, combing the blades with my fingers. At first, I don't notice Ethan. I'm sketching a patch of wildflowers along the shore, light blues and yellows, petals swaying delicately in the wind. Taking a break, I stretch backward, embracing the sun's warmth on my skin, appreciating the way she casts a twinkly haze on the water. Hearing footsteps behind me, I turn, locking eyes with Ethan. Quietly, he walks over, sits down next to me, saying nothing.

For several minutes, Ethan and I sit together, watching the water peak and fall with the wind. Watching the boats gliding in the distance. Close, but not touching. Gradually, our hands edge closer to one another as we languish in the grass.

Ethan runs his finger along the lines of my right hand. Gently, he traces the backside of my hand, moving slowly toward my wrist, drawing invisible diagrams from one tiny freckle to the next. His fingers are like feathers, raising the hairs on my skin, spilling warmth across my skin. I'm lost in his touch, absorbing oranges and sunshine from the heat of his body near mine. My entire body tingles, set afire with anticipation.

We don't speak aloud: instead, thoughts hover between us like soft, golden orbs. They float between our bodies, pulling the air together like an unstoppable force. Suddenly, I want him so badly. I want his body close, his chest pressing mine, his eyes spearing mine with the truths we don't dare say aloud. Dizzy, I drink in the smell of his skin, feeling cool, mint breaths line my arm as he traces.

Electricity buzzes between us, tingling the edges of my consciousness, and I can barely stand it. I am here and not here. All I can see, smell, taste, and touch is Ethan, but it isn't enough. I am restless, counting each breath: quick, uneven. Suddenly, I notice something different. The way Ethan's fingers lift and land on my skin, like he's sketching something...

Letters. I feel the familiar swirls and loops of words. He's writing to me. *Y...o... u...* I lean back on my left arm, resting my weight there, wayward curls fall across my forehead. *A...r...e...* Closing my eyes, the sun's rays wash over me. *S...o...* The air is deliciously still. *S...e...x...y.* I peek at Ethan, finding his eyes on mine. He's so close.

I draw myself upward, reaching to push the curls out of my face, meeting Ethan's hand there instead, brushing hair behind my ear. In one smooth movement, he pulls me to him. Our eyes connect, inches from one another. His sweet, minty breath exhales once across my lips, tingling. So close. Delicately, I wet my lips, leaning closer. And then... his soft lips pursue mine, arms pulling me tight against his chest. Strong hands cradle my head: permission to fall. So I do. Ethan's soft, warm tongue finds my own, slowly teasing. My stomach flutters, frenetically rising and falling in electric surges: butterflies on crack. I breathe him in.

Loud buzzing broke the moment: the bell. I jolted, pulling back my hand. I couldn't believe I'd been daydreaming this whole time. Ethan laced his fingers together and stretched them out in front of his body. "That wasn't so bad, was it?" he asked.

You have no idea. I smiled in response. "No, I guess not. So, see you tomorrow?" I asked, trying to come back to Earth.

"Or sooner," he winked. "I think there's a meeting for Mr. Westlake competitors after school today. Not planning on missing that one, are you?" Ethan stood up, watching me as he pushed the wooden chair close to the large, metal table.

"Oh," I blushed, "I guess I will see you then." I straightened my shoulders and gently tossed my hair over my right shoulder, making room for the strap of my bag.

"Hey, Andie," Ethan called back as he walked ahead of me out the door, "For the record, I think it's cool. What you're doing... And, by the way, you promised me a movie- don't think I've forgotten." With a wink, he turned and sauntered down the hall, leaving me surprised. Ethan was the first guy, besides my friends, who actually seemed to like me *more* because I'd entered the competition. Most guys were describing my run as some kind of Femme-Nazi siege against "The System." Which it was, I guess. Minus the reference to the most heinous terrorist group on Earth.

As the day wound down, I became more nervous about this meeting. Honestly, I'd forgotten all about it. All I could concentrate on before today was the announcement and how people would react. The meeting was far from my mind.

For the most part, kids were acting okay. I received a few snickers in gym class when we separated by gender for a basketball game. Two meatheads on the wrestling team thought it'd be funny to pretend that I was on their team instead of playing with the girls. Then there'd been a minor incident in Statistics when two geeks, thinking they were hilarious, had decided to calculate the odds of me winning if I competed against a group of terriers, calling it the Mr. Westie competition. I suppose they were taking the term *bitch* a little too literally there. But really, that was it. I was kinda hoping to get more words of encouragement from the girls, but I knew that what I was doing might have been a little reminiscent of Veronica's run last year. Why get their hopes up when I might quit just days before the competition? So many girls had invested their time and energy into Veronica's campaign, it'd been a huge let-down when she'd backed out. *Especially* when that was followed up by the whole sex tape scandal.

So when it came time to walk into the front conference room for the meeting after school, I was feeling pretty good. No one had shouted at me or mumbled comments about my sexuality under their breath. Compared to the break of the article a week ago, this was nothing. I'd take a little teasing any day if it meant I could do something bigger than myself. It was really only the comments intended to be cruel that got to me. Ignorant words did little to rile me up.

Brauer was setting up a coffee station when I walked in, serving Brad Kingsbury the first cup. Of course. After the little meeting I witnessed in the hallway last year with Brauer and Brad's mom, I wasn't surprised at all to see him sucking up to our current student council president. I was curious about how Brad qualified to run if this was some kind of student council initiative, but I'd long learned that the UTs did what they did to suit their own needs, regardless of logic or ethics. I still fumed thinking about the horrible things Brad's mom had said about Veronica and her student council campaign. Even though Jared was still the evil monster in that whole situation, the constant fight from his friends and their parents *had* to have influenced his dirty deeds.

After everyone had filed in, Brad stood up to speak. "Hi guys." A dozen heads nodded at him from around the giant oval conference table. Hamilton Smith actually had his feet up on the table at the other end. He raised his fist to Brad in a gesture of approval. "Thanks, man, but seriously, we don't want to waste your time, so we----"looking at Brauer as he talked, "just have a few guidelines to go over and then we'll see you in a week for the judging."

Phew. A week. I forgot how short this whole thing was. On the one hand, that was great. Less time to stress and less time to anticipate my surefire, grand loss. But at the same time, I was kind of excited.

Brad continued, "Basically, the deal is to find out who's the big man," he looked at me, "um, or woman," I heard a few snickers at his correction, "on campus." You're here because you've been nominated *and* you agreed to a little shameless promotion and humiliation in front of your peers." Everyone laughed. It was so weird to be part of this boys' club moment. I'd never realized how little they took themselves seriously.

Brauer jumped in, "Gentlemen...and lady," He glowered at me, "We really only have one or two things to remember and then the floor is yours for any questions. First, all contestants must have an escort for the fashion walk." He air-quoted the last two words, rolling his eyes at something he obviously found lacking in importance. All around me, guys were showing one another their biceps and talking about who had the best abs. *Wow. Were guys really this full of themselves?* I snuck a glance at Ethan to see how he was fitting in, but he was just staring at Brauer, listening.

Brauer went on, "And second," He waited for the room to quiet. "You must all present a speech about your merits. Remember, this is a scholarship opportunity, so the speeches will be the most important part of your competition." The guys exchanged looks with one another, clearing indicating how little they thought brains would factor into the final judgment. Great. I'd entered some sort of backwards beauty contest. For men. I slumped down in the chair, crossing my arms. Now it was going to be insulting if I didn't at least make it to the final three.

"Okay, guys, that's about it. Any questions?" I had a million, but I wasn't about to raise my hand with this group. I'd talk things over with Cressida and then just approach Brauer later. He'd be much less likely to snarl at me if his pretty boys weren't standing there, peering over his shoulder.

Brad scanned the room. "'Kay. Looks good. See you all next week, but don't work too hard. You know I'm going to be the one in the winner's circle," he boasted. That declaration prompted a round of 'No way, man' and 'I've got a way better strut than you do.' My favorite was Anthony Montano's proclamation that *he* had moves that no one had ever seen. Yuck. Not what I needed to think about. I was still trying to erase last year's sweaty embrace with him and Jensen Bell out of my mind. Luckily, it was very, very dark in that bedroom in Jared's house, but still, seeing a breathless, shirtless Anthony running into the hall to shut the door was way more than I cared to see of any of these ridiculous jocks.

After that, the next few days passed quickly and, soon, the competition was only forty-eight hours away. I'd been practicing my speech with Jon and Cressida, who by the way, had listened when I'd told her to "Back off." Every time she got a little too pushy, Jon just gave her a look and she calmed down. I was focusing on the idea of breaking through walls. That we all hoped to break through walls someday, but this was a chance for the women of Westlake to finally be represented as a significant body at our school. At first I'd tried to get all historical, but everyone who read that speech gave it a big thumbs-down. This wasn't a run for mayor. This was just a school contest. So keep it in perspective.

Plus, it was hard to ignore the things Cressida kept yelling at me, "Baby steps, Andie. Baby steps. Jeez. You'd think you were trying to cure cancer or something, as serious as you get. Laugh, okay." She'd smile at me in that, 'You're a pain in the ass, but I love you' way and then I'd be fine again.

The hardest thing now was just keeping my parents out of it. Mom kept telling me with tears in her eyes how proud she was. After all my academic honors, it was a little surprising that *this* is what brought tears to her eyes. Dad had even gotten into the game, joking with me about how I was the son he never had. He thought that was particularly funny, but all it did was remind me how boneheaded so many of the guys are at Westlake, so I barely gave those comments a courtesy laugh. Mostly, Dad just got a lot of glares.

Jesse had gallantly stepped up as my escort, which had sent Lonzi into a pouting session until he was reminded that *he* would not be the one who got to trounce up and down the catwalk: I would. At the thought of not being able to hog that spotlight, especially in regard to something as critical to Lonzi as fashion, he easily gave up the job. Plus, a part of me was excited to have such a catch on my arm when I was competing against Ethan. I didn't want him to think that I was some kind of loser who had to sucker her gay best friend into serving as her escort. That's the last thing I needed. I was curious to see who Ethan would bring. And a little jealous. If he hadn't been a contestant himself, I'd have asked him. Well... At least I would've fantasized about it. Whether or not I'd actually have the nerve is something else entirely.

Twenty-eight.

On the morning of the competition, I woke up late.
Sunlight streamed into my window and I could hear
Kermit scratching furiously at my door. *What time is it?*
I rolled over to grab my purple alarm clock- one I'd
had since my seventh birthday---and gasped. *9:20?*

Crap. I was supposed to be at the school for mike
checks by 10 am. Calculating the time it would take to
drive over to Westlake, not to mention gather the
armload of "supplies" Cressida and Janika had made me
stuff into the faded, Adidas duffel bag I'd snagged from
my dad's closet, I had exactly 20 minutes to shower
and try to corral my crazy hair. Not much to work
with.

Just as my feet hit the cold, pine floor, I heard
banging on my bedroom door. "Andie!" The knob
wiggled and I silently thanked God that I'd had the
forethought to lock it last night. "Andie! Open up!
Now!" Nothing like the bracing sounds of Cressida
Maas to wake you up in the morning. Remind me to
tell her not to *ever* take a job in P.R.

"Jus' a minute" I mumbled, throwing bright, pink
pajama pants on beneath my oversized Redskins t-
shirt.

The knob rattled again. "Andrea Mancini! If you don't open this door right exactly now, *immediately*, I will personally kick it in! Chuck Norris doesn't have anything on me!"

Irritated, I shuffled to the door, reluctantly moved the lock, and flung it wide open. "Yes?!" I responded grumpily. Cressida was standing with her hands on her hips, a giant shopping bag on her arm, and a guilty-faced Janika behind her. Janika waved.

"Yes? Is that all you have to say you little imp? This is *only* the day we've been working toward for the past few weeks. The day we show Westlake that her women are *not* going to just stand by while the *boys* of this town slowly take over *every* opportunity we've ever had. Only that. And *you*," pointing a finger in my chest while moving determinedly into my bedroom, "*you* are not even remotely ready." Scrutinizing my outfit up and down, she grimaced like she'd just taken a whiff of rotting garbage. "Ugh, Andie. This," waving her arms the length of me, "is pathetic!"

Janika whispered hello, following behind the tornado that was Cressida. I shook my head and ruffled the lopsided pile of hair on my head. "I woke up late," I moaned.

Janika grabbed my hands and led me toward the bathroom. "It's fine," she soothed. "I can work my magic in 10 minutes flat. Promise." She winked.

"It's NOT fine," Cressida retorted, pacing the room. "We have NO time now to rehearse your speech and, no offense, but your hair looks like some kind of dishrag mop." She frowned, but relaxed a little when Janika shot her a fiery look. "Okay, I guess your hair's not *that* bad," Cressida relented, "but we really don't have much time." She reached into her bag and began flipping through a stack of papers. "I'm just going to go through a few talking points while Janika's, uh," air-quotes, "working her magic."

I saw Janika glare at Cressida again, but she'd already started pulling at my hair, thrusting it into giant roller curls while she forced my head in front of the sink, scrubbing furiously at my skin. "Ouch!" I felt a pinch when one of the rollers pulled the hair too tight on top of my head. Meanwhile, the face scrubbing session was rubbing my skin a little raw. "Okay, okay." I pulled away from the sink. "I think my skin is definitely clean. Let's move on."

Janika rolled her eyes, "Haven't you ever heard of exfoliating?"

"Yeah, there's exfoliating and then there's removing several layers of skin. I think we're moving dangerously close to giving me that whole burn victim look." I stared at Janika, waiting for it to sink in. "And I'm running out of time." I glanced at the clock, alarmed to see that it read 9:30.

"Trust me, Andie," Janika easily replied, "Your skin is great. Now I only have a few tiny things to add…" She reached down into her makeup case to pull out containers of eye shadow, tubes of mascara, and some

sort of glittery powder. "…and you'll be just perfect."
She moved her fingers deftly across my face, lightly
adding this and that, biting her lip and periodically
squinting one eye in concentration.

Feeling a wave of nostalgia, I closed my eyes. It
was hard not to think of Veronica today. She would've
been the one here with me, offering words of
encouragement and telling me how *fabulous* I was going
to be. V would understand how nervous I felt, but
she'd push me through it anyway. I missed her so
much. By now, my anger had faded from an angry red
wound to a pale scar; all I really felt was sadness.

Fifteen minutes later, the three of us crammed into
Cressida's car and headed toward the school. We were
late, but Cressida drove like a maniac, so the
likelihood that we'd make it on time was still pretty
good.

Twenty-nine.

Opening the door to the dressing room behind the stage, I was startled to see Brad and Anthony seated on two wooden stools, elbows balanced on a small table between them, arm-wrestling in their shirtsleeves, black bow ties dangling loosely from around their necks. Grunting from exertion, they reminded me of two squealing pigs. Smiling at how fitting that image really was, I pulled the door shut, wondering where I was supposed to wait. They'd probably arranged some janitor's closet- or worse- for me to prepare.

"Looking for me?" It was the voice that haunted my memories. The one I tried to escape when I closed my eyes and pretended that so many things had not actually happened. Facing the door, my back to the hallway, I took a breath, dreading the moment when I had to see him.

Jared didn't give me the chance to wait. Sliding up behind me, stretching his arms to reach either side of the doorframe, he was forcing my hand. To get away from him, I'd have to squeeze my body between his and the wall. "Seems like we keep running into each other…" Jared grabbed my waist, spinning me around.

I panicked. Every fiber in my body screamed in disgust, sensing the tight grip Jared now had on my waist. A grip that threatened to shift downward if I couldn't escape.

Jared placed his lips near my ear, whispering, "It's so obvious you're still hung up on me…the way you keep trying to find your way back." I squirmed in his grasp, trying to slide my body to the right, toward the hallway. "Just like she did."

Veronica. At the mention of her, I felt a wave of fire rise within my chest. Summoning all my strength, I stomped on Jared's foot sharply with the point of my high heeled shoe.

"Bitch." Cursing in pain, Jared loosened his grip on my waist just enough for me to duck under his arms and sprint down the hallway. Waiting for the sound of footsteps barreling behind me, I was surprised to hear a very different sound. The sound of laughter.

Jared's sharp laugh echoed eerily down the narrow hall, followed by a warning. "Just wait, Andie. Just wait."

His words rang in my head: loud warning bells clanging together in sync with my hurried steps. Nearly tripping in my heels, I slowed my pace as I exited the cavernous hall of the theater wing, searching for a place to rest, to hide, to…

I didn't want to imagine why he was laughing. Today was important to me. As much as I'd fought it, as much as I'd convinced Cressida and Janika that it was all about sending a message, that it was all about rebellion…it was also about me. Today was an opportunity to change my story, to present- for the first time- the truest version of myself, the girl I'd always been too nervous to place on public display.

Looking up, I realized I'd been wandering in a circle. The hallway leading to the stage, to the dressing area, to the moment I'd just been trying to shake off was squarely in front of me. The only difference now was the presence of a familiar figure leaning against the wall. Distracted by an image on his phone, Ethan was oblivious to my gaze, which was a blessing because I couldn't keep myself from staring. Ethan looked hot. So hot I could feel every beat of my heart pulsating like a snare drum threatening to burst through my chest. Every nerve along every inch of my body buzzed with energy. He wasn't just wearing the deep blue Italian suit: he was *owning* it. Shoulders resting along the wall, right foot casually pressed against it, right hand hooked inside his open jacket: he was the picture of understated confidence. Sleek lines of brushed cashmere in midnight blue hugged the contours of his broad chest, narrowed to define the trimness of his abdomen, crisp white shirt accented by the dark charcoal of his silk tie. He could have stepped from the pages of a glossy, fashion magazine. Or my sexiest dreams.

Ethan lifted his head, smiling out of the corner of his mouth. I blushed as his eyes flickered across my dress. "You clean up nice," he appraised, smiling wider. As I walked close to where he was standing,

Ethan slid his cell phone into his left pants pocket and glanced at his watch. "So, Andie…are you ready for this?"

I blanched, eyes widening, mortified that he might be able to guess exactly *what* I was ready for. Reminding myself that there was no way he was actually able to read my mind, I tried to regain my composure.

Amused, Ethan raised an eyebrow. "You look terrified." Leaning toward me with meadows in his eyes, he soothed, "Hey- it'll all be over before you know it." He smiled and I breathed in the confidence of his voice, considering his words.

"Andie…" Ethan stepped closer. Comfortably close. The space between us could be measured in inches, but I would've settled for centimeters. Nervous, I glanced down at my feet, hoping I wouldn't stumble in my never-wear heels and pink-painted toenails. Deep auburn strands tumbled across my forehead as I fidgeted with the silky fabric of my dress.

Ethan brushed the hair that had fallen across my face, twirling a single strand around his finger. "We could always just get out of here." I held my breath, afraid to break the spell of his hand's barest touch, radiating dizzy, heady waves through the tumble of my hair. He waited for me to look up, continuing as I did, "Find a pond…" Here, Ethan started smirking, just a bit, obviously encouraged by the quizzical expression on my face. "You know- catch a few frogs…" Unable to contain his amusement, Ethan smiled widely now, "Study their anatomy…" Raising an eyebrow, Ethan prodded, "What do you say?" Barely missing a beat, he added, "Everybody's doing it."

I smiled back, remembering how embarrassed I'd been that day in the library, pretending to search for something deep and original, NOT boring and scientific about, of all things, frog bodies. I was trying to be so cool when all I really ended up doing was acting like a total idiot. And now, the idea of Ethan teasing me, of laughing *with* me and not…okay, I guess he was laughing *at* me, but this felt so monumentally different from the cruel snickering of Brad Hamilton and Jensen Bell. Of every other everyone who'd made a game of toying with my confidence. This so-close-I-could-kiss-you kind of teasing, this I could get used to.

Racking my brain for a witty retort, I settled on the ever-sophisticated, "Oh really?" Eyes glimmering, I attempted my best flirty voice, well, as flirty as I was used to never using, so who knew…but Ethan wasn't running away, he was looking over my shoulder. Wait-looking over my shoulder?

Turning, I could hear the sharp click of heels as Ethan stepped backward, letting go of my curls. Suddenly, a breathless, "Andie!" echoed as Janika appeared next to me, leaning on my shoulder as she paused to catch her breath. "Andie, we found your dressing—."

Sensing she'd interrupted something, Janika smiled awkwardly, backing up. "Yeah, so, I'll just catch up with you…" She gestured around the corner, "You know…when, uh…it's a good time."

"WHEN IT'S A GOOD TIME?!" Cressida's presence now filled the hallway. I was surprised that I hadn't heard her coming until I noticed her bare feet. Cressida's red peep toe heels were dangling from her left hand. "I've been practically *sprinting* through this *maze*." Her tone was accusatory, insinuating this was most definitely my fault, as if I had designed the map of Westlake myself. Barely catching her breath, she continued, "Just to find you and tell you- get this, Andie- they expect you to share a dressing room, well, maybe not share because I guess they don't have anywhere else, but the *guys* have a place to hang because OF COURSE they don't actually care about anyone else winning and----."

I had to interrupt her. Who knew how long this diatribe would continue if I didn't intervene? Besides, Ethan was looking more than a little amused, and if Cressida saw him laughing at her, wild dogs wouldn't be able to restrain her from giving him a loud, obnoxious piece of her mind.

"Okay, okay…let me just come with you, then." Resigned to the fact that apparently Ethan and I were destined to *never* actually be alone, I shrugged my shoulders in defeat. Ethan winked, and I sighed, wishing I could stay to find out just exactly how long it would take for the tiny space between us to completely dissolve. I glanced at Cressida, ready to stall her, even just a little bit, but the spell of the moment with Ethan was already fading. Now I didn't know how to say goodbye. Somehow, *I'd like to kiss you in the moonlight and run my hands desperately through your hair* seemed a little over the top. Even if it was all I could think about right now. "See you onstage, I guess," I murmured, smiling over my shoulder as I walked toward Cressida's now retreating footsteps.

"Sure- in the winner's circle." Ethan grinned and I melted just a little bit more. He was so fun. I mean, yeah, he was undeniably sexy and the way he seemed to be looking out for me was sweet, but what I liked best was the way he reminded me to laugh. Without Veronica, I'd been laughing a helluva lot less- with Ethan, it was nice to think funny again.

"Hello?" Cressida stopped walking long enough to wave in my face. I must've been tuning her out, but right now, I didn't much care.

"Yeah?" There was a definite edge to my voice, one that didn't escape Cressida's notice.

She unfurled her eyebrows and softened the purse of her lips. "Andie...I know we kinda barged in just now..." She paused awkwardly, nudged onward only by Janika's elbow to her ribs, accompanied by a very stern expression. "So yeah, we're..." Janika raised an eyebrow. "I mean, I...am sorry. Okay?"

It wasn't great, but for Cressida- who never apologized- it was pretty significant, so I'd take it. "All right…now what was so critical you had to interrupt the most romantic almost-moment of my life?"

Both girls raised their eyebrows this time, surprised to hear me talk about something we never did: my dating life. Janika smiled wide, eager to hear more. "Details, Andie….and don't leave anything out." She grabbed my arm, linking it in hers, drawing us close.

I blushed, not sure what to say. How could I explain my complicated feelings for Ethan? That I hated how I couldn't get over his connection to Jared or how I daydreamed about him so often I was messing up the most basic tasks like washing my hair? That he's funny and playful and smells like summer mornings? That he's so comfortable in his own skin I can't imagine a moment he isn't truly, completely himself? In fact, the more I thought about it, the more I realized how ridiculous I've been, how much time and energy I've been wasting. For what? No one can keep Hurt at bay. There was no Unbroken Heart guarantee.

Mid-epiphany, Brad Hamilton appeared at the end of the hall. He marched toward me with purpose, "Andie, baby, don't want to miss your cue. Curtain call in five." He smirked, turning on his heel, disappearing into a door that led backstage.

"Yeah, okay," I grumbled, annoyed that his voice was the one to interrupt my thoughts. Maybe it wasn't too late to catch Ethan before the show. "Hey wait," I caught Janika's eye, "I've gotta take care of something." I turned around, headed back toward Ethan. "I'll see you in a minute, okay?"

Cressida opened her mouth to protest, but Janika just smiled, placing a finger over Cressida's lips. "It's cool, Andie." I could hear Cressida squawking a little, gearing up for a mini tirade, but Janika was insistent, pulling her forward.

Relieved, I walked as quickly as I could back to the spot where we'd been standing. Ethan was gone. I began searching the halls, weaving and winding through the maze of classrooms and store rooms and seating areas surrounding the massive auditorium. *Where could he be?* Running out of time, I stopped to catch my breath, certain that it was too late. The show was starting any minute and I'd miss my chance to talk with Ethan.

Resigned, I turned back toward the hall that led backstage, passing the costume chamber on my left. Suddenly, a hand reached out and pulled me through the darkened doorway. I panicked, certain it was Jared, until the smell of summer wafted through the air.

"Seems we were interrupted back there," Ethan's voice was soft and low, tingling up my spine. I couldn't see him- the room was too dark- but I could sense the heat of his body, tantalizingly close.

"Oh, I don't know…what else did we really need to say?" I teased, matching the quiet of his voice. Gently, but fervently, my heart pounded. The blackness of the dark room began to fade to a comfortable slate gray as my eyes adjusted, taking in the comfortable presence of Ethan's tall, strong form.

"Hmmm…" Ethan's words slid like silk across my skin. "Maybe you're right. Maybe there isn't anything left to *say*…"

His kiss. Ethan's mouth caressed my lower lip, pulling so gently, prompting the tiniest sigh escape my lips. I melted into the warmth of his body, tingling as his lips lay claim to my own. Slow and measured, the heat of his kiss teased every nerve in my body. I could barely breathe, dizzy with the tumble of his hands gradually arching along the curves of my neck, playfully tugging at the hair tucked behind my ears. *I could do this forever.*

"Andie?" *Apparently, forever was a lot shorter than I thought.* At least Ethan's hands were still playing with my hair.

Breathlessly, I murmured, "Mmmhhhmm?"

"I think we have a contest to win." I could hear the grin in Ethan's voice, "Well…at least I do." He grabbed one of the curls closest to my chin, yanking slightly.

Back to reality. "You might win…" I taunted, "but I'm still going to be the prettiest one onstage."

Ethan laughed, leaning forward to murmur in my ear. "Don't count on it—you haven't seen me in heels."

I shoved Ethan playfully, pushing against his chest. Quickly, he covered my hand with his own, holding it to his heart, pulling me back toward him. "Wanna bet?"

"On the contest?" I grinned, raising an eyebrow, "Didn't realize you were such a gambler...you know you're going to lose miserably, right?" On the surface, I practiced the fake bravado of my certain win, but truer words were never spoken. I might not have a chance in hell of winning this thing, but let's face it: neither did Ethan. The only ones who ever won anything at Westlake were the Brad's and Jared's of the school. I felt a little sad for Ethan just then-it was only a matter of time before the Powers-that-Be unearthed his golden heart, and kicked him out of their kingdom.

Ethan squeezed my hand a little tighter. "Little did you know...I've got an 'in' with the judges..." He leaned in conspiratorially, whispering in my ear, "Mrs. Fitzheimer can't resist my world-famous foot massages."

"Gross," I shuddered. The image of Dean Brauer's mother-in-law, lounging on a couch, eagerly thrusting her pale, rheumatic soles into Ethan's waiting hands was nauseating...and genius. Just enough to break the spell of our Steamy Closet Rendezvous. "But I do have a bet for you…" I teased.

"Oh yeah? What's that?" Ethan murmured distractedly.

I yanked open the chamber door, flooding light into the room. "Bet I can beat you to the stage." Giggling, I shut the door quickly behind me and took off running down the hall.

Seconds later, I heard the door reopen as Ethan stumbled through, "Not fair if you get a running start," he yelled after me.

But I didn't care because I knew what I had to do. Now that the tension with Ethan was finally broken, I could focus. I had a job to do. Not just for myself, but for Westlake. It was time to run with the big dogs. Let's just hope I wasn't about to fall on my face.

Thirty.

The lights onstage were blinding. It helped not to look at the audience. I could hear murmurs, so I knew they were there; I just didn't know how much they might be staring at me. I willed myself to breathe. *You can do this.*

I gripped Jesse's arm fiercely. He winced. "Sorry," I whispered, straightening the fabric on my blue silk dress. Janika had forced me into a knee-length dress with dark blue silk fabric that shimmered delicately in the lights. I had to admit: it *was* stunning. The line of the dress fit my body like a glove, softening my figure. The bodice was cut into a subtle 'V' with straps that wound around the back of my neck, extending down my back in a dark blue silken braid. I felt soft in this dress. Even beautiful. Again, I thought of Veronica and a knot lodged in my throat. Once upon a time, she would've been standing in the wings, whispering silly comments to make me laugh, willing my nervousness away.

Dean Brauer was still in the middle of his opening remarks, but I'd tuned out long ago, partly because he was unbelievably boring, but mostly because he was going on and on about Westlake's long history of tradition. Yeah, the traditions of misogyny and aristocracy are real bragging rights. If only Veronica had succeeded last year, things could've been different as a senior. No more feeling like the forgotten. We could've had a voice.

But I guess she'd been too enamored with the prospect of becoming one of the remembered, one of the chosen crowd. If I was really honest, a part of me got it. Everybody wanted to be wanted. Everybody wanted to feel important. She saw her chance and took it. Unfortunately for Veronica, they were only playing with her. They didn't really want her.

My heart ached with that thought. How much had it killed her to know that Jared was toying with her? How small had she felt sacrificing her best friend's dignity for a chance to be in the spotlight, if only for a moment?

I imagined her in my memories: brilliant and beautiful. All these months, I couldn't get past the hurt, the betrayal, so for just a moment, I chose to remember her as I'd always loved to see her: laughing, head tilted to the side, flashing a row of shiny, white teeth, grinning from ear to ear. I saw her...

My head snapped up. I saw her.

I gasped, and Jesse whispered, "Hey. You okay?" He turned his head ever so slightly, trying not to catch Brauer's eye. "Andie?" I couldn't reply.

I saw her. Veronica. She was there- in the audience. I squinted through the lights, expecting a mirage. No. It couldn't actually be her. We hadn't seen each other in months, hadn't talked for even longer. She wasn't even supposed to be here. If Brauer caught on, if anyone caught on, she could be arrested. But there she was- sitting in a chair on the right side of the auditorium. Close to the right side of the stage. Close to me.

*Why was she here? And how did she even know...*Lonzi's face flashed in my mind. *Of course.* He'd never understood why Veronica and I stopped talking because I didn't have the heart to tell him the truth. Why tell him? It would only destroy his image of her and after she moved anyway, what was the point? Besides, not talking about it almost made it seem unreal, and I didn't want it to be real. Telling Lonzi...I'd have to fully face it myself.

Ow. I felt a tiny, sharp sting on my left forearm: Jesse was pinching me. "Hey!" I whispered, grimacing at his touch. "What was that for?"

"You're spacing out," he whispered through his teeth. I focused on the front of the stage. *When had Brauer stepped down?* I noted Brad Hamilton at the podium. Tuning in, it sounded like he was talking about the program, but I couldn't concentrate.

My palms were sweating, heat rising up along the sides of my neck, and I was starting to feel dizzy. I breathed out hard through my teeth. I knew that I should be listening to Brad, that I was probably missing my cues. But I was so distracted. *What did Veronica want?*

Suddenly, all the couples were standing. Jesse pulled me to my feet, trying once again to wake me out of my dazed state of mind. Hearing my name, I turned to the left and saw Cressida frantically waving me down. "Andie! Wake up!" She whispered loudly, attracting the attention of three of my competitors.

I shot her a look of death. All I needed was more attention on myself. These other guys on stage already thought I was crazy to compete with them in an all-male contest. Having Cressida breathing down my neck didn't exactly help me blend into the crowd.

I walked slowly across the stage on Jesse's arm, trying my best to smile, but I know it probably only came out as some frozen half-grin. *Get it together.* I willed myself to focus, but all I could think about was the girl sitting in the audience. The girl who used to know me better than I knew myself. I felt a catch at the back of my throat again. *Don't cry. This is absolutely the worst place to break down. The worst.*

I could hear our names being announced as we paced across the stage, circling back to our chairs. Suddenly, Jesse released my arm, walking down the steps to sit with the other escorts. *Oh, I guess it's time for my speech.* I processed the thought in my brain, but it just didn't make sense. *Speech? How could I give a speech?*

I felt someone staring at my face. Someone onstage. Blearily, I turned my head to the right and Ethan caught my eye. He smiled warmly.

My stomach danced a little, remembering our kiss moments ago. It soothed me a little to return his smile, but not enough. In a moment, well, actually *now*, all eyes would be trained on me. A not-so-friendly laser beam intended to scrutinize every miniscule sound and movement I made. My heart palpitated and I heard my stomach growl. Loudly.

Brad stifled a snicker as he turned to face me on the march toward the podium. Of course I was going first. Anything to make me more uncomfortable. There would also be no chance to repudiate anything said about me afterward. Pretty slick when you think about it. For all my repugnance of pretty much *every* one of Brad's qualities, I had to admit that he was smart. In fact, it was almost a shame, really, that his mother was such a calculating wench. He actually had potential as a bonafide human being, a successful one at that. But now everything he did would be tainted by the stain of his mother's influence.

I squelched the rising quake in my stomach and flashed him the biggest grin I could manage. Brad's face shifted for a moment, but just a moment. He recovered by whispering as I passed him, "Good luck, M..m..mandie".

Screw him. Forget every thought I'd just had that might possibly resemble consideration because throwing back that awful nickname was psychological warfare. So I threw back the only thing I had in my arsenal.

"Same to you. Wouldn't want to disappoint Mama…" Leaning in so no one else could see, I mimed a sucking thumb, "…would we?"

His face reddened instantly and I knew that if we weren't onstage in front of hundreds of watchful eyes, Brad Hamilton would have let loose a stream of obscenities and spiteful commentary right then and there. Remembering himself suddenly, he straightened his jacket and walked back to his seat.

Phew. I breathed out gently, trying to settle my rapidly beating heart. *I'm on.* Reaching the podium, I gripped the sides, sliding my hands along the polished, wooden surface. The lights were hot and bright in my eyes but they couldn't mask the expectant faces in the first few rows. Dean Brauer's words rang in my ears as I readied myself for the speech Cressida and Jon had been drilling into my consciousness for the last week. We'd switched the tone from breaking down walls- voted down for its intensity and similarity to a history lesson- to equality and perception. Now, it was supposed to be about how the way we treat youth in a society shapes the way those young people will perceive their world. It was about the responsibility of schools and communities to teach fairness and equality at all costs.

But I suddenly felt very tired of fighting. Seeing Veronica here unsettled me. It was hard to feel angry as I looked at her face in the crowd, shining with pure, unadulterated pride. *What was this all about anyway? What was I really fighting for?*

As I thought about what to say, about how to begin, the crowd shuffled in their seats. I started to panic, realizing that I only had a moment to make a decision: to share the words I'd practiced with Jon and Cressida all week, or to go rogue...to speak from the heart. Soon, I'd have lost the audience, doomed to repeat the embarrassment of that spelling bee long ago. I took a breath, knowing what I had to do.

Suddenly, a gasp erupted from a section in the back of the crowd, and I could feel Cressida's eyes burning into me from the wings of the stage. When the murmuring grew to a roar, I noticed how many eyes *weren't* focused on me. They were very clearly trained *behind* me. Terrified, I turned around.

Thirty-one.

It was huge. Not giant: gargantuan. All I could see was my face looming on the screen. My face with a giant red circle around it. And the words scrawled across the bottom...

*Put the **Man** in Mancini. Vote for Andy: Westlake's #1 Dyke*

I couldn't breathe. My ears rang and the crowd's noise dimmed. All I could see were the words on the large projector screen above my head, pasted over a photo I'd never seen. Me, shivering in a wet, silk dress, drenched with snow and ice and humiliation. The image loomed overhead, cruelly pronouncing every detail from that awful day four years ago. But that couldn't compare to the ugly words. And my first name...purposely misspelled, hovering above Brad's head, casting a glow on his sick, smirking face. It was all too much. Too much to even cry. My body felt hazy, numb.

From the corner of my eye, I could see Cressida nearly mauling the AV guy, trying to get him to move faster, trying to get my image off the screen. But it didn't matter. The damage was done. No one would ever think of me as anything more than the awkward girl who didn't go to parties and loved spending time at the library. Students here would never see me as attractive, funny, or creative. They saw what they wanted to see: someone who didn't fit in. Someone who was the butt of a cruel, cruel joke.

I stood onstage, rooted to the spot just past the podium. All around me students were talking and moving. But I didn't care. Nothing could break me from this reverie.

And then, a loud cry echoed across the stage.

I looked up as Brad's chair flew out from beneath him, nearly hitting Jared, who was standing close behind. Brad lay flat on the floor of the stage, holding his face. Two thick crimson streams ran down either side of his fragmented nose. He groaned, trying to stem the flow of blood. My stomach lurched, sick at the gory sight.

Standing over him, Ethan was on his feet, shouting down at Brad, barely held back by both Jesse and Anthony. Jared stood still, open-mouthed, watching his cousin rail on Brad. Shouting. Shouting about me. And I understood, then, that Ethan had punched Brad in the face. That chair flying across the stage was the result of every ounce of force in Ethan's body, trained on knocking Brad squarely in the nose.

Blood continued to run steadily down Brad's face, and I realized, with no small satisfaction, that he was muffling tears behind his red-coated hand.

I sucked in a breath, knowing how much trouble Ethan was in, how his name couldn't save him on this one because he'd picked a fight with one of the Untouchables. He was completely screwed. And here I was, at the center of the mess.

I let that sink in. Ethan risked this for me. I looked at him, straining to break free from Jesse and Anthony, face bright red, eyebrows scrunched together in anger. *He did this for me.*

Taking a deep breath, I shook my arms a little, willing the blood back into them. It was time to face the music. I walked toward Ethan, knowing that I was also walking toward the rest of the guys, walking toward the people who'd most likely masterminded my humiliation. But then there was Ethan. The one who stood up for me in the most public, dangerous way of all. I had to show him what that meant.

As I grew closer, the noises onstage slowly faded. I could feel every eye in the room trained on the center of the stage. Every ear tuned to the words I would say.

But I didn't have anything to say. At least, not about the photo. It wasn't worth my time to yell, to scream, to comment on their cruelty. I couldn't waste that kind of emotional energy on such lowlifes. My words were only for Ethan.

He saw me coming toward him and lessened his struggle on Jesse's and Anthony's clutches. Ethan turned his body to the right, reaching out, starting to speak.

I cut him off. "Wait!" My voice echoed across the stage, and just as soon, I felt every eye pause in my direction. The shuffling shoes, the whispers, the craning necks in the aisles suddenly stilled in the most unsettling way. Here it was- the attention I'd never craved, the attention I'd tried to avoid my entire life focused in now like a giant unrelenting scope, magnifying everything.

I felt a flush creep up my neck, hot and fuzzy. I could've walked away- no one would have questioned it; no one would have expected anything but tears. But what would that accomplish? Nothing. Nothing. Nothing. I'd be right back at square one: helpless to the powers that be: a mouse.

"Wait…" I softened my tone, looking only at Ethan. "Please don't say anything. You don't have to say anything." I shook my head. "They're not *worth* it." I heard Jared snort in disbelief, but I didn't even look in his direction. My attention was with Ethan.

"Andie, you can't give up. You can't let them *win*." Ethan wiggled free from Jesse and Anthony, who had almost completely released their hold on his arms. He walked toward me, staring earnestly into my eyes. "They may not be worth it, but you *are*."

I blushed at his words, but still, I couldn't be distracted. All I wanted was to thank him and leave. To leave the stage with as much dignity as I could manage. Behind me, I could hear Dean Brauer on the intercom, trying to settle the audience for the rest of the show.

"Ethan, thank you so much." I could hear the tears at the back of my throat, threatening to break through. "I'll never forget this." As I reached out to grab his outstretched hand, I noticed a figure striding across the stage with purpose. At the same time, Jared came into view, calling out to his cousin. Was he defending Ethan?

Everything happened at once. Suddenly, I wasn't alone. Someone grabbed my arm, pulling it back from Ethan's. Jared swung forward, calling out to Ethan as he launched his fist at his face, but before he could make contact, he doubled over in pain. Sucker punch to the gut. And one very tiny, very angry blonde snarling in his face.

Thirty-two.

"V!" I could hardly believe it. Making a quick escape was her only way out of trouble with Brauer, but she hadn't left. She was here, making Jared Bronson a *very* unhappy guy.

"If you *dare* lay one tiny *finger* on Ethan or Andie or anyone else I care about, I will *personally* see to it that every girl in school gets a specific rundown of all your little tricks *and...*" Here she paused for effect, throwing Jared a wicked little grin. "I'll release my own little video...emphasis on the word 'little'"

All color left Jared's face. He stammered a little, in between groans, trying to appeal to Veronica. "V, baby, you wouldn't do that. Not after all we've been through..." He smiled innocently, projecting his large blue eyes upward from his crouch on the floor.

"Yes. I. Would." Veronica's voice was cold and clear. She meant business.

"Bitch!" Jared lunged forward, trying to pull Veronica down on the floor with him. She sidestepped his advance, causing him to fall on the floor. "You're nothing but a slut, pissed off because you couldn't ride me to popularity. Don't you get it?" He shouted as he rolled away from her, pushing himself angrily to his feet.

Jared stepped back, brushing his jeans furiously, trying to fling every ounce of Veronica from his body, trying to separate himself from the mess he'd so obviously helped create. "You. Don't. Matter." Jared smirked as he punctuated each word with the tiniest pause, just enough to complete the sense of detachment he hardly worked to reveal.

It was a gut punch. Again. The hurts were compounding and it was hard to breathe with this thick perversion swirling in the air. *How could he be so indifferent?* Before all this, before I'd lost my best friend, I'd believed in the simplicity of emotion. You love or you hate. You accept or you reject. Before, I didn't see the layers and layers of feeling that crossed between opposing forces. I didn't have to. I'd lived a protected life. But when Veronica betrayed me, I loved and hated her. Then, the more I missed her, the more I didn't want to see her. I'd spent months trying to fathom how two opposite ideas could coexist. *How could it be so complicated?*

I guess…because it just *was*. I was tired of fighting the feelings I'd been having from the feelings I want to have. Veronica, Ethan, myself…I loved and hated them all, depending on…depending on everything.

Watching Jared's face shift from annoyed to aloof was unsettling. His indifference was a card I could never play: it wasn't in my deck. As much as I sometimes hated the way my emotions fluctuated wildly, I wouldn't trade them for the coolness of safe ground in a second. Sometimes, smiles were just expensive.

Before me, Veronica and Jared were still facing off. She perched one hand on each hip and met Jared's remote gaze. "Look- I don't care what you think of me. Not one bit." She opened and closed her right hand in the air, dismissing the idea. "But…" Veronica paused dramatically, turning loose one of her brilliant grins, "you DO care what your stuffy little friends' parents think, especially the ones who're writing your recommendation letters to Harvard."

Jared's eyebrows lifted, but his expression remained unchanged.

"What would Mr. Hamilton say if he knew about your little…" here she dropped her voice conspiratorially, "…*extra-curriculars?*"

Jared's face colored immediately. "You don't…" he stammered, "…you don't know what you're talking about." He straightened his shoulders nervously, shifting his eyes toward Ethan and Brad.

"Oh don't I? What about the way you've been slumming it? How would mommy and daddy feel about that?" She winked at Jared, clearly enjoying his squirms.

"Look," Jared reached out to take Veronica's arm, trying to steer her away from the group. Surprisingly, she didn't resist. They talked in low voices, while the rest of us burned with curiosity. *What could she know that would have Jared Bronson willing to negotiate?*

I took the moment to turn toward Ethan. Since Veronica had launched herself at Jared, I hadn't paid much attention to him. Ethan was gazing at me with those gorgeous eyes, filled with concern. How could I have pushed so far before, when he was clearly a great guy? I smiled at him now, small but pure. "Thank you," I mouthed.

He shrugged, as if to play it down, but then he smiled back at me, and for one moment amid the chaos, I felt happy.

Jared and Veronica returned to the group. All eyes turned toward them expectantly, but for a moment, neither said a thing.

Then Jared spoke. "I think that..." His face contorted, as if he was about to choke on his words. "I think that we can clear up these, uh, *misunderstandings*," here he looked pointedly at Ethan and Brad, "by just, um, calling it even."

Brad exploded. "EVEN?!! My FACE is broken, you bastard!" He looked heatedly at both Jared and Ethan. "Just because he's your COUISIN does not mean I'm NOT going to personally rearrange his DNA." Brad lunged toward Ethan, but Jared stepped between them.

"HEY!" Dean Brauer's voice carried across the stage. "That's enough!" Brauer had finally managed to exit the rest of the student body- having determined that the show would most decidedly *not* go on- and was just now returning to the scene onstage. "Haven't you boys had enough drama for one day?"

Brauer stomped across the stage, grabbing Brad by the arm. "YOU had better calm down, Hamilton. I just spoke with Arthur Longeton, and he seemed very eager to report how you bribed him to broadcast Andrea's picture during her speech. Something about a date with your sister?"

Brauer raised his eyebrows at Brad, and then shook his head in disbelief. "I imagine your mother would be *quite* unhappy to hear about how easily you offered her daughter as bait, not to mention your involvement in such a *public* harassment scheme."

Brad's shoulders slumped immediately, sucking all bravado from his demeanor. He mumbled assent.

"So, do I need to call in the police, or are we done with this mess?" Brauer looked from Brad to Ethan to Jared.

Jared quickly agreed. "Thank you, Dean Brauer. We will, uh, handle this on our own." Brauer quickly raised his hands to object. "WITHOUT any fighting." Jared hastened to add.

Brauer turned to me. "And you? Are you, uh…all right?" I'd never seen Brauer so uncomfortable. He shoved his hands into his pants pockets nervously.

Before I could answer, though, he spotted Veronica and his face fumed. "YOU! Ms. Linwood, you know the terms of your expulsion. Stepping foot inside these walls is completely unacceptable. I'm calling your *escort* right now." Brauer smirked at Veronica, "Come with me!"

"NO!" I shouted, not caring that I was yelling at an administrator. Brauer frowned and began to chastise my tone, but I cut him off. "To answer your question, I'm definitely NOT all right." Brauer started to look uncomfortable again. "But…" I paused, lifting my chin, "I think that I might be willing to drop any *charges*," I look pointedly at Brad, "if Veronica's allowed to leave on her own."

Brauer's jaw hardened at my request. I could tell he really hated this idea, but the prospect of not having to deal with Mrs. Hamilton in a battle for her son's clearance was too tempting to pass up.

He sighed. "In the spirit of *charity*," he glanced disgustedly at Veronica, "I think I can do that. On the condition that we will never, EVER have to speak of this again." He looked at each of us in the group, pausing to meet eyes with everyone. "Agreed?"

A chorus of "yes's" circulated the group. Brauer sighed again, straightening his suit jacket and walked determinedly off the stage.

I let out my breath heavily, hardly realizing I had even been holding it.

Veronica turned toward me, eyes wide. "Andie. I can't believe you did that." She looked over her shoulder at Brad, frowning, "Are you really okay with letting him off the hook?"

I laughed a little. "Well, watching how long it takes for his face to heal will take the edge off quite a bit."

She laughed, flashing that grin I knew so well. And then…silence. We stared at one another, alternately looking down at the polished wooden stage, then back toward the other. The chaos of the past ten minutes had been a protective wall around our disconnection. Now, we had nothing between us. Nothing, that is, except for a large chasm carved in hurt and betrayal.

Veronica spoke first. "Do you think we could get coffee sometime? Just…" She paused, choosing her words carefully. "To just talk a little?" She looked at me hopefully, face so open and vulnerable, taking a risk that I'd shut her down.

I could do it. I could shut her down. The wounds were still raw, and trusting again would be so hard. But not trusting was eating away at me. What was worse? The anger, the hurt- it was lonely. Lonely and sad.

More than anything, I hated feeling bad about my situation. Like it was some kind of pathetic burden to bear. What was the purpose in holding onto the past when I couldn't change it? I couldn't promise that things would be okay, but I could promise her a conversation.

Thirty-three.

"Cappuccino, please."

"Add a salted caramel latte, and put it all on my tab." Veronica walked up to the counter, lightly touching my shoulder for confirmation. "Is that okay?" She scrunched one eyebrow quizzically.

"Yeah," I answered softly. "It's okay." I smiled, a half-smile, uncertain how to proceed and feeling awkward that I didn't know how to act in front of the girl I had once known better than anyone.

"It's weird, huh?" She stated it for me, acknowledging the atypical quietness between us, bouncing lightly on her feet in the habit I remembered so well.

I drew a breath across my lips, pushing them outward nervously, biting the bottom lip. "Yeah." Looking sideways at her profile, I was grateful she'd said it. One thing about V, she was always honest. Sometimes brutally honest, but it was a relief to slip back into some sort of pattern. She prodded, and I responded.

"Let's sit," she prompted, grabbing the two steaming cups of coffee, drawing many admiring eyes as she sauntered across the café, settling on an overstuffed chair by the window. I perched awkwardly on a straight-backed chair across from her, three feet away, the tips of our shoes nearly touching.

Here we were, face to face in the aftermath, no clear way to navigate these new waters. I opted for the lightest of the issues first.

"So what kind of crazy secret did you have on Jared anyway?" I tapped my foot a little on the floor, trying to find a comfortable groove for our conversation.

Veronica laughed bitterly. "Oh- it's a good one: believe me." She leaned in, looking from one side of the café to the other, lowering her voice to share. "He's sleeping with Mrs. Hamilton *and* the maid."

I nearly spit out my cappuccino, trying to process such a juicy secret. "No way! Does Brad know?"

"Are you kidding? If he knew, Jared's face would've been rearranged long ago. Though I don't know if Brad's going to be getting into too many fights anytime soon." She snickered, "He looked pretty destroyed after Ethan played the knight in shining armor." She smiled knowingly at me, falling into our old banter pattern.

"Yeah." I smiled back, smaller. It was nice to see her joke, but it felt hollow somehow.

Veronica noticed my hesitation, settling back a little. She took one, long sip of her latte, setting the mug down on an end table nearby. She looked at me, waiting. Waiting, but smiling. I had so many other questions, but there was really only one question that mattered. The one I was afraid to ask.

"Why wasn't I worth more to you than Jared?" I let the question slip out. It loomed between us, large and quiet.

For a moment, neither of us spoke. I didn't look up. If I looked up, I'd know. Or worse, I'd see pity. I'd rather lose her friendship than lose my dignity. Without dignity, it wouldn't mean anything. *I* wouldn't mean anything.

She coughed once, and I looked up. "I thought..." she paused, furrowing her brow, "I thought that I was someone I wasn't. I felt so...jealous."

She looked intently at me, flushing at her words. "I was so *jealous* that Jared wanted to be with you. Jealous that you had one more thing I'd never have, and it just...it made me feel crazy." She rolled her eyes in exasperation, resting her chin on her left hand, leaning toward me.

I tried to process her words, but they just didn't make sense. *Veronica- jealous of me? Beautiful, confident, adventurous Veronica- envious of my world? What kind of world was that?*

She continued, "In that moment- in that stupid, ridiculous moment- I just wanted to be someone *else*: one of those girls who doesn't care. One of those girls with everyone falling at her feet. *Untouchable.*"

Veronica looked at me, tears in her eyes. "To say I wasn't thinking is so small. It takes away from everything I did, but if I *was* thinking, if I had any idea of the *cost*...Andie..."

Tears dripped down her nose, but she didn't push them away. They branded her. I started to speak, but she reached across the feet between us and grabbed my hand.

"Andie- he could never mean more to me than you. He never did, and I was a fool to think that I could have you both. To think that I could lie to you, and worse, that I would care for someone who hurt you...it was the worst kind of thoughtlessness. The worst." She let the tears continue down her nose, rolling across her now-ruddy cheeks.

She drew a deep breath, settling back against the chair, giving me space to consider. Reminding me of my own role in the story. "I should've..." I sighed, looking down at my hands. "I should've told you about Jared right away. I thought I was protecting you, but to see you with him and just *pretend*...that wasn't fair either...would it have made a difference?"

V tapped her fingers absentmindedly on the arm of the chair. "Honestly, I don't know. I was in this low place, this vile, jealous place. Talking about it then...I think it might've just been this explosion between us. This awful, honest fight. I was...insecure."

I felt so conflicted. I wanted to be open, but I wanted more than this too. Jealousy? Jealousy didn't make sense to me. I'd always been the one envious of her. In what alternate reality, did I have something she didn't?

"V…" I opened my eyes wider, raising my eyebrows in surprise. "I guess I just don't understand. You've always been the center of everything we do, everywhere we go. Why would you think…" I paused, looking for the words. "Why would you think you needed anything else?"

Veronica raised one eyebrow, laughed shortly, and then shook her long blonde hair. "Really? You just don't see it?" She leaned forward, drawing my attention toward her.
"Andie- do you ever wonder why I push you so hard?"

"No," I looked down, "I mean, no, I don't know, so yeah…I always thought it was about me catching up. About trying to keep up with you." I fiddled with the silver bracelet on my right arm, rolling each tiny bead between my fingers, a way to focus. I looked up and Veronica and sighed. "I'm not like you. Confident. Adventurous. So certain about everything."

Veronica scrunched her face in consternation and then burst out laughing. Tears started rolling down her cheeks and I felt my face flush. I'd come here to move forward, not be embarrassed. If she thought this was funny-

"Fine. This obviously isn't working." I stood up angrily, grabbing my brown leather satchel from the polished wooden floor, pulling it so quickly that the strap was now caught on the leg of the end table, threatening to topple as I yanked on the edge. Veronica's latte shifted dangerously, but she reached out suddenly, grabbing not only the mug but my arm as well.

"Andie- I'm not laughing at you. I'm laughing at myself. I *promise*. Please. Sit." She gestured to the overstuffed armchair right next to her, dismissing the spot I'd been using as too far away. I resisted, but Veronica increased her grip on my arm and I felt myself sinking toward the plush seat.

I was tired. All I wanted was for life to slow down a bit, for things to return to some normalcy. That's what this whole visit had been about, anyway: I'd spent so much time trying to rearrange my life without Veronica when all I really wanted was to mend this hole in my heart. But now, I was questioning this whole process. Maybe we were meant to grow apart. Not all friendships could endure, I guess. I'd just been hoping so hard that I was wrong about this one.

"I'm not laughing at you," Veronica repeated. "I'm just stunned that you have it so wrong, so backwards-" she rolls her eyes to the ceiling, emphasizing her surprise.

Where did she get off telling me that I was wrong? I flushed again.

"---Because all this time you thought I was trying to get you to catch up when I was really just trying to catch up to you."

This didn't make sense. Veronica was the strong one. She was the wave-maker. Not me.

"You never needed anyone to push you. You never needed anyone to...*validate* you." Veronica spoke softly, looking down at her hands, folding them delicately in her lap. I'd never seen her so small.

I started to speak, ready to contradict her, but she stopped me. "No. Don't make it better. That's another thing," she laughed bitterly, "you always try to help me, even when I'm being...well, when I'm being me, I guess."

I just looked at her. I didn't really know what to say, because this was foreign territory.

She continued, "It's not easy being so close to someone who doesn't need you as much as you need them. It feels...inconsequential. I never felt neglected or unimportant, just that...that you don't really need me, Andie."

I stared at Veronica blankly, finding it hard to take in what she was saying.

"Look at you this year. Writing that blistering editorial. Standing up to Brauer. Running for Mr. Westlake," Veronica shook her head, smiling. "At the same time I've never been prouder to know you, I've never realized how much you can do on your own, and how great you are without me distracting you, or whatever it was we used to do together."

Tears were forming in her eyes.

I processed what she was saying. *Was it true? Was I better without her?* Before she left, I'd always used Veronica as a sounding board, but mostly, I'd followed her lead. Since we'd been apart, I'd relied on myself more than ever before. Yeah, I could see it that way. Being alone forced me to stand a little taller, forced me to reconsider my boundaries. But it was also lonely.

Looking across the table at Veronica, I realized that the thing I'd been missing so much wasn't her support but her company. I liked *sharing* with her. I missed having someone to be silly with, to laugh with, to understand the inside jokes because she was there when we made them. And the trust, well, the trust might not ever really come back. I believed how sorry she was. I believed that she would change things if she could. But it never would change because we couldn't go back, and a part of me would always wonder now, always question- just a little bit- when she called or when she made a suggestion.

I breathed in and took one last look across the table. It would never be the same with Veronica because I would never be the same. But for the first time in a long while, that didn't make me sad. I couldn't trust Veronica again, but I *could* trust that not everyone else in my life would betray me. I could trust that it was time to let new people in my life. To really give them a chance. Ethan's face popped into my mind. I had been keeping him at arms' length, but watching the way he defended me in front of his cousin, it was hard not to feel a surge of warmth, a desire to welcome the possibility that a truly great guy was standing right in front of me.

But that was the future. For the moment, I was still locked in the past. Veronica. She looked at me, eyes red from tears of laughter and tears of sadness. Maybe it didn't have to be so defined, she and I. Maybe...

"V," She smiled as I called the nickname only I ever used, "I know that things are different between us, and I wish that we could go backwards, but we can't."

Her face fell, anticipating the meaning of these words. "It's hard for me to see things as the same, even after putting all this," waving my hands across the space between and around us, "together."

She opened her mouth to speak, and then closed it just as suddenly. I could see her mind working furiously, trying to think of the perfect way to solve this.

I continued, "I'd like to hang out---." Her eyes sparkled. "-with Lonzi...and maybe others, I don't know, but I want to see you. Not seeing you...it's been lonely."

"Me too! Oh, Andie, I'm so excited. We'll have a party or maybe just a movie marathon weekend. I don't know, something great---."

I cut her off. "---It's not going to be the same, though... Okay? I can't...I can't be the same Andie with you now. I miss you, but I just can't be close like we were…"

Veronica's face deflated, but she still managed a small smile. "I think I can do that. I'm not pretending it's all I want," she assured me quickly, "but it's something." Suddenly she grinned wickedly, "But I'm NOT promising to be satisfied with just that, so you know. I'm gonna keep at you, Andie Mancini." And I knew that she would.

I smiled back, but inside, I knew that we'd never be best friends again. We'd never even be close friends- that door had closed. Reflecting, I could almost see the future before us. The time between phone calls stretching from a day to two to a week. Languishing visits. Busy schedules and time for everyone else but each other.

Thinking of "everyone else" brought Ethan to mind again. That was one door I was about to fling wide open.

Thirty-four.

Sunday morning dawned cloudy and cool, unseasonably groggy for the end of October. As I stretched my legs, detangling them from the crisp, cotton sheet, I thought about my plan for the day. Yesterday, after Veronica and I had awkwardly hugged goodbye, I'd felt such resolve about today, but now, all I could feel was a nervous pit in my stomach.

Was I really going to tell Ethan how I felt? Every ounce of courage seeped out of my body as I stared gloomily at the darkening clouds outside my bedroom window. Was this some kind of karmic sign?

My phone buzzed on the oak stand beside my bed. Lonzi. "Get your ass out of bed and go get that boy!!!" I had to laugh at how well he knew me, bringing back my lonely feelings from yesterday. Veronica and I might never be close again, but that didn't mean I was friend adrift. I had plenty of good friends to support me, and maybe, something a little more...

"Okay, okay," I grumbled to myself, swinging legs out of bed, stumbling toward my bathroom and a much-needed shower.

As the water ran down my back, I thought back to the first time Ethan and I had met. It figured that he had to be related to the biggest jerk at school. But still, he'd caught my attention even then. His smirk, teasing me. His deep, reflective eyes. His perception. I mean, yeah, he was smokin' hot, but once he started talking, it was hard not to focus on everything *else* about him.

Before I knew it, the water was running cool, marking the end of my series of daydreams. Now, it was time to face reality. To stop being so afraid of what might happen and just let something *actually* happen.

Thirty-five.

"Hi," I smiled shyly as Ethan stepped out of his car. The paint of his deep blue Chevelle sparkled beneath the crack of sunlight peeking through the clouds. It was the shine of a fresh wax, which on a day like today would have been really impractical...unless someone was trying to impress someone. I smiled wider.

"Hey," Ethan replied, walking toward me. I felt that rush of butterflies again. The one I got whenever I heard his voice or breathed in his delicious scent.

"Is this okay?" I gestured toward a worn, wooden bench at the edge of the clearing. Ripples from the lake shone on the water, a glint in my eye. I squinted, shading my face with one hand, watching Ethan slide onto the bench easily. He always moved in synch.

"You ready for tomorrow?" Ethan looked across the water, giving me time to respond.

Silence grew warm and comfortable between us, as I realized- for the first time- that I didn't feel anxious next to him. Excited, yes. Anxious, no. Out of the corner of my gaze, I studied his profile. Strong jaw. Calm, determined expression on his face. He exuded strength, a kind of certainty in himself that drew me to him like a plant thirsting for water.

"I don't know." It was the most honest thing I could say, and also the most disappointing. The combination of the past betrayal and current humiliation was nauseating. I wanted to be a pillar, but the thought of that was so exhausting....it just didn't seem likely. "I'm fine, but then I think of it all again and..." I stalled, looking into Ethan's eyes.

"I know it must be hard," Ethan paused, running a hand through his chestnut hair. "But you don't have any reason to be scared." He leaned closer. "Look- I don't know if you realize this, but I haven't exactly made many friends since I've been here."

I crinkled my brow, "But you've got----"

Ethan interrupted me, "Yeah, there's always a crowd, or just people saying 'hi'- I get it- that looks like something...but it's not real. It's not—I haven't made any actual friends, Andie. No one knows me here...no one..." He sighed, "But that's not the point. The point is that I don't want to know anyone."

Shoulders slumping, my heart deflated as the words "I don't want to know anyone" rang in my mind. "I see..." I turned away.

"No—I'm not saying it right." Ethan shook his head. "You still don't see it, do you?"

I waited, holding my breath for whatever idea had suddenly taken hold of him. He seemed upset, crinkling his brow as he gathered his thoughts.

"Andie, you're one of the strongest- and most stubborn---" Ethan smirked at that- "people I've met.

The way you just…hesitate, sometimes…" waving one arm away from his body, gesturing impatiently, "…it's so unnecessary." Ethan looked intently at me.

"How is that…?" I sat back against the bench.

"Andie, listen to me." Ethan placed his hands on my shoulders, turning me toward him. The feel of his strong hands on my skin was soothing, instantly calming. "Just please let me get this off my chest."

"Okay." Worried about what he needed to say, about what was so urgent, I sat still. Ethan dropped his hands from my shoulders, gently sliding them down the length of my arms to rest on the bench. I resisted the urge to shiver, but I couldn't hide the tiny trail of goose bumps his warm fingers left behind.

"Your strength is one of the things that drew me to you. When I see you wavering from that because, I don't know…. maybe you don't see what others see in you…." Ethan sighed, sweeping a hand across his forehead to push soft, caramel hair from his eyes. "I know this is hard, and I don't really understand what you're feeling." He shook his head gently. "I won't pretend that I do. What I *do* know is that you can get through it. Jared…" He hesitated here. "Jared told me some things about last year. About you."

My face was on fire. If Ethan thought that Jared and I had been *together*…or whatever awful things he could make up…my mind raced to think of the consequences.

"I…" I could feel the panic written all over my face.

"Hey," Ethan raised an eyebrow pointedly, "you haven't given me a chance to finish."

Using every ounce of restraint I could muster, I clamped my mouth shut, determined to at least hear him out.

"Jared told me that you *wouldn't*…" Ethan paused, clearly uncomfortable, "that he came onto you and you pushed him away."

I raised my eyebrows in shock.

"He wasn't trying to be honorable- though he could stand to try that once in a while." Ethan rolled his eyes, "Really, he was just drunk and blubbering about how a girl could actually say 'no' to him- God, he's disgusting." Ethan shook his head in exasperation.

"But anyway- the point is that I know a little bit about what happened with you and Jared and you and Veronica." Ethan turned his gaze squarely on mine. "Andie, you've already been through a lot and you didn't give up. So all this with the campaign," he shrugged his shoulders, "is just another bump."

Ethan leaned toward me, crashing a wave of sweet citrus and summer rain into my skin. "Just don't let them get the best of you, okay?" I could see the concern in Ethan's eyes, the way he locked in on my gaze and then gently furrowed one brow.

This was the moment I'd tell him the truth. That I *did* care about him and was sorry I'd been pushing him away. That I was hesitant to trust someone with my heart, but seeing him stand up for me in front of Jared and Brad and all the other guys at school was the moment I was confronted with how honorable, how compassionate he really was. The moment...

"Andie?"

I blushed, thinking of the emotional blathering I'd been doing in my head. Regardless, I could only avoid this conversation for so long. Better to just bite the bullet.

"I've been thinking about something," I paused, gathering courage, "but I'm nervous to share it with you."

A puzzled look crossed Ethan's face. I hastened to reassure him. "It's not a bad thing, not at all...I mean, I guess it depends on how you feel about," blushing, "me." I blushed even harder, hating how I was stammering and carrying on awkwardly. This was *not* how I wanted to talk to him. Why did I have to become this flustered mess whenever I was around him?

Ethan was staring even harder now, waiting for me to finish my thought. He stretched his long legs, so at ease on the worn, wooden bench. So at ease anywhere, now that I thought about it. He never seemed uncomfortable or uncertain. Ethan was always so confident- a quality that I admired and found daunting at the same time.

"Ethan…" I stretched out his name a little, enjoying the way it rolled off my tongue, so soft and warm. "I really like you." I searched his gaze for some sign of encouragement. "I've been avoiding that…getting close to you, I mean, and I don't want to do it anymore. The truth is that I want you." I breathed out in a rush, nervous about the vulnerability of my revelations.

The moment of truth. No turning back. I bit my bottom lip, looking down, looking anywhere besides his face. I could feel his gaze on me, but I couldn't look. I was too afraid of the rejection. Now that I'd been completely honest, there was so much to lose.

The water lapped the shoreline, a sound I usually found soothing, but now it only matched the ebb and flow of my stomach, turning somersaults.

"Andie…" I couldn't read the tone of Ethan's voice, and I wasn't ready for this to become something *less than*. My heart could only register *more* and the possibility that he wouldn't see that was agonizing.

"And I want to kiss you right now." I stared down at my hands, blurting the words that had been burning in my chest. "I want to kiss you madly, and swim in your chameleon eyes, and run my fingers through your hair, and drink in the scent of soap and rain and palm trees that seem to follow you everywhere. I want to--"

"Andie, can you look at me?" Ethan's voice was low and soft.

I looked up. His eyes were swirling green and brown, two pools of disquiet.

Too afraid of his rejection, I straightened suddenly, "Look, it's fine, okay. I'll just see you at school tomorrow." I reached for my bag, leaning toward the cool, green grass. As I pulled the chocolate brown handles together, two large liquid spots appeared suddenly on the silky fabric between them. Puzzled, I ran my fingers across the wetness, looking for a leak inside my bag. The spots quickly multiplied as rain fell with certainty now, steadily soaking my body. I leapt up from the spot, ready to run toward my car, when I felt strong arms around my waist, anchoring me.

Ethan reached forward, running a hand through my dampening hair, wiping the rain from the sides of my face. His fingers stopped, gently, on my lips, tracing their outline.

I couldn't breathe. His touch was warm beneath the cool rain.

He stood, wrapping me closer, sheltering my body from the brunt of the shower. I longed to kiss him so badly, the memory of his lips on mine just days ago fresh and intense.

Ethan whispered into my hair, "I don't want you to leave." He pulled back to look into my eyes, "Madly, huh?"

I frowned, feeling the weight of the rain on my face, "You're making fun of me?"

Ethan was quiet for a moment. I wondered what he was thinking, but I couldn't bear to look at his face. Too much was riding on my confession. Then I heard him chuckle softly.

I started to speak, but before I could say a word, Ethan leaned in, so close. I was engulfed in his scent, full of summer & soap & trust, melting my resolve. Very gently, he swept damp curls from the nape of my neck, a place to press his lips in the barest of kisses, scarcely touching skin. Tiny electric sparks cascaded down my arm. I could feel the faintest brush of his eyelashes on my cheek.

Ethan examined my face. I blushed, feeling so exposed. He didn't seem to notice, lightly tracing a raindrop down my nose with the tip of his finger. I felt the heat intensify between us, heady and thick.

I thought about his lips, how much I wanted to kiss him again, this time, for more than just a moment.

"Do you think you could show me?" Ethan's voice was a silken whisper.

"Show you?" It was so hard to concentrate with Ethan's hazel eyes swirling inches from my own.

"What madness looks like?" Ethan gazed down at my lips, my flushed cheeks. The seconds expanded, building between us. *Just breathe. Just breathe. Just-*

Ethan stilled my thoughts, lifting my chin just enough to meet his lips, soft and sweet, then gently hungry, pulling me into his arms. I wrapped my hands around his neck, into his hair, sensing his heart beating so close to mine. The rain fell steadily: sweet, cool water quenching the heat of his lips. I fell into his kiss, falling, and falling until I wasn't sure I could ever come back.

Gently, Ethan drew away, arms still holding me, so strong. He looked into my eyes. "Still scared about tomorrow?" I saw a glimmer of his smirk, but mostly, his eyes were warm & true.

"Walk me in?" I tilted my head, glancing up beneath my lashes.

Ethan grinned, "If you're lucky."

"I think you've got it all wrong," I smiled slyly, "You're the lucky one."

Thirty-six.

Give yourself with every fiber,
lift your eyes to the horizon

-Eberhard Arnold, "Man"

I'd thought about leaving. Moving on to another
school without the history, without the same pressures
and expectations and open wounds. That would've
been the easiest thing to do. But these days, I wasn't
satisfied with easy. Easy was accepting the status quo.
Easy was a stationary life. Easy was ignoring the thing
right in front of you because the cost of reaching seems
too great.

I've wondered many times how I would've felt
walking in those doors if Ethan wasn't beside me. If I
hadn't been brave enough to show him my heart. The
stubborn part of me wants to believe that I would've
been okay anyway. That I would've gone back to
school and faced the humiliation with grace and
strength.

Maybe I would have. Maybe it would've been
okay. But one thing I know - my heart had been on life
support for too long. Edging around the people in my

life had taken more energy than facing my fears, facing mistrust.

Which is why it meant everything to know that I could trust again. Just knowing that all the hurt with Jared and Veronica and Brad hadn't crippled my spirit was a seed of something good. Something to build upon.

I knew it wasn't going to be perfect: an empty part of me would always miss Veronica's friendship. But I also knew that I had changed. The heaviness that had followed me like an angry cloud had slowly lifted. I felt free. It was hard not to believe that no matter what kind of craziness lies around the corner, at least for today, I was feeling just a little bit...untouchable.

Acknowledgements

Because this is my *first* novel, my gut reaction is to acknowledge every person who has ever influenced my writing, but that list would be LONG ☺ and I don't want to minimize, in any way, the special individuals in my life who have invested the most time in being supportive, honest, and loving. You are my writing inspiration.

This novel would have never *been* without you, Liliana Key, my beautiful, fiery daughter. In the journey to find you, to become a mother for the first time, I found my voice. Thank you for being incredibly stubborn, infinitely creative, and absolutely worth the wait: the time spent wishing and hoping for just the *idea* of you ultimately pushed me to write.

To Charlie, my sweet little guy, your birth completed my heart, encouraged me to return to this piece, to really *finish* what I'd started years ago. Thank you for sweet morning hugs & skin that always smells like cookies. You reminded me that boys can be both fiercely affectionate and incredibly strong. Ethan thanks you too.

To my crazy *first* family- Sisters Unite- Jackie & Jessica, thank you for being the first to show me what real friendship is. I will never laugh harder or cry harder than with you two. There are pieces of us here- I'm sure you didn't have to look hard to find them- so

I thank you for that and for getting excited along with me as I wrote and wrote and wrote. Jessica- thank you for staying up all night to finish the first copy. I found the ending to Andie's story while talking with you.

Mom & Dad- you were the *very first* to read my *very first* stories. Mom, thank you for taking us to the library practically every week, traveling to the Bookmobile when the library was too far, filling our hearts and minds with a love for stories. Dad, thank you for teaching me to persevere even when it gets really hard.

To Jamie, my most thorough editor, and closest friend, you invested such incredible time and energy sifting through my words, delving into my characters. Your honest, thoughtful advice and gentle critique has been invaluable. I entrusted you with my third child, and you took the greatest care. Talking about this book with you has been a joy to share. Not to mention all the moments I channeled our friendship and collective high school stories to help me find the path of Andie's friends and foes.

To my YHS Creative Writers, you have and will always push me to write Real- to try new things and stay connected to what is Now. Reading your words has catapulted my drive to write. Thank you for reintroducing the immeasurable FUN to writing. To Jenna, thanks for reminding me of myself, for writing romance & emotion so authentically. To Sam S., thank you for infusing poetry into everything, encouraging me to find that crossover between poetry and prose. To Heather, thank you for your depth of characters & emotion. To Sam G., thank you for writing "no holds barred." To Rachel, thank you for knowing exactly how to write Funny and reminding me how endearing a character's awkwardness can be. To Amanda, thank you for your bravery & honesty—the way you never stop stretching toward the land of Better. To all my writers, thank you for inspiring me every day. I couldn't do this without you.

And most of all, to Craig, my best friend, husband, and crazy partner in this crazy life. You never let me settle. You remind me of my strength when I become discouraged. Your unwavering dedication to pursue personal greatness is beautiful and inspiring. The best in Ethan is the best in you. Thank you for showing me what it means to go all out, to love fiercely, to actually enjoy Hemingway, to live adventurously, to know without a doubt that what is great is what is difficult, and to always tell me the truth, even when I don't want to hear it. I love you.

ABOUT THE AUTHOR

Jennifer grew up surrounded by stacks of irresistible fiction-
thanks, Mom- and has been a writer at heart since the early days
of enjoying Nancy Drew and Babysitter's Club. Reading and
telling stories evolved into a deep curiosity about *why* people do
what they do, so she ventured into Psychology. Jennifer
graduated from the University of Illinois with a degree in
Psychology and then set her sights on the zaniest psych ward
known to man: *High School*.

Earning her teacher certification from North Central College
and her Masters in Counseling from Northern Illinois
University, she has spent the past umpteen years working as an
English teacher/counselor/creative writer to hordes of fourteen
to eighteen-year olds, whom she loves dearly. Though--
sometimes daily--she wonders when the men in white coats will
arrive to cart *her* away, the laughs, audacity, and tenacious teen
spirit keep her coming back to the classroom again and again.

Jennifer lives with her brilliant, adventurous, creative husband
in a lake community with their two bold, free-spirited, hilarious
children who simultaneously set her world on fire and,
well...*set her world on fire.* She and her husband love to travel,
especially to the Florida Keys, and dabble in Foodie-ism and
Craft Brew Drinkie-ism because what other hobbies require you
to really *indulge?* Jennifer loves spending the summers with her
Tiny Dynamos, charting new waters of lovable insanity.
Untouchable is Jennifer's first novel but certainly not her last.
She has *loved, loved, loved* every minute writing it.

***Seeking a little wordapy? Visit jenniferwaldvogel.com.